The King of the Coral Sea

by
Robert Louis DeMayo

11/21/23

Available on Amazon, ACX,
Ingram, KDP, and other retailers.

Published in print, hardcover, eBook & audiobook.

Edited by **Alison Starratt**
alisonstarratt@gmail.com

Cover Design by **Andrew Holman**
www.andrewholman.com

Illustrations & Maps by **Tom Fish**
tfishart@yahoo.com

Audiobook narrator **Edmund Bloxam**
www.edmundbloxamaudio.com

This book is written in Australian English.

Michael Fomenko's Journey (March 1958 – December 1959).
Illustration by Tom Fish.

Odysseus and the Sirens.

Maps

Table of Contents

Michael's Story

Michael Fomenko at Weary Beach, Bloomfield, in the 1980s.
Photo courtesy of Harold and Ingram Jung.

Steve Douglas.
Photo courtesy of Sally Douglas.

for

Steve Douglas

In 1998 while visiting the Douglas family in Cairns, Australia, Steve introduced me to Michael Fomenko's story. He later brought me to a place where I glimpsed the illusive *Tarzan* — almost got run over by him, if I'm being honest.

A few years later, Steve sent me the excellent book by Peter Ryle: *Michael Fomenko – The Man Who Dared To Live His Own Exotic Fantasy*. After reading more of the truth behind Michael's story, I was hooked. I thought about it for years, but it took me a while to get the narrative straight. Now that I've finally written this book, the first person I want to thank is Steve.

I first met Steve Douglas in southern Israel in 1986. We were both part of a community of broke travellers who congregated in Elate, by an extension of the Red Sea called the Bay of Aqaba. We were both twenty-one years old and full of adventure. I lived in a shack in the hills. He slept on the beach. He was a great person to travel with: resourceful, entertaining, funny and tough. A good guy to have on your side.

Some of the travellers begged for money, but we never did. I remember Steve doing card tricks for tips when times got challenging. We lived hard back then, on the fringes, and I could see why he was drawn to — and understood — part of Michael Fomenko's life. I felt the same way. Sometimes it's worth giving up luxuries for a greater good.

Steve eventually lent me a pair of pants so I could get through English customs. Later we met again in India when he travelled with his future wife, Sally, and their nine-month-old Sorcha.

Over the years, we kept in touch. I visited him in Cairns with my family, and he dragged his to Arizona. Through it all, I learned that Steve Douglas is a very unique individual.

In the "real" world, Steve is a self-taught visionary business strategist and entrepreneur. He started and operated multiple successful travel accommodations and nature-based adventure tours across Far North Queensland. If you ever stayed at *Dreamtime Travellers Rest* or *Tropic Days* in Cairns, or *On the Wallaby,* up on the Tablelands, you'd remember Steve and his Irish accent.

By his side for much of this, his lovely wife Sally is equally dynamic and an essential part of all they've accomplished. Together they are an inspiration, as are their three children: Sorcha, Shay and Kiera. Spending time with the Douglas family has been a lesson in how to bring community together and live sustainably.

Steve has also encouraged children, young adults, and adults to commune through physical activity and healthy sporting culture. For fifteen years he has volunteered as Football Coach, President and Chairperson at the Edge Hill United Football Club. He led the club to build first-class facilities, football fields and professional match quality lighting.

People who meet Steve remember him, and because he introduced me to this story, I wanted to make sure you remember him too.

Thanks, Steve!

Michael Fomenko on the train after his Odyssey. 1960.
Photo courtesy of Harold and Ingram Jung.

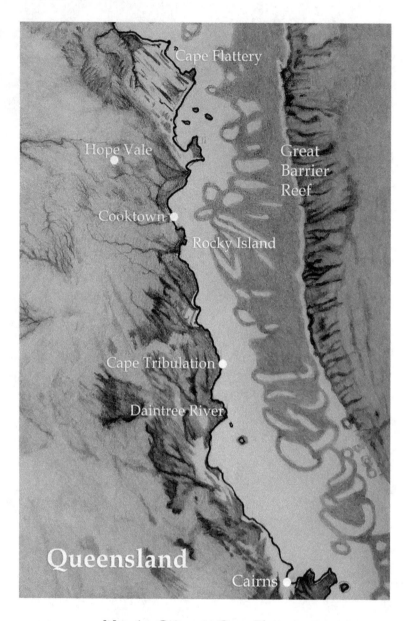

Map 1 – Cairns to Cape Flattery.
Illustration by Tom Fish.

Chapter One

The Odyssey I – Daintree River
(March 1958)

Michael made a deep stroke with the paddle to set his canoe in motion, the bow pointed out to sea. The muscles of his frame were robust and rippled with the effort. He stood just under two metres, weighed close to ninety kilos, and at twenty-seven, his body seemed made for the job.

But despite the force behind his endeavours, the boat barely moved.

The craft was more than seven metres long and made from a hollowed-out cedar-like tree called blushwood. An outrigger was firmly attached to the hull, hanging off the starboard side, and a thin mast of bamboo stood in the middle with a hessian sail wrapped tightly around it.

Behind him, he had tethered a smaller craft. It was only four metres in length, and because it had no outrigger, it swayed unsteadily.

Both canoes were heavily stowed with supplies for a long sea voyage: plastic water jugs, spare sails, rope, netting and dried meat. Plus, he had coconuts, mangoes, pawpaws and a basket of crabs.

Next to his sandalled feet was a wooden crate filled with tools and materials for repairing the boats, including a chisel, an axe, and a cane knife. A rifle, wrapped tightly in plastic, was lashed to the big canoe's inside wall.

It had taken him a year and a half to make the boats and collect the supplies, and now he was ready to begin his adventure.

Finally, he thought, *the time has come. There's no reason not to be gone. I'm as ready as I'll ever be.*

With determination, he tightened his grip on the paddle and dug the blade into the water again.

And again.

Finally, after a half-dozen strokes, his small fleet began to crawl forward.

He had set out early in the day, exiting the Daintree River, just as the high tide began to ebb. After allowing the freshwater flow to casually pull him seaward, he paused and stared back at the shoreline.

Behind the sandy beach, a wall of mangroves and rainforest faced him head-on. The Alexandra palms swayed despite there being no wind, and the emergent blue quandongs leaned his way like jurors anxious to reveal their verdict. The river flowed at him like it was sneaking away from the jungle, and he felt in some ways he was doing the same.

A mass of grey clouds hovered over it all, blocking out the sun, and obscuring Mount Windsor to the northwest. Its summit, Thornton Peak, was the third-highest in Queensland and he'd often thought of climbing it.

A flicker of lightning lit the distant sky. The oppressive heat swallowed the thunder.

Looks like the wet isn't ready to quit, he thought, knowing an early end to the rainy season was wishful thinking. There would still be plenty of storms for the next month or so, but after that, the northwesterly winds would reverse — and then he could try out his sail.

The ancient thriving wilderness of the Daintree beckoned him, and for a moment, he questioned his destination.

Why leave this? And for what? To travel over a thousand kilometres through treacherous waters?

He thought of his intended route up the northeast coast of Australia along the Cape York Peninsula and then across the Torres Strait to Dutch New Guinea.

And beyond that, where would his fancy take him? The Solomon Islands? Or maybe Maluku in Indonesia?

Sensing how much effort was required to move the boat just a few paces, he hoped he possessed the strength — mentally and physically.

A random wave splashed over the port side and soaked his feet.

Sweat seeped out of his curly black hair and rolled down his forehead. His skin had a slight olive sheen to it, a Slavic remnant of his father's Cossack blood.

A shell dangled from a leather cord around his neck.

Michael peeled off a short-sleeved button-up shirt, leaving him only in a pair of worn khaki shorts.

He stared out over the water, contemplating his journey.

Suddenly it seemed too far. A surge of fear gripped his gut.

It would be much easier to just camp along some Queensland river where the fishing was good, and there were plenty of wild pigs and bush turkeys.

The voices of those who thought his proposed voyage was crazy echoed in his mind. He stared out to sea and imagined the perils: black brewing weather, sudden cyclones and boiling, rolling mountains of water.

It was true that he was on a voyage of uncertainty, with no exact destination other than a distant land. But still, he felt compelled to set off.

He flexed his hands, cracking his knuckles. He wouldn't quit before he'd even had a blister or muscle cramp — or felt the pangs of hunger.

I have to go. I don't care if it's reckless, he thought as he let his eyes sweep the seemingly level water. He knew if he didn't complete this tale of endurance, he would only be half alive. Around him, a flock of silver gulls screeched and squawked, and he found it reassuring.

He chuckled. *You get me.*

He thought of his father, Daniel, who was his greatest supporter. His father understood why Michael had renounced civilisation and why he felt he must test himself.

But even he had been daunted by what Michael planned to attempt. "You'll be all alone," his father had warned, "with no help at all. In Queensland, there are strict laws that regulate the lives of the Aboriginals. They can't drink alcohol or vote, and their every movement is recorded and regulated by the police. Most of all, they are highly discouraged from fraternising with Europeans — especially in the bush towns."

Michael had chuckled. "I'm sure I can find somebody not being watched."

Daniel shook his head. "If you go off and form a friendship with one of the Aboriginals living on a mission up there, you'll most likely get him thrown in jail."

In the end, his father had given his blessing, but others still tried to convince him to settle down and give up his epic dreams. Michael shrugged them off. He'd already decided he would complete the journey, and their worries meant little to him.

Rather than succumb to those small-minded voices that still darted through his head, he thought of his father again, during happier days.

He leaned forward and paddled harder.

Slowly, the canoes ploughed through the water.

Snapper Island rose on his right, and he cut between it and the mainland on a northern route.

Over the next week, he sluggishly followed the coastline, more interested in getting a feel for handling the boats than covering a great distance. With all the supplies, the canoes lay incredibly low in the water, and he soon found they were vulnerable to every change on the surface. Several times a short, choppy wind had half-filled both boats with water, forcing him to hightail it to shore.

The winds were still blowing in the wrong direction, too, coming at him from the northwest. But even if they hadn't been, he wasn't ready to try the sail. He was not an able seaman, and he had not fared well the few times he'd experimented with wind power.

Still, he had faith that in time he would learn the skills he needed.

He would ride the tide out, make what distance he could, and then pull ashore with the high tide later in the day.

He travelled slowly, enjoying the coastline and islands — exploring the magnificent rainforest and reefs — and letting his curiosity flow where it would.

Even though he was overstocked with supplies, he busied himself to gather more coconuts and replenish his water. He also walked the shoreline, searching for shellfish or crabs.

Can't be too safe, he thought. *Never know when I might run along a barren stretch of land.*

Sometimes he would venture into the rainforest with his rifle and hunt for birds. After the constant crashing of waves, the quietness of the prehistoric forest enchanted him. He sensed that the place was aware, and he often felt a desire to lay down and sleep — or maybe rest silently.

He spent hours reclined on the forest floor, amongst the herbaceous shade-loving plants and saplings, while he watched the birds, butterflies and insects pollinate the flowers in the canopy and understory.

He often thought dying there would be a perfect death; slowly decaying until he became part of the ancient rainforest. Maybe a small bush or tree would sprout from his remains — a pink evodia perhaps — with its vibrant fuchsia flowers sharing a last remembrance of his awareness.

And yet, his journey would not let him relax long. The only timepiece he kept was an internal clock that whispered this voyage was his chance to do something exceptional.

Although a casual pace was alright, that clock would start ticking when he camped in the same location for too many days.

He continued, always pushing north.

He passed Cape Tribulation, where British navigator James Cook's ship ran aground a reef in 1770.

Michael had a grudging respect for Captain Cook, who had chartered over three thousand kilometres of the Australian coastline. The explorer once said, "I had ambition to not only go further than any man had before, but as far as possible for a man to go."

That sounds like a bloke who doesn't give up easily.

Cook had named this place Tribulation because he said, "Here begun all our troubles."

Michael hoped he would not share the same fate.

The big canoe was turning out to be too cumbersome. It was unwieldy and almost impossible to steer in tricky winds, so when he passed the Bloomfield River, he headed into it.

In the estuary, he camped for a few days. He thought of how slow his progress had been during the last few days, and during that time, chopped off a metre from either end of the big canoe.

He also took the opportunity to fit a piece of wood across the inside of the hull for support, just behind the mast. The thwart strengthened the craft and also offered a place to set his feet when he paddled. He'd noticed a small crack had developed where the outrigger connected to the canoe and caulked the fitting with tar and animal fat.

Lastly, he carved a turtle design on the port side of the bow. It wasn't a sea turtle, but a land tortoise—a joke regarding his slow progress. He stared at it and the boat, proud of his hard work, and hoping his modifications would help him make better speed.

"I dub you *Tortoise!*" he said.

When he went to sleep that night, he did so, feeling confident that the next day would be a good one. But in the night, an offshore squall blew in.

He awoke to pelting rain. Immediately he got up and tied the big canoe to a stout log he'd hammered into the sand. Then he pulled the smaller canoe further ashore, flipped the boat over, and crawled under it for shelter.

At dawn, he rose to discover the larger boat had floated away in the night. The stake in the sand was gone too.

He cursed the squall. *So much for wishful thinking*.

He should have waited until the seasonal storms were over, but he'd wanted to be well on his way when the winds reversed and the southeasterlies began.

He walked up the coast for an hour—and then down it—but didn't see the larger canoe anywhere. It had vanished. The clouds had moved on as well, and in the early morning sunlight, a brilliant rainbow arched overhead.

He returned to his camp, spent the day outfitting the smaller boat the best he could, and the next day continued up the coast.

A few days later, disaster struck again. Michael had started paddling early that morning, the sun glinting at him from the soft, indigo horizon.

It was a clear morning, but a steady breeze made the water choppy. He had trouble controlling the smaller canoe, which still lacked an outrigger. He covered little distance.

Slowly, Rocky Island came into view, rising out of the water on his right. He could see he would pass over a large coral reef. He checked the tide.

Going out, he thought with a sinking feeling, *that shoal will be exposed before long*.

He glimpsed an outcrop of rock that the retreating water had already revealed. On it, a flock of gulls squabbled over what looked like a carcass of some small animal.

Suddenly, a sea eagle dropped out of the sky on one of the birds and sent the flock scattering.

He tried not to look at the scene as an omen and reassessed whether he should attempt crossing the reef. If he had had the larger canoe, he might have tried his sail to see if he could scurry past quickly.

But he didn't, so he was left with either calling it a day and heading to shore or going for the open water beyond the reef. From where he rocked on the water, it looked like the route to the beach was equally troublesome with exposed rocks, so he decided to continue.

Initially, he made good progress, but as he rounded the bend, he encountered a headwind that kept blowing him back. He leaned hard into his strokes, trying to force his way forward with brute strength.

Around him, more outcroppings of coral began to appear, and he worked hard to avoid being smashed into one of them. The pull of the water tugged his craft closer and closer to danger.

He held his breath when the canoe's hull scraped over a slab of submerged coral.

Suddenly, a retreating wave revealed a deep pocket in the reef, and the nose of his canoe dropped into it. With a sickening crunch, the bow wedged tightly into the shoal at a forty-five-degree angle.

The force of the impact threw him into the air and straight into a large chunk of hard rock.

He screamed in pain as the sharp edges bit into his flesh.

Before he could grab hold of the rock, another wave forced him underwater, where he smashed the right side of his head against the coral.

He floundered underwater, unsure of which way was up.

Repeatedly he was flung against the coral, which tore at him, burning and stinging.

Somehow, he surfaced and glimpsed his canoe, the stern still projecting out of the water at a steep angle. The next wave moved him closer, and he managed to grab the side.

With a herculean effort, he flopped into the boat.

Blood flowed into his eyes and blurred his vision.

He sank into the craft and passed out.

Hours later, he was pulled from sleep by the whispering of his mother in his ear, "Wake up, Mikey... Wake up."

And then the sound of wood cracking and splintering brought him fully around. The side of his face ached painfully; he couldn't see out of his right eye.

He glanced around, uncertain of what had happened.

He slowly discerned that he'd been unconscious for some time.

The tide was now coming in. The shore was further away — twice the distance of what he remembered.

He was up to his waist in water and was surprised he hadn't been washed out of what was left of his canoe.

The constant force of the waves had destroyed the boat. A strong sense of despair overcame him as he realised that the remaining supplies had been swept away.

With the next wave, he launched himself in the direction of the shore. And it was only then that he discovered how badly he'd smashed his shoulder.

He barely made it to the beach, and after he finally dragged himself onto the sand, he passed out once more.

The following day, he woke up feeling like a corpse. He still couldn't see out of his right eye. He gingerly probed the area with his fingertips to find it caked with scabs and dried blood.

He could barely move his right arm.

Angry red patches covered his body where he had slammed against barnacles and fire coral.

He sat up and tried to regain his senses.

I'm not even a tenth of the way to my destination, and I've lost everything. He stood and brushed himself off, trying not to think about the efforts of the last eighteen months — all that work preparing.

Still, he knew he could not quit. He couldn't go home.

What home? he asked himself. He glanced up and down the beach and thought: *This is my home now.*

He let his eyes sweep the shoreline around him, hoping he might spot at least one item from his supplies. Yet only sand, shells and clumps of seaweed along the highwater mark decorated the beach.

I have nothing left, he thought.

Suddenly, he remembered his father saying the same thing on the eve of his family's flight from Moscow. He had been barely a year old and couldn't possibly have that memory, but still, he could hear his father's voice clearly.

"We will stick with our plan," his mother had replied. "We have each other."

Chapter Two

Michael's Story – Age One
(Moscow 1930)

Michael bounced along in the arms of his sister, Inessa. He had just turned one, and she was only three but determined to carry him whenever she had a chance. He gripped a toy dog in both hands; it was carved from pine and covered in soft black fur.

Later in her life, Inessa claimed to remember everything about that day. As a result, Michael's memories were tinted, at times, by a three-year-old's supposed observations.

In her version of the day's events, Michael's new toy dog played a significant part, though neither of their parents had ever mentioned it.

Daniel and Elizabeth marched ahead of their kids in their nervousness, not realising the little ones were having difficulty keeping up. They were trying to leave Moscow, and if things went wrong, both parents would be imprisoned—and who knew what would become of the children.

Daniel Fomenko looked like a ghost as they approached the Yaroslavsky Train Station. At twenty-nine, his hollow cheeks and sunken eyes made him look much older than he was.

In his hand, he clutched their tickets and identification papers, which stated that he currently worked in the Bank of Foreign Trade of the U.S.S.R.

His other hand gripped a worn suitcase with barely a change of clothing for each of them. Their valuables had all been sold or pawned off over the last few years, and they now travelled lightly.

His wife held a smaller suitcase, similarly packed with garments, and a cloth sack with bread, cheese, and fruit. It represented all they could scrounge up after purchasing the train tickets. Her stomach rumbled, but she knew there would be no tapping into their meagre supplies now — they had a long way to go. One glance at her daughter's thin frame would suck her appetite away anyway. What they had would go to the children.

According to Inessa, they *did* have a remaining piece of jewellery hidden away — not much, but enough to buy passage to safety when the train reached the end of the line, in far off Vladivostok. It wouldn't help them now.

The last ten years had seen a radical transformation of the Russian Empire into a communist state. The Soviet Union was dedicated to Vladimir Lenin's version of Marxism, which promised a socialist utopia that would destroy capitalism and the elite who had prospered from it. This need to find people to blame had caused problems for both of Michael's parents.

Michael's mother, Princess Elizabeth Matchabelli, came from a long line of Georgian nobility. And his father, Daniel, was a Cossack — another group that had been singled out. Their social status had caused the family problems over the years, and now they feared arrest daily.

Daniel was visited regularly by the Soviet Secret Police, who disapproved of his lectures at Moscow University. He was a Professor of the Comparative History of Western Literature.

It was Elizabeth who noticed the children lagging. She grabbed her husband's arm, forcing him to pause. He took a breath of the cool night air and forced a smile. Soon they stood huddled together, like a small grove of willowy trees.

Daniel glanced down at young Michael, who was oblivious to the current dangers because of the toy dog he'd been given for the journey. A clever fellow professor had carved it as a parting gift.

The toddler stuck the dog's nose in his mouth and then gave a wide grin that showed off a mouth full of stubby little teeth.

"We have nothing left, only our lives," said Daniel to his wife, as if trying to convince her. "If we remain, they will take even that."

Elizabeth nodded calmly. "We have each other."

A train whistle blew in the night, followed by a burst of steam into the dark sky.

"That's us, children!" exclaimed Daniel, trying to show bravado.

"How far will we ride it?" asked Inessa.

"This is the longest railway line in the world," he said hollowly. "We will cross eight time zones and travel over nine thousand kilometres."

The enormity of the journey appeared to sink in as Daniel glanced at his family, and Elizabeth sensed he might falter. If arrested, they may never see each other again, but there was no turning back at this point. She put an arm around her husband.

They headed towards the station gate, where two sentries waited.

The guards watched stone-faced as they approached. One was fat and slovenly, the other tall, wearing an anguished expression like he had a splitting migraine. Inessa always referred to them as Fatso and Headache.

Headache requested the papers.

Daniel looked over the man's uniform and said, "Here you go, Capitan."

The man nodded. "You were in the military?" he asked.

Daniel said, "Yes, in the War I fought in the army against the Ottomans in Turkey."

Fatso motioned for Elizabeth to place her suitcase on a sturdy wooden table. Inessa excitedly gazed at the steam engine now in full view while Michael snuggled with his toy dog; even a steam train wasn't enough to pull his attention away.

Fatso pawed through the contents of the suitcase. His tired expression said he'd found nothing of value. He flipped the case upside down, emptied the contents on the table, and then banged it loudly.

Headache winced and gave him an evil look. Then he turned to Daniel's papers again and said, "I see you not only work at the bank, but you lecture at the university."

Daniel nodded meekly.

The Captain motioned for Daniel to hand over his suitcase to Fatso. "This one might be hiding something," he said with a nod at Daniel.

Fatso flipped open the suitcase and began rummaging through it.

Headache finished examining the tickets and handed them back. He looked over the identification papers again. Time stretched then, for so long, that even in their memories, it was interminable. Daniel looked ready to pass out.

Fatso searched for hidden compartments in his suitcase, banging it despite the nasty looks from the Captain.

"And what subjects do you lecture on?" asked Headache.

The colour flowed out of Daniel's face like a retreating tide.

"Economics and geography," whispered Daniel.

"You. Come here!" ordered Fatso while motioning for Daniel to come forward. Daniel stepped closer on shaky legs, and the guard began a methodological search of his clothes and body. Elizabeth started to quietly place the clothing back into the suitcases.

Headache creased his brows, and his voice had an edge as he asked, "And maybe world economics? Maybe world politics?"

Suddenly everyone grew quiet. Daniel stared at Headache while Fatso patted him down.

"No," he said, "only Russian economics."

"And why are you going to the far end of the empire? It seems to me that you might be trying to flee your homeland," said the Captain while his eyes bore down on Daniel.

Fatso finished searching Daniel and stared unflinchingly at Elizabeth. The children now sensed that things had turned serious. Inessa clung to her mother's leg; Michael was standing unsteadily by their feet. Elizabeth scooped up the child and cradled him protectively in front of her.

"No, sir," stammered Daniel, "I have secured a job teaching at the Eastern State University in Vladivostok."

Fatso noticed the toy dog Michael was so enamoured with and grabbed it just as Headache was about to speak.

Michael let out a howl like the end of the world had arrived.

The guard laughed and called the Captain.

"Look!" he shouted. "See how much he wants it."

Headache clamped both palms over his ears.

Fatso was about to tease the boy some more, but Elizabeth snatched the toy dog from him and returned it to Michael, who still screamed bloody murder.

"How can you tease a child so?" she scolded.

The guard leaned over her, and suddenly she realised her maternal instinct might have ruined everything.

Fatso glared at her, but the Captain had had enough of the screaming child. "Let them go," he said. "Get them out of here!"

Later that night, in the safety of their cabin, the family sat in a tight circle. Elizabeth broke off a piece of bread and handed bite-sized portions to each of her children.

What happened next was related to him countless times by Inessa. Maybe it was because he'd been told the story from such a young age that he remembered it clearly as a real memory. He'd often argued with his sister that at age three, she could hardly have remembered the event either, but that never stopped her from telling the story.

When Michael accepted his next morsel, Daniel casually took the toy dog away.

The toddler appeared ready to cry out, but his father gave him a disarming smile — followed by a wink — and Michael satisfied himself with eating.

While he watched, Daniel unhooked a secret compartment in the toy dog's belly, and a moment later, a glittering necklace spilled into his palm.

Elizabeth met Daniel's gaze calmly and breathed a sigh of relief.

He handed her the necklace, and she spirited it away into a secret fold in her dress. That night, the clickity-clack of the train moving over the seemingly endless line of tracks floated through their dreams, promising a better future.

Chapter Three

The Odyssey II – On Foot
(April 1958)

*M*ichael looked north up the desolate beach, though he wasn't sure to what end. In theory, he could follow the coast on foot all the way to Cape York. However, the numerous rivers he would have to ford on the way were inhabited by crocodiles.

And without a boat, he couldn't cross the strait to Dutch New Guinea.

Travelling that distance without support would be nearly impossible — his family and friends had used the very word when he mentioned the idea of this voyage. And that's when they imagined him doing it in a boat.

"That's impossible!" they'd shouted unimaginatively, "maybe in a sailboat with a crew, but not by yourself in a crude man-made craft." Even his father had come up with a shortlist of genuine dangers: drowning, starvation, shipwreck, sunstroke, sharks and saltwater crocodiles.

He was so mad at himself for trying to cross the reef with the low tide approaching that he blocked out all those voices — and perhaps his common sense — and simply stood up.

He wore only a pair of shorts; his shirt and sandals lost in the wreck. A leather cord circled his neck, although the shell had smashed off. When he looked down, he was shocked to see that he still wore his cane knife in a sheaf around his waist. Somehow it had remained with him through his desperate swim for shore.

Perhaps some luck was still with him because a short way up the beach, he spotted a floating coconut rolling in the surf. He walked to it and picked it up, wondering if it could be from his supplies.

Nervous energy kept him on the move that day, and he walked through the afternoon and into the soft twilight. Dusk found him on the shore of the Annon River as it spilled into the Coral Sea. There he smashed the coconut he'd been carrying on a rock and picked out the pulpy flesh with his knife.

He was still hungry after that but too exhausted to search for more food.

After checking the river for crocodiles, he waded up to his waist and then crouched and tried to wash away some of the dried blood.

A mirror would have helped, but he was afraid to look at himself and see his damaged face. He felt hideous, like a revenant.

He wondered if he'd ever see again out of his right eye.

At least his shoulder had become less troublesome. He figured he'd dislocated it and then somehow knocked it back into place. He knew it would be a while before he regained full use of it.

On the bank sat a large boulder with a flat top. He climbed it and slept there—out of the reach of any crocs that might be attracted to the smell of his blood in the water.

In the next day's first light, he surveyed the river cautiously. By its mouth, a sandbar extended out into the water, and if he walked out onto it, he'd only have about half the distance to swim before reaching the other side.

He knew there were a lot of crocs in the river but felt confident they would be further upstream under the shelter of the mangroves.

He stared long and hard at the crossing. Even though he was a strong swimmer, one of his arms was currently useless. On the school team, he had averaged about forty strokes when competing in the fifty-metre swim. That worked out to about fifty strokes per minute. Some swimmers had more strokes per minute, but Michael took deep long pulls with his arms.

He stood there for a lengthy moment, contemplating before he finally entered the water. *If my shoulder weren't injured, I'd guess it to be about two hundred strokes to the other side – but who knows how many in my current state.*

He waded in until the flow was up to his neck and then, using his left arm, did a modified crawl.

Halfway across, he began to panic as the current pulled him out towards the sea. But he pushed on and eventually breathed a sigh of relief when his toes brushed the sand of the far shore.

Two days later, the sandy beach gave way to the rising tide. Michael hopped from rock to rock along the shore, the waves smashing loudly at his feet. He followed Quarantine Bay with Mount Cook National Park on his left.

He moved in a daze, his mind free of thought.

Another few days after that, he was surprised when he came upon buildings and streets and other signs of man. He had been alone for a while now and hadn't talked to anyone for weeks.

"I bet I look like an ogre," he said out loud.

He figured he had reached Cooktown and hid among some large boulders on the edge of town until evening. When the sun had set, he tried to slip past the town undetected, not wanting anyone to see him in his current state.

As he approached the Endeavour River, he heard music and voices along the waterfront. He hid again.

Later, in the dead of night, he swam across the river. The thought of encountering people had scared him so much that he'd forgotten to check for crocodiles before making the swim.

Over the next week, he continued following the coast on foot. He scanned the beach for shellfish as he went, eating them raw each time.

At night he lay in the sand, wishing he had a fire. *What I would give for some dry matches,* he thought.

Sometimes the beach disappeared, and the steep shoreline prevented further progress. Then he had to wait for the tide to go out before he could continue.

During those times, he scrambled along frantically, fearful that the returning tide would find him in a tight spot with no way to higher ground.

The days blurred until one afternoon, he found himself walking along an isolated beach. If asked, he wouldn't have been able to tell you his location. Later, he discovered he had covered about a hundred and fifteen kilometres since his accident by the Rocky Island reef.

At this point, he'd travelled a little over two hundred kilometres since paddling out of the Daintree River.

He was treading along the beach, his hunger driving him to find food, when he saw a large tree trunk half-buried in the sand.

Since he had left the Daintree River, he had seen no trees that were suitable for building another canoe. He had no appropriate tools either, so he couldn't cut down a tree if he wanted to — his cane knife was too thin.

But now, in the sand before him, he noted that this tree trunk was just about the right size. He crouched before it and began digging around the tree.

After about a half-hour, a peculiar feeling came over him, and he moved to the far end of the trunk. He scraped away the sand.

There he found a carved image of a turtle.

I don't believe it, he said to himself. He had found his large canoe, the one he had named *Tortoise.*

He sat back on his haunches and laughed.

His eyes scanned the area around him. The beach extended back to a cliff, and by its base, he spied a cave.

He approached it and stared into the darkness.

Chapter Four

Michael's Story – Age Three
(Manchuria 1933)

*D*aniel crouched by a low fire, warming his hands. A thick forest of pines and spruce sheltered them, hiding the shadows cast by the flames, but still, he placed several stones around his small blaze to conceal it even more.

Now that night had fallen, he couldn't be too careful.

Elizabeth crept to where the two children slept on a pile of pine boughs and gently roused them. It was late in the fall, and with the sunset, the temperatures had plummeted.

Inessa sat up first, rubbing her eyes. She was six now and aware that the mountainous terrain they were traversing contained dangers. She glanced around warily at the small, concealed area where they had taken shelter for the day.

Michael, now three, didn't seem too ready to get up. The child was very skinny — his ribs visible through his clothing — and Daniel prayed that they could get some healthy food into him when they completed this journey.

Elizabeth's voice came out in white puffs as she shook him gently. "Wake up, Mikey... Wake up."

Daniel wished they could all cuddle under a thick blanket and sleep for a hundred years. The last two years had seemed to take an eternity, as if their personal hourglass had moist grains of sand in it, that from time to time, stuck.

They had somehow managed to stay on the train from Moscow to Vladivostok in far eastern Russia, where he had secured his job as a professor at the Eastern State University. But the Soviet Security Service continued to harass him, and he felt it was only a matter of time before he was arrested.

The family still needed to escape the Soviet Union if they ever hoped to experience peace.

Finally, after two years of being watched, Daniel was put in contact with two men who would smuggle them across the border into China. The guides were Chinese, of the Tungusic people, and he had no idea if he could trust them, but he had run out of options.

Their immediate destination had been Jilin City, about five hundred kilometres away, in Manchuria, China. From there, they would travel another two hundred kilometres to the city of Harbin. Manchuria's area is split between Russia and China; the Russian part is called Outer Manchuria, and the Chinese region is known as Inner Manchuria.

After a terrifying sprint across the border, the family journeyed through Inner Manchuria on foot. They walked at night, across a vast forest of taiga and pine, and hid during the day. They existed on the meekest of provisions.

Even after putting some distance between the border and its guards, there was still plenty to fear. This area was home to Siberian tigers, Amur leopards and brown bears. In the daylight, they saw their tracks, as well as those of wild boar and deer.

Daniel added a few twigs to the fire and wondered when the guides would return from scouting the trail ahead.

Michael walked to his side and stared at the flames, still sleepy-eyed. Aside from being thin, what concerned Daniel was that the boy rarely uttered a word. At three, Inessa had been a chatterbox.

But as a toddler and now a three-year-old, Michael rarely spoke — and it was only then for something he wanted badly.

Soon the two men returned. One was older, in his late fifties, with a mop of white hair. He spoke a little Russian and had told Daniel his name was Dorgon, which meant Badger. He looked like a badger with his white hair, so that's what they called him.

His companion was Nikan. He was in his thirties and spoke very limited Russian, which made him seem aloof. Badger was in charge, and Nikan followed his lead.

Nikan proudly dropped a dead rabbit by the fire, then began heaping wood on the timid flames.

Daniel feared the resulting blaze would be too high, but Badger calmed him with a hand gesture and said, "We are far enough way. We no longer need to fear the Russians."

Elizabeth breathed a sigh of relief.

Inessa watched Nikan gut and skin the rabbit. Her hungry eyes held both fear and hope as she asked, "Are we going to eat that?"

Badger nodded. "Yes, we'll have a warm meal before we continue, and after tonight we travel during the day."

Soon the rabbit was sizzling over the fire. They all watched silently, listening to the wood crack and snap while the meat cooked.

With a warm meal in their bellies, they all felt recharged, but even still, Inessa had a dizzy spell when she stood. Earlier on their journey, she had been passing out regularly due to malnutrition. Daniel had resorted to holding her upside down by her ankles so that the blood would flow to her head.

Now, he wondered if he was even strong enough to lift her thin frame.

They hiked late into the night, eventually taking shelter by an uprooted tree. The next day, with the sun on their faces, everyone's spirits began to improve.

The land changed too, and they moved through oaks and elm trees and occasionally along tranquil rivers. Finally, the cold weather tapered off for a few days, and they delighted in a brief respite.

Late one afternoon, when the sky was alight with colour, they came upon a cave where Badger informed them they would spend the night.

Nikan lit a fire, and they had all just moved inside when they heard a tiger roaring in the nearby hills. Elizabeth turned white and herded the children far back into the cave.

Michael didn't want to be stuck inside. He anxiously looked to the cave entrance, and then in a tiny voice, said, "*Tigr.*"

He walked to Inessa, tugged her shirt, and said, "Inessa, *Tigr.*"

Badger stepped outside with Daniel and listened to the cat moaning and calling out from the east. He smirked. "She is in heat. She is only looking for a male — we have nothing to fear."

In response, another tiger cried out from a different group of hills to the west. "There is Old Grandfather," said Badger.

Elizabeth crept to the cave entrance, with Michael trying to sneak around her legs. "Is there any danger from the tiger that keeps roaring?" she asked.

"I don't think so," replied Badger, "she has bigger things on her mind." He winked at Inessa and added, "She's looking for a boyfriend."

Elizabeth nodded but didn't look convinced. The cat continued her vocalisations — which had a tone of desperation to them. Michael seemed eager to get outside, but she steered him back into the cave. "*Tigr,*" he said again.

"Yes," said Elizabeth, who continued to pale. "Now, back inside."

Badger tried to help console her by saying, "Tigers generally try to avoid people — it is much more likely that you would be killed here by a wild boar or wolves."

That only made things worse, and as they entered the cave, Daniel did his best to soothe his wife. Nikan tended his fire while Badger skinned another rabbit he'd shot late in the day.

During the busyness, nobody noticed Michael creep out of the cave.

The memory of what happened next stayed with Michael, vividly, for the rest of his life. Not because it was violent or traumatic, but because it was an experience that embraced his soul, awakening something inside of him.

A nearly full moon shone behind a stand of swaying firs, greeting him when he stepped out of the cave. In what seemed a matter of heartbeats, the sun had set. A chilled breeze ruffled his hair. Behind him, he could hear a host of comforting sounds: his father reassuring his mother; Inessa singing a lullaby; the fire crackling; and somebody splitting wood.

The forest had turned silver in the moonlight, and the trees danced in the wind as if celebrating the end of the day. Michael found himself drawn away from the cave's entrance.

After a dozen steps, he paused and peered into the murky, magical forest. He sensed something there. It seemed there was a pattern to the wind; it was as if the forest were breathing. Or maybe it was the chirp of the insects combining with the calls of the nightbirds. It all seemed linked together.

His three-year-old brain didn't overthink it like an adult's. He just smiled because he suddenly felt that the night was aware — and it was aware of him.

Another roar rippled through the woods, this one further away. He frowned — he wanted to see the tiger. He stood there in the chilly night air, feeling something special whispering in the wind.

Just then, a twig snapped. It was a sharp crack that hinted at a large animal. Michael let his eyes sweep over the forest.

Perhaps he felt a little fear, but mostly he was filled with love and awe. There was a magical presence all around him — a sense of mystery and vastness. Everything felt connected.

From that day on, he carried the knowledge that a place could be aware, and somehow, he was a part of it.

Over the years, Michael became convinced that when he'd left the cave on his own that night, a male tiger had been hiding in the shrubs right in front of him. It may have started as a hunch, but over time he pulled more details from his memory, and as an adult, he became sure of it.

He imagined the tiger crouched low in the ferns below the pines. He pictured the pale pelage of its coat blending with the dull earth, while the cat watched his every move.

He later learned that male Siberian tigers grew to over two hundred and twenty kilograms. He often thought of how that cat would have dwarfed his younger self.

Michael could clearly imagine the tiger observing him; curiously, and maybe a little hungrily. He saw the narrow black stripes swaying with the wind and the trees — all of it connected.

And over the years, it all mixed together: The magical forest swaying in the moonlight, the tiger observing him, and the feeling that the forest was aware.

Sometimes he felt he was the tiger watching the young boy, and other times, he was the forest observing them both.

Perhaps because of that experience, and his formative time in Manchuria, Michael found he was drawn to the natural world as he grew older. He often yearned to be alone, battling and testing himself against the elements.

He was terrified by lightning storms in his teenage years, but he would still stand outside and confront them, staring up at the heavens when one came through.

One time Inessa found him doing that and escorted him back inside. She'd asked him why he did it. He had shrugged, later realising that when he defied the storm, it was the only time that he felt he was looking at the world through the tiger's eyes again.

Chapter Five

The Odyssey III – Cape Flattery
(May 1958)

John Caldwell sailed his yacht, *Outward Bound,* along the coast of Australia, heading north by northwest up the Cape York Peninsula. The 14-metre ketch cut through the water smoothly, an easterly wind filling both the main and mizzenmast sails.

Caldwell sat at the helm. His wife and two boys reclined behind him, out of the wind in the cockpit. It was an idyllic day with almost perfect conditions for sailing; wind at his back, about 8 knots, smooth seas, and clear skies all around.

Regardless, he kept a constant vigil, continually watching the water ahead—all too conscious of how easily and quickly things can go wrong when sailing.

He studied the rugged coastline and pondered how dangerous it might be to approach it if they suddenly had to abandon ship. Or, for some reason, race to land.

They passed a long stretch of beach, and he glanced at his chart to see that it was called Elim Beach. There was little coral here, and he felt he could get closer to land without wrecking his boat if he had to. Caldwell was an American and not familiar with these waters, but it was more than that. He regularly did this, imagining disasters — the habit a result of his past.

Ten years before, Caldwell had been sailing from Panama to Australia when his sailboat, *Pagan*, had been damaged in a hurricane. On the edge of starvation, he had drifted without food for forty-nine days. Even after washing up on an island in Fiji, it had taken him months to reach his wife in Australia.

The episode had done little to discourage his passion for sailing, and in fact, he'd written a best-selling book about his misadventure. But it had highlighted the dangers. Now with his family on board, he took extra care.

He noted the shallow bay, numerous sandbars, and distant flatwater lagoons when passing Cape Flattery and thought it a place best avoided — even at high tide. He was sure he'd get stranded in the low water if he ventured closer.

Then beyond the breakers, he spied a man walking along the isolated beach. In the distance, the man rippled like a mirage.

"Mary!" he called to his wife, "pass me the binoculars, please."

She stepped to his side and handed him the glasses.

"What do you see?" she asked.

He chuckled. "I thought I saw a man walking near the water."

"What's so strange about that?"

He scanned the shoreline. "Well, it wouldn't be so odd to see an Aboriginal — but I thought it was a white guy."

A flicker of movement caught his eye, and when he focused on it, sure enough, there was a man. The man had long, unkempt hair, wore no shirt, and his ragged shorts dangled in tatters above the knees.

The man's skin was deeply tanned, his face covered by a thick beard, but he was still decidedly white.

"I wonder what he's doing way up here," Caldwell mumbled.

Mary laughed. "I guess we'll be dropping anchor?"

He gave her a knowing look. "You know me pretty well, don't ya?"

Mary smiled. "It doesn't take a genius to know that you wouldn't sail by someone that was possibly stranded."

An hour later, Caldwell was in the dinghy, rowing for land. He had left *Outward Bound* anchored safely offshore, with Mary and the boys playing checkers. The high tide was coming in, and he figured he would stay ashore for an hour or so, departing before it started going out.

He saw no sign of the lone man as he approached, eventually riding the crest of a wave as it spent itself on the shore of the Cape.

He pulled the little boat out of reach of the waves. A lone croc lay sunning itself by the highwater mark. He skirted around it and walked along in the soft silica sand until he came upon the fresh tracks of a man.

The footprints led to the southern end of the Cape and into a cave in the cliff wall. Driftwood logs had been piled across the ingress, preventing Caldwell from seeing inside.

By the entrance, a dugout canoe lay propped on several logs.

A grove of coconut trees provided dappled shade.

It seemed like an ideal location, but something about the cave gave him an ominous feeling. Like it was the home of some sinister mythical being.

Caldwell paused by the dim entrance, cupped his hands in front of his mouth, and hollered, "Hello!"

No voice answered his call, but he heard a hollow banging from inside — the man he'd seen was in there.

"Hello!" he tried again.

The pounding of the surf behind him, and the constant wind, were the only sounds.

Caldwell stood there uncomfortably, waiting, but eventually, his curiosity got the better of him, and he crept his way into the cave, which was filled with swirling shadows.

"Go away!" a voice bellowed. "Leave me alone!"

Caldwell peered into the gloom. It seemed more than one person was hiding back there. His eyes slowly adjusted, and eventually, he made out a spectre crouched near the back of the cave. The figure swayed from side to side as if trying to see him from different angles.

"Forgive me," said Caldwell. "I saw you walking down the beach and thought you might need help."

"I don't," the voice roared. "Leave me be!"

Caldwell sensed that he'd stumbled on a recluse who wanted nothing to do with him. And this guy seemed big and intimidating.

He began backing out of the dark cavern.

But he had angered the man, who stepped forward, a shaft of light revealing a face with one eye covered by tattered bandages.

"I think it's about time you were on your way."

Caldwell nodded, but the man's rude demeanour had grated his nerves, and he threw out a parting shot as he backed away.

"Settle down, Polyphemus, I'm going."

Outraged, the man stormed forth, shaking with anger. He stopped a short pace away from Caldwell. He smelled horrible, and his body, although large, looked emaciated.

By his waist, he wore a cane knife stuck into a rough sheath.

"You come here, uninvited, and now you make fun of my injury!" cried the man. "You dare call me a cyclops?"

Caldwell's face suddenly burst into a grin.

"My apologies," he stammered, "but I would not have guessed in a hundred years that you would have known the name of the cyclops in *The Odyssey*."

The man spat into the sand. "So only uneducated men should inhabit the caves of Queensland — is that it?"

Despite the angry man in front of him, Caldwell laughed.

"That's not it at all — I just didn't expect it."

Caldwell extended his hand in friendship.

"Come, let us try again. My name is John."

The man appeared afraid of the hand and backed up a step.

"You think because we've both read *The Odyssey* that you can just walk in here?"

Caldwell chuckled. "Yes, in fact, I do. And I bet I can do it with a single word."

42

The ragged man watched with distrust as Caldwell leaned forward and whispered a lone three-syllable word into his ear.

And then he sighed.

The man's hand moved slowly — as if from a great distance — until it paused in front of Caldwell. When Caldwell shook it, the man said, "My name is Michael."

They stepped outside and sat on a dune that looked over the water. The light reflecting off the waves was dazzling, blinding them both for a moment. There had been a heavy feeling of dread inside the cave, and they paused while it slowly dissipated.

Caldwell had felt that there were others in the cave, but it became apparent that Michael was alone. Soon Michael began to talk, and with the surf as a metronome, he told his tale.

At first, he was upbeat, describing his two canoes and all the supplies he'd stored for the long journey. He had spoken to no one in months, and the words just flowed out. But as he recounted losing one boat after the other and then the long walk to the Cape, the weight of the journey settled in, and the light faded from his eyes.

"And that's how I ended up here with nothing, unable to continue my travels," he mumbled in the end, his head held low.

Caldwell stood and brushed the sand off his legs. He looked back at the cave, still sensing something ominous about it.

He glanced at the canoe propped on the logs and said, "But you have a boat right here — where did it come from?"

Michael chuckled and gestured at *Tortoise*, "This is one of the canoes I lost earlier. I found it washed up on this beach. Thought my stars were changing, but without tools, the repairs have been slow in coming."

Caldwell walked around the boat, examining the craft. It didn't look like any repairs were going on at all. Michael had mentioned his earlier canoe had a mast, sail and outrigger, but this boat had none. It seemed Michael had stalled on his journey.

"You said you arrived here in May? So, you've been living in that cave for three months?" asked Caldwell.

Michael seemed unable to process that fact and stared at the craft in front of them. He had been following the tides and the moon — but time had stretched painfully in the cave. And it was a strange place, too. Sometimes he would wake in the black night to hear someone crying. *Best not to mention that right now,* he thought, *or this bloke will think I've gone bonkers.*

Beyond the breakers, *Outward Bound* rode the waves. They could see several figures on the deck, peering their way.

"That's my wife, Mary, and my two boys, John and Roger," said Caldwell.

Michael grunted, his eyes more concerned with the yacht's rigging and the cut of her bow.

Caldwell asked, "And what is the purpose of this voyage? Do you have a destination?"

Michael was quiet for so long that Caldwell didn't think he was going to answer. The waves pounded and hissed.

Eventually, he said, "I'm trying to get to Dutch New Guinea — maybe the Solomons after that."

Caldwell stared at the rough, dugout canoe and had to bite his tongue. His first thought was that it'd be impossible in that craft.

Instead, he asked, "Why?"

Again, Michael remained silent for a long time before speaking.

"I wanted to do something extraordinary," he eventually said, softly, his voice barely audible behind the wind.

Now it was Caldwell's turn to remain silent. He thought of the long journey across the Pacific and how his brush with death had turned into a guiding light. In his mind, that ordeal had created a separation between those living ordinary lives and himself.

"Something extraordinary?" asked Caldwell.

And then, after a beat, he added, "Like the journey of Odysseus?"

Michael stared him dead in the eye but didn't speak. Instead, almost imperceptibly, he nodded.

Caldwell looked at the shell of a man sitting next to him and doubted he would ever be a clerk or postal employee. Even though he could see that Michael was still a young man, he knew he was destined for an unorthodox life.

It also dawned on him that Michael was about the same age he had been when making his ill-fated crossing of the Pacific. He wanted to help the twenty-seven-year-old but wasn't sure Michael was ready for it. Afraid of the look of despair in Michael's eyes, Caldwell changed the subject.

"How do you get by here? Did you manage to salvage any of your supplies?"

"Almost nothing," answered Michael, shaking his head. He patted the sheaf by his side. "All that was left in the boat when I found it was my rifle and another cane knife that I'd converted into a stabbing spear."

Michael pointed to the base of a tree where the rifle now leaned. "The gun is useless — rusted beyond hope."

Then he picked up a long stick with a cane knife mounted to the end. The flat blade was about a foot long with a slight hook at the tip. The material was not thick, but the edge looked sharp.

"It's been useful for hunting and foraging along the shore." He patted the cane knife in the sheath by his waist. "The other one I keep close in case of trouble."

"And food?" inquired Caldwell.

Michael nodded at the surf. "Oysters, fish, coconuts — anything I can find along the shore. Sometimes I dig for crabs in the mangroves."

He looked down and rubbed his left foot. "A few months ago, I stepped on a stonefish and couldn't walk for a few weeks — but it seems to be all better now."

Caldwell nodded. He knew he should go soon but didn't want to. For some reason, he didn't like leaving the man to hide in his cave alone. It seemed like the kind of trap that could do a man in.

They talked then about the progress Michael had made since moving into the cave. About digging out the canoe and dragging it to the cave's entrance, about scavenging up and down the beach looking for suitable logs for a replacement outrigger, and the fruitless search for cloth for a new sail.

"I've even hiked over to Elim Beach. There's a Mission there, although I tend to avoid the people. But they have good mango trees and don't mind if I take a few from time to time."

Caldwell glanced at the tide and saw that it was going out. He asked Michael to walk with him to his dinghy. They strolled quietly.

On the way, they passed a small tidal pool where two small whiting fish were stranded. Michael snagged one quickly and stuck it in his mouth, eating it raw. He grabbed the other one a second later and plopped it in his mouth too.

A little further down the beach, he picked up a floating, green coconut that was rolling with the surf. He tossed it in the air like a rugby ball and then dropped it in the sand when they came to stand by the dinghy.

"I would like to leave you with a few things if you don't mind," said Caldwell as he stared down at his small craft.

Michael was appraising the little boat and barely heard him.

Near the bow, on the inside of the hull, Caldwell had fastened a plastic first aid kit. Below it, two plastic jugs filled with water sloshed around. Caldwell retrieved the water containers and handed them over.

Michael's eyes lit up as he saw them. He accepted the water gratefully, and Caldwell wondered which he valued more – the freshwater or the plastic jugs.

Then Caldwell opened the first aid kit to reveal bandages, gauze, safety pins, iodine, aspirin and scissors – as well as another small bundle wrapped in cloth.

While displaying its contents, he said, "My mother was a nurse, and she always insisted I travel with a first aid kit. I've got a bigger one on *Outward Bound*, but I always keep the dinghy stocked too."

Opening the small bundle of cloth revealed a glass jar filled with wooden matches. The younger man's eyes lit up.

"I've missed the warmth of a fire."

Caldwell's eyes gleamed. "I bet."

Then he added, "Maybe with a fire for cooking, and after some attention to your injuries, you can finish your repairs and continue on your journey."

Michael stared at the beach, his eyes drifting to the north end where his journey lay ahead. Caldwell sensed the younger man imagining the distance that stretched between him and his goal. He knew how important it must be to him.

Caldwell said, "You have to keep moving. Mark my words, if you stay in that cave too long, your dreams will die—and pretty soon after that, you will too."

Michael nodded but remained silent. Something bothered him. Finally, he said, "I don't know if I can take all this."

Caldwell saw now that Michael was proud and didn't want to be considered a refugee despite his status. With a cold shock, he realised the young man might walk away from aid because of some moral reason. Caldwell thought of his own state of mind when he had been starving—paranoia mixed with desperation—and wanted to avoid it now.

He remembered *The Odyssey* and shrugged. "You have been my host, and I simply want to acknowledge that with a gift."

Michael shook his head. "I've been a poor host."

Caldwell held his tongue, choosing his words carefully.

"You said you are heading up Cape York? Then you will pass Horn Island eventually."

Michael nodded.

"Well, I'll be in that area for the next six months or so. When you arrive, you will be my guest—and you can entertain my family and me with stories of your adventures."

Still uncomfortable, Michael nudged the green coconut with his toe. Then his face lit up, and he grabbed the coconut and handed it to Caldwell.

"Take this with you, so I feel like we truly exchanged gifts."

Caldwell smiled. "Happy to."

He glanced at the skies and added, "And get to work right away — you really should be on the water in the next month or so if you want to take advantage of the southeasterlies. I can imagine it would be a miserable voyage if you try to do it when the rains arrive."

Michael nodded, then helped Caldwell drag the dinghy to the water's edge.

Caldwell had one leg in the dinghy when he suddenly stopped. "I can't believe I'm not leaving you with any food."

Michael shrugged. "You've given me more than enough."

"No, I haven't," said Caldwell. "We're heading to port — our stores are just about depleted. And I can't linger in this area."

The news had little effect on Michael, but Caldwell couldn't let it go. He'd been so hungry on his crossing that he'd boiled the soles of his shoes and eaten them. In his eyes, the worst thing you could do was leave a man hungry.

He said, "When we stop at Barrow Point, I'll have a friend — Bill Hudson — come by and drop you some supplies. He's got a fishing boat and passes this way from time to time."

Michael appeared not to have heard but instead asked, "Would you mind doing one thing for me?"

"Anything," said Caldwell.

"When you are safe in port, give my dad a call. It bothers me that he might be worrying about me."

Caldwell frowned. "I'm glad you have a dad that cares — mine was an alcoholic and left when I was fifteen."

Michael was overcome with melancholy. "My dad would be with me right now if he could be — he's my biggest fan."

"It is a wise child that knows his own father," said Caldwell, quoting *The Odyssey*.

Michael held the bobbing dinghy while Caldwell scribbled down the phone number. Then he pushed him over a wave, out to sea.

Back onboard the *Outward Bound*, Mary was anxious to hear about her husband's excursion. His young boys crowded around him while their eyes searched the shoreline for Michael.

"So, what was your *Wild Man* like?" she asked, jesting, not realizing she'd come close to the mark. The boys were wide-eyed.

Caldwell laughed nervously. "Quite scary, at first. I was on the verge of fleeing when I first found him."

"But when I watched you through the binoculars, you boys were laughing like old friends—how'd you pull that off?"

Lifting his eyes to meet her gaze, she noticed a slight twinkle.

"You wouldn't believe me if I told you," he said.

"Oh, really?" she asked. "Now I have to know—how did you bring him around?"

Caldwell grinned. "You know how I'm always talking about Homer's *Odyssey*?"

She rolled her eyes. "I respect how you value that silly old book—but really, I find it one of the most boring stories I've ever read."

He pointed at the shore. "Well, he doesn't find it boring—or silly. On the contrary, I suspect he guides much of what he does by that book. And I think the only reason he opened up to me is a concept in *The Odyssey* called *xenia*."

"What the heck is zeenmia," asked his oldest son, John, who was now eight.

"In *The Odyssey* are lessons regarding how a host should, or should not, behave," Caldwell replied. "The Phoenicians called it *xenia* or guest-friendship, and they had all sorts of rules regarding how a host should act."

"John, are you telling me he likes you because you both are obsessed with a two-thousand-year-old book?" asked Mary.

Caldwell laughed. "That's precisely it! *Xenia* governs how you treat a guest—feeding them, offering a place to sleep, giving gifts, allowing them to leave when they want—it's all there in the book."

Mary shook her head and chuckled. "Well, that's all very interesting. I'm glad you made a new friend, but I'm sure we'll never see him again."

"On the contrary," interjected Caldwell, "I'm sure we'll see him when we stay at Horn Island. I invited him."

"And what makes you think he'd travel all that way to see you?" asked Mary while raising an eyebrow.

Caldwell was enjoying himself now and chuckled as he replied, "*Xenia*."

Chapter Six

Michael's Story – Age Ten
(Sydney 1940)

Daniel Fomenko proudly walked his son across the stately grounds of the Sydney Church of England Grammar School. The second semester had just begun, and Michael would soon be a student there.

The previous year, Daniel had secured a position as a schoolmaster, teaching economics, ancient history and geography. He also coached cricket. He was excited about the job but more enthused for his son. The school was commonly referred to as Shore, and the professors at the elite establishment aimed to produce the next generation of Australia's leaders who excelled at learning and sports.

It was precisely what he believed Michael needed to feel accepted in their new country. Daniel had applied for residency, but it would be years before any Fomenkos were officially citizens.

Daniel bit his tongue, trying not to overwhelm the ten-year-old with too much info, and didn't tell his son the school motto:

"They hand on the Torch of Life."

But he could barely control his enthusiasm as he pointed out the various buildings and courtyards. "That's the War Memorial

Chapel," he said. "Eight hundred and eighty Old Boys served in the Great War, and one hundred and twenty-two gave their lives."

Michael gave him a blank stare, and he added, "Old Boys are what we call graduates of Shore."

On the pathway ahead of them, an older man with a black robe approached. "That's L.C. Robson," said Daniel. "He's the Senior Mathematics Master and acting Headmaster."

Michael nodded, and his father quickly added, "You stay on his good side—he's been here seventeen years, and not much goes on at Shore that he doesn't know about."

Michael meekly let his eyes fall as the man approached and noticed them. "Hello, Professor Fomenko—this must be your son."

Daniel nodded. "Yes, this is Michael."

Michael shook his hand and mumbled, "Hello, sir."

"Well, hello, young mister Fomenko," began Master Robson, "I'm so excited to have you with us. You look like a rugged young lad—I hope to see you participating in some sports. Shore men are quite accomplished in all the sports—rugby, cricket, sailing and cross country running."

Michael timidly whispered, "Yes, sir," which caused the man to laugh loudly. Daniel fidgeted nervously. His son was adapting well to Australian life, but he was shy and didn't speak often.

Robson thought a moment and then said, "Out of all the lads we have here, I believe you are the only non-Australian but don't worry, we'll find a place for you."

"Thank you, sir," said Daniel, both agitated and relieved by the comment. He didn't like his pending citizenship brought up, but the man had sounded genuine.

He stepped aside so the older man could continue on his way.

Robson gave Michael a parting glance as he passed and said, "Don't worry—we'll make an Old Boy out of you yet."

Michael would not begin classes until the next week, and Daniel had a lesson in ten minutes, so his son would accompany him and audit his first lecture at Shore. While they walked to the hall, Daniel thought of the last few years.

It had taken eight years for Daniel to get his family from that cave in Manchuria, China, to Sydney, Australia, and it hadn't been easy. For a while, they had been happy in Harbin, China. Daniel had found employment lecturing at the University, and the children were healthy and well-fed.

Soon after their arrival in Harbin, Elizabeth had discovered that she was pregnant, and that February, the Fomenkos welcomed their second daughter, Nina Oom.

When hints of war in the Pacific began to emerge all around them, both Daniel and Elizabeth thought it best to move on.

Next, they lived in Japan in the countryside around Kobe. According to Inessa, it was a magical place filled with beds of violets, but Michael only remembered skirmishes with local boys who didn't like outsiders. When in 1937, Japan invaded China to initiate the Pacific War, the family began their immigration to Australia.

Daniel came first, and his reputation as a Soviet dissident landed him work delivering talks on the ABC radio under the heading, *An intellectual under the U.S.S.R.* He spoke primarily about Russia, its political situation, and its people.

He was an astute intellectual and proficient in several languages, including Russian, French, German and English. And having been partly educated in England, he understood his audience and how to entertain them. Later talks included: *Vladivostok, The Elements of Aesthetics in School Life,* and *I Follow Marco Polo.*

When Hitler attacked Poland in 1939, Daniel was called upon to comment on Russian affairs and Russia's place as an ally in the fight against the Nazis. He was proud of Russia's progress in many scientific fields and the military contributions in the war against Nazi Germany. Soon he was a well-known commentator, and it was partly this reputation that landed him the job at Shore.

Daniel was glad the first lecture that Michael would attend was on *The Odyssey* by Homer. He had a sneaking suspicion that Michael — a reclusive boy even at ten — would enjoy it.

The classroom was filled with about fifteen students when they arrived, all upperclassmen and older than Michael. Several gave him inquisitive stares. It was a few minutes before the hour, and most were seated already or just sitting down. Michael was relieved to find an empty chair in the back of the room.

Daniel walked to the chalkboard, erased a few notes from the previous class, and wrote: *The Odyssey* in large, cursive letters. The students all settled down, and by the time he turned around, they were faced forward and silent. Even as a ten-year-old, Michael detected that the kids liked his father and respected him.

He jumped right into the lesson. "Good morning. Today we will again discuss the story of Odysseus, king of Ithaca, and his journey home after the Trojan War. Can anyone tell me one of the central themes in the story?"

One student in the front row quickly blurted out, "Homecoming!"

"*Nostros* — homecoming," said Daniel, nodding, and quickly asked, "Another?"

"Wandering," offered a different student.

"Yes," said Daniel, "there is definitely a lot of wandering in the story. How about one more?"

After a slight pause, someone said, "Guest-friendship."

Daniel responded, "Good! *Xenia* — guest-friendship."

He turned to write the word *Xenia* on the board while speaking.

"*The Odyssey* is filled with lessons on how a host should, or should not, act. It's easy to see examples of people who do not exhibit *xenia*. For example, Polyphemus the cyclops did not exhibit *xenia* when he moved a massive boulder to seal the entrance of his cave and proceeded to eat Odysseus' men."

A few chuckles erupted from the back of the room.

"And neither did the witch-goddess Circe when she turned half of his men into swine."

Daniel looked over the young men and asked, "Now give me a few examples of good *xenia*. What are some of the things a good host does?"

This subject was not new to the class, and they began firing answers at him: "Providing food and drink... bathing... giving fresh clothes... entertainment... offering a place to sleep."

Daniel nodded at each answer. Then, when the students had quieted down, he walked to his desk and picked up a copy of *The Odyssey*.

"This book was composed in Homeric Greek around the 8th or 7th century BCE—can anyone tell me why themes like *xenia* are in it, and why they are still relevant today?"

Michael found himself drawn into the lecture, even though he didn't know any details of the story. He watched as a student in the front row answered his father's question.

"Is it because how we treat guests hasn't really changed in the last few thousand years?"

Daniel gave the lad a rewarding smile. "That's it exactly. How we treat guests is still very important. And not just how you greet and entertain them—what does *The Odyssey* say about the end of a visit?"

The students began throwing out responses again: "There's an exchange of gifts... the guest is granted a safe journey home... and you can't keep the guest longer than they wish."

"All good answers," said Daniel. "What we need to remember is Homer's story of endurance is about a man who was alienated and mistreated by most of the people he encountered. And despite how strong and clever Odysseus was, he never would have completed his epic journey without friends—without *xenia*."

Suddenly Michael couldn't wait to read this mysterious book.

Map 2 - Cape Flattery to Princess Charlotte Bay.
Illustration by Tom Fish.

Chapter Seven

The Odyssey IV – Cape Flattery
(September 1958)

*O*ver the coming weeks, Michael pulled himself together. With a crackling fire, the cave didn't seem so bad. In fact, with a few improvements, it began to feel like home.

He made a lamp out of a coconut shell, filling it with the fatty oil from ripe coconuts, then floating a wick of fibre in it. Next, he cut bundles of beach grass with his cane knife and used them as bedding.

He still occasionally heard the crying at night, but a careful search had only revealed some Aboriginal drawings near the back.

I must be dreaming, he told himself.

The most significant improvement came from the medical kit Caldwell had given him. He washed his face with soap and hot water — boiled in a tin can over a flame — and bandaged his head wound properly.

He still had no mirror, but his fingers told him that the months since his accident had been enough; he had healed properly. There seemed to be no permanent damage to his eye.

One day he found a length of fishing line wrapped around a drifting buoy. He salvaged what he could, crafted a fish hook out of a shell, and began dedicating a few hours a day to fishing.

Before long, his cave smelled of sizzling groper or coral trout, and he began putting the lost weight back on.

The weather was picturesque, serene even. It lulled him into afternoon naps, and a part of him wanted to simply enjoy the new comforts of his home.

But deep down, he knew he should be on the water. Whenever a big gust of wind came through, he imagined it filling a sail. *Those southeasterlies won't last forever. I should be moving.*

Restlessly, he began with the repairs to his canoe.

He crafted another thwart and mounted a sturdy pole as a mast. He still needed to make another outrigger, requiring a couple of sturdy logs. And he had to find some rope. Without rope, he couldn't lash the outrigger together or hope to keep a sail rigged properly to the mast.

He found a mysterious chunk of metal that would serve as an anchor, but again, it would be useless without a rope.

His wandering led him again over the peninsula to Elim Beach, to the Lutheran Mission. On his first visit there, he had watched the residents from a distance, hanging back in the shade of a palm tree. He knew several of them had seen him, but nobody waved or acknowledged his presence.

Then he remembered his father's warning: His existence would be noted, and anyone who helped him might come under suspicion.

After months in isolation at Cape Flattery, it felt strange to be around people. But a side of him yearned to talk to someone — anyone. Since meeting the sailor named John, he'd had no other visitors; the shallow bay made the location unfavourable to boaters and local fishermen alike.

On subsequent visits to the mission, he hung back in the shade of the banksias by the beach. From there, only a few people could glimpse him, and under those circumstances, the local Guugu Yimithirr mob who lived at the Mission seemed friendly enough. They waved discreetly and sometimes motioned for him to help himself when he glanced at the mango tree full of ripe fruit.

They appeared to know who he was, and Michael guessed they had known he was living in the cave for a while. One day when the Mission courtyard seemed just about empty, an old man approached him, crouched by his side silently, and soon confirmed that belief.

"That cave you're in is a sad place."

Michael figured he was referring to living alone and said, "Oh, it's not so bad."

The old man shook his head. He looked deep into Michael's eyes as if trying to decide how much he should say. His skin was wrinkled and worn, and he looked like he'd seen a lot of life.

He began, "Long time ago, twenty-eight men and thirteen women and children were all killed at Cape Bedford. They hemmed in the women and kids in a narrow gorge, and shot 'em, and then shot the men on the beach."

Michael listened, wondering why the old man was telling this tale. A sea bird landed between them and hopped around. They watched it silently for some time.

Eventually, the man continued. "Four of those men swam out to sea and were never seen again. They say they drowned."

Michael's parents had immigrated to Australia when he was a boy, and his family bore no connection to past massacres of Aboriginals. But still, he felt guilty.

In school, he had learned of the hundreds of massacres throughout Queensland in the 1800s. Most were supposedly reprisals. The victims often included women and children.

The old man gave a weak smile, "Some say those four men didn't drown at all—but they made it to Cape Flattery, and they lived in that cave for a spell."

Michael thought of the cave and how he'd often heard crying and sensed others there at night. *Now I know why.* He pondered on how much sadness those men must have been filled with after all their families had been killed.

Michael began to fidget, and the old man sensed his disquiet.

He patted the sand as if saying the earth was not offended and said, "It's okay for you to stay there for a while, but even those men moved on eventually."

One afternoon, Michael made an excursion to the rural town of Hope Vale, located a few hours' walk beyond Elim Beach. The town had about one hundred and forty people, and that turned out to be too many. When Michael came upon a paved road, he stopped and huddled in the bush beside it, as if the black tar was the body of a giant snake.

He feared encountering the folk of Hope Vale more than the resident Aboriginals at the Elim Beach mission. Even though his body had healed, and he no longer looked hideous, he still felt certain that if anyone saw him, they would alert the authorities.

Living the way he did, Michael was no stranger to people calling him a vagrant. If he'd had something to trade, he might have pushed on and entered the town, but as it stood, he could only beg.

Before he left, he paused by a home with sheets fluttering on a line. He knew the thin fabric would never work as a sail; they weren't strong enough. And the clothesline wasn't ideal either, but at least it was a rope. He watched the sheets snap in the wind for a while before moving on.

As desperately as he wanted to be back on the water, he wouldn't let his journey turn him into a thief. *That's just what the police would like — then they could haul me back to Sydney as a criminal.*

When he returned to the Bay, Michael found a man waiting on the beach next to a wooden box. He was in his forties, a fisherman from his looks, and appeared uncomfortable just standing there. A small dinghy lay tilted on its side, close to the water.

Further away, in the deep water beyond the bay, Michael saw a fishing boat anchored.

It was apparent the man was there for Michael. He didn't know if he hadn't spotted his cave or had simply decided to remain in the open. His tracks showed he hadn't gone far.

Michael waved and walked over to him.

The man waved back, looking a bit relieved, and when they were closer, he said, "My name's Bill Hudson. John Caldwell asked me to stop by and drop off some things—you Michael?"

Michael nodded, "I am."

"Well, this here's for you," said Bill as he lifted the lid off the box.

Inside were two plastic water jugs, a bag of rice, one of sugar, several loaves of bread, a big stick of salami, a large chunk of cheese, tea and several thick chocolate bars.

While Michael looked it all over, Bill fished in his pocket and pulled out a note. He cleared his throat and read it, "*The men then landed on shore and entered the cave of Polyphemus, where they found all the cheeses and meat they desired.*"

"Does that make any sense?" asked Bill. "He made me promise to read it."

Michael chuckled, "It's from *The Odyssey*."

Bill gave him a confused look and said, "Who can figure the mind of a writer?"

Michael creased his brows, "A writer?"

Bill nodded. "Sure, he wrote a book about being lost at sea. I never read it—but I'm pretty sure it was called *Desperate Voyage*."

Michael's laughter shocked Bill at first. He'd read the book while still living in Sydney and dreaming of adventure.

Michael quoted, "My boat was in her trim, and rearing to be off on her long, ill-fated voyage," and then added, "That bloke?"

"Well, how should I know?" answered Bill.

Bill kept glancing at his boat, and Michael knew he'd be off soon, so he hit him with a question before he left.

"You ever hear about the Cape Bedford massacre?" asked Michael.

Bill rubbed the back of his neck while staring at his shoes. After a minute, he said, "The one back in 1879? Yeah, I know about it."

Michael asked, "Do you know what caused it?"

Bill nodded. "I heard two white men got speared, so they killed forty-something blackfellas in response."

Before Michael could ask another question, Bill had already turned back to his boat.

He yelled over his shoulder, "Caldwell said you'd be heading north soon—woulda thought you'd already been on your way—but when you pass by Barrow Point, you're welcome to call in."

Sheepishly, Michael nodded he would.

Three months after the initial visit by John Caldwell and seven after he first arrived at the cave, Michael was finally getting his canoe closer to being seaworthy. He had no calendar, but the way the sky had begun to cloud up again was a clear sign the rainy season was imminent.

A log washed up on his beach that was suitable for the outrigger, although it needed to be cut in half. Unfortunately, he only had his cane knives, which, although sharp, were thin. It took two days of little patient chops before he cut the log to length.

He had scoured the area for green coconuts and wove baskets from the palm leaves, eventually filling them with mangoes, crabs and oysters. He still had the four plastic jugs that Caldwell had given him. Three he filled with freshwater; one had developed a crack near the top, and Michael decided to use it as a bailer.

In an abandoned house near the Mission, he found a small length of rope. Not enough for the sails or anchor, but sufficient to lash the outrigger together.

An odd piece of driftwood turned out to be perfect, once carved up a bit, as a paddle. He'd considered putting in oar locks and trying his hand at rowing, but the outrigger prevented that.

He should have been happy and excited about his progress, but the darker the clouds became, the more he felt he'd missed his window. He should have been on the water months ago.

Maybe I'd be better off just staying in the cave until the rainy season passes. That thought battered around his head like a ship lost at sea, tormenting him. For a sailor tossed in a storm, land is not a friend, and he began to look at the cave the same way — a safe home is not the friend of the man on a journey.

As if on cue, the clouds began to roll in. Michael stepped to the mouth of his cave and watched them fill the sky to the horizon.

He drifted around the cave, kicking objects out of his way, cursing the monsoon. The thought of travelling in that weather depressed him, and he decided to wait it out.

He woke one night from a dream. In it, four Aboriginal men had stood by the entrance at dusk and slowly said goodbye to the cave. They looked healthy, although sad, but as they walked away, he detected a look of hope in their eyes.

In the inky blackness of his shelter, he lay awake thinking. In the back of his mind, he heard Caldwell's voice warning him, "Mark my words, if you stay in that cave too long, your dreams will die — and pretty soon after that, you will too."

Michael knew the man had spoken the truth. *I might not die physically, but whatever I consider dear to me will.*

A deep rumble of thunder drifted over the water and entered his cave. The power of it shook his chest.

Is that a challenge? Are you daring me?

He stepped outside and noticed a flicker of white by his boat. He walked to it and saw somebody had left a coil of rope. There was no one around, but he glimpsed bare footprints leading away.

He thought of the old man he'd talked to by the Mission. Had he decided to risk everything and help Michael?

I guess it was pretty obvious I needed rope.

He looked back at his cave, which he'd fixed up quite nicely. A fire was burning in the corner. Plenty of food. Dry shelter. If he stayed, he would be fine. *But there's more to life than comfort.*

When the next lightning bolt lit up the sky, Michael began pushing his canoe towards the water.

North of Cape Flattery, Russel Jervis was piloting a motorboat through rough seas. The 9-metre launch, *Myrenia*, was open, with no cabin, but thankfully the forward deck was covered so they wouldn't take on a lot of water unless conditions got worse.

With his eyes glued to the white-capped seas ahead, he was surprised to see another craft out in the bad weather. At first, he thought he'd sighted a drifting tree, but on closer inspection, he discerned it was a dugout canoe being paddled by a large, determined man.

The man was battling like hell, fighting for every bit of forward progress against the heavy winds.

He thought the man might need rescuing, and when they got closer, he prepared a line. But upon seeing the launch approach, the man—Michael—raised a hand and gestured that he was okay.

Russel turned to his mate and said, "That bloke has to have the devil breathing down his neck to be out here."

The last they saw of him was his paddle flashing on a backdrop of monstrous, black-bellied clouds descending from the north.

The folks at the dock all took a good gander at Michael when he paddled into Barrow Point. The late afternoon had blackened with another storm closing in. He pulled ashore as spidery lightning flickered across the skies.

A foot of water sloshed around the bottom of his canoe, several coconuts and a plastic jug floating in it. Gone were all the supplies he had meticulously collected—either eaten or washed away.

After tipping out what water he could, he dragged the craft above the highwater mark. He then walked away unconcerned.

I dare someone else to try to pilot that boat.

He entered the town and got a few strange looks for his ragged appearance. His shorts—the last piece of clothing he owned—had finally fallen off.

He was now completely naked except for a roughly made loincloth, the type the locals called a laplap. It had three parts: a front flap, a back flap, and a cord tied around the waist.

His lack of clothing seemed to shock people as much as his wild appearance. He had not shaved or cut his hair in ten months — he hadn't even combed it. And there was a look in his eyes that seemed to dare people to challenge him.

Those he encountered were all too happy to point him to Bill Hudson's house and get him off the street.

Bill looked a bit stunned when he glimpsed Michael on his doorstep. When they'd met at Cape Flattery, the young man hadn't appeared quite so untamed and out of place as he did now.

Standing in his doorway, the man looked absolutely feral.

His wife, Doreen, stood behind him, and he didn't know how to break it to her that this was the bloke he'd invited to stay with them.

Having been a fisherman's wife for many years, Doreen wasn't squeamish. She took one look at Michael and invited him in.

Michael seemed to enjoy the shock he'd caused. He glanced down at his loincloth, chuckled, and said, "Maybe the laplap's too short, and I should make a grass skirt for when I come into town."

"You'll be right," she said while running a hand over his long mane of hair, "but we have to do something about this."

His head was covered with shoulder-length black hair that strayed in unruly curls over his warm brown eyes. His thick eyebrows looked like caterpillars attempting to crawl into the tangled mess on his head.

Michael might have resisted her efforts to groom him, but the steaming bowl of fish chowder she put in front of him provided ample distraction. Compared to what he'd been living on, the food was extraordinary, and he scoffed it down in a daze.

Over the next hour, while he ate three bowls of chowder and chatted, Doreen cut his hair.

Before the next day was over, she'd encouraged him to shave with Bill's razor too.

At breakfast, Bill dropped a copy of *The Cairns Post* on the table and said, "Looks like you're famous!"

Michael seemed unconcerned with the paper, but Doreen picked it up and read the first few paragraphs.

"Michael Peter Fomenko, age twenty-seven, of Sydney," she read out loud. "That's you?"

Michael nodded timidly. "I'm twenty-eight now, but yes."

Then Doreen's face broke into a wide grin.

"They say the locals call you The King of the Coral Sea!"

Michael met her gaze, a twinkle in his eyes. "Now that has a ring to it."

He stayed with them for two nights. When he woke on the third day, Bill tried to get him to stay longer.

"You should rest a bit more," he said, "it's blowing its guts out… it'll be miserable on the water."

Michael shook his head, "No, it's time to move on."

As he said goodbye, Doreen took in Michael's unique and easy way of being. She would miss him and the stories about his journey. By watching his eyes, she could tell that every interaction he had with nature was sacred in some way for him. Since his arrival, she had noticed how he would stare off across a room, and regardless of where he was, you'd feel he was looking at some distant horizon with the sun glinting in his eyes.

Bill had other concerns, and before he let Michael paddle away, he pulled him aside. "The Cold War has this country bound up in fear and mistrust," he said. "I don't know how to say it, so I will: people might think you're crazy."

Michael couldn't stop the laughter that burst out of him.

Bill shook his head. "I'm serious. Heck, last week, some bloke got roughed up at the theatre for not standing when they played God Save the Queen. Folks fear any deviation from normal — it threatens the good order of society."

Michael placed his hand on Bill's shoulder and spoke earnestly. "I can only be true to myself."

Bill nodded, feeling like he had somehow let the young man down. "Then you best avoid the coppers."

When Michael paddled north that morning, the sky was ominous, but he was smiling and upbeat. Bill talked him into accepting a pair of shorts.

"Just in case you have to go into a town," he said. "Don't give them a reason to haul you in."

Before he was out of sight, the clouds obscured the sun. The Hudsons wondered if he would make it to the next town, let alone Dutch New Guinea.

Bill worried about how the people further along the Queensland coast would treat him. He'd held back when talking to the young man and wished Michael had read the article, which debated his controversial journey. A lot of Australians weren't ready for a man like Michael. What would happen if everyone wanted to shrug civilisation and live in the wild?

For his part, he was glad some people still wanted to make their own way, and he wished Michael luck.

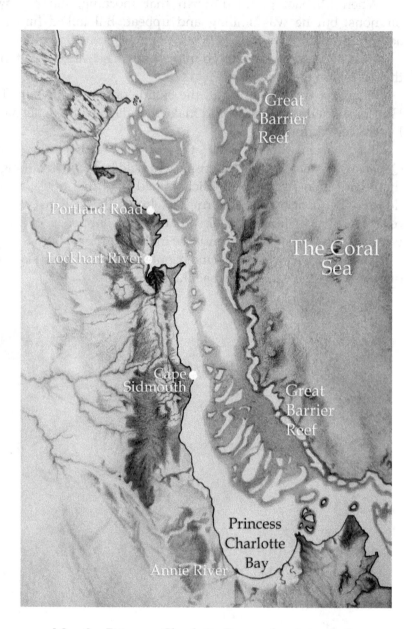

Map 3 – Princess Charlotte Bay and points north.
Illustration by Tom Fish.

Chapter Eight

Michael's Story – Age Nineteen
(Shore 1949)

*I*n the nine years since arriving at Shore, Michael had made a name for himself in sports. He was now a highly competitive athlete and regularly placed in the top three ranks in competitions for the shot put, discus, high jump, broad jump and decathlon events.

His body resembled a Greek warrior of old. Tall and lean, with chiselled shoulders and a lanky, muscular lower frame that made hurdles and the long jump appear easy. It seemed he was a league ahead of the competition.

The state medals kept piling up, and he enjoyed the slight fame his brawn and skill brought him while somehow remaining the quiet, shy boy he'd been when he first arrived.

One morning in March, his father greeted him at the breakfast table. "Here's our champion!" he shouted over a conversation between Elizabeth and two of his daughters.

Michael had three sisters now, Inessa and Nina Oom, plus a third one—Renee—born shortly after the family arrived in Australia. She was eight now and currently teasing Nina about a boy. Inessa was not around, most likely already off to work.

Daniel held up *The Sunday Herald,* and Michael asked, "Did they run anything on yesterday's meet?"

Daniel grinned. "They sure did." He cleared his throat and read a line, "Michael Fomenko won the State Junior Broad Jump title with a jump of 6.7 metres."

He offered Michael the paper so he could see a photo of himself soaring through the air. Behind his flying self, he noticed a classmate, Campbell, standing there watching him.

"I beat Campbell by a full metre," said Michael.

Daniel nodded. "I saw that," he said, "and his father didn't look happy about it."

Campbell's father was a well-known donor at Shore, and Daniel hoped this wouldn't lead to any trouble.

Later that day, Michael was in the Chapel attending a lecture from Father Gilfeather. At thirty, he was one of the youngest priests at Shore and a favourite of the students. Michael was a senior now and comfortable with many of his professors, but he preferred the young priest to most.

"Shore, at its heart, is a Christian school based on biblical foundations," he began. The other students sat back and relaxed; they'd been to these lectures before and knew it wasn't all going to be about religion.

"And we express our dedication to God through Chapel services, Christian studies, our community life and curriculum here, and one other thing... can anyone tell me that thing?"

A boy in the back raised his hand, a slight smirk on his face, and asked, "Sailing?"

Father Gilfeather beamed benevolently. "That's right, sailing."

The young men began to smile and loosen up as the priest continued, "Shore was the third Sydney school to take to the water, and since the 1890s, we've been rowing in the GPS Competition to great results. And we've also produced some great sailors!"

Several boys in the back dared *woop* encouragement.

Father Gilfeather stole a fleeting glance at the heavens and said, "And it is my firm belief that if Jesus were here today, he'd be a sailor, and that when you are on the water — wind in your hair, waves parting before you — that you are closest to God."

Now he had their attention. Father Gilfeather was often tasked with giving odd lectures — subjects that didn't always fall into traditional classes — but everything always looped back to God and sailing. Sometimes, half the fun was figuring out where he was going.

On the wall was a map of Australia, with a good portion of Asia visible above it. Father Gilfeather walked to the map and, using a wooden pointer, indicated Sydney on the continent's lower right-hand side.

"Here we are at five o'clock — and then up here," he said, pointing to the top middle of Australia, "is Darwin at twelve o'clock. The Australian monsoon — or the wet — occurs when a trough develops over northern Australia and then drifts south. We get over three-quarters of our annual rainfall during this time."

He next pointed to the top of the map, far above Australia, and said, "But it doesn't begin there. The low-pressure zone starts way up in Asia, eventually drifting south by Sumatra and Borneo, then descending to the Philippines and Java, and finally passing Dutch New Guinea and northern Australia to drift down to us."

He stopped and looked over the dozen boys sitting before him and said, "These storms affect the currents and the winds — and why is that important to us?"

"Because wind and current are important when sailing," ventured a boy sitting next to Michael.

Father Gilfeather nodded. "That's right — and sailing brings us closer to God."

He took the pointer and followed the route of the monsoon down through Asia to the Arafura Sea, then west into the Coral Sea, and finally along the east coast of Australia and into the cold southern depths by New Zealand and Tasmania.

"For nearly half the year, the currents run clockwise around Australia, bringing moisture and northwesterly winds — but when the monsoon is over, they reverse, and the southeasterlies arrive. And why do we love the easterlies?" he asked.

This time several students answered at once, "Because they let us sail!"

He nodded. "Okay, I see you get it—you bloody well should being Australians. My point is, the southeasterlies are coming in the next few months, so let's get ready for them. Be smart on the water."

Michael stared at the map and asked, "What would happen if you tried to sail up there during the monsoon when the northwesterlies were blowing?"

Father Gilfeather shook his head. "Well, there'd be storms and a few cyclones to deal with—and heaps of rain. All the rivers flowing out to the sea would be overflowing. But the biggest problem would be the currents and wind trying to blow you south."

"But *could* you do it?" asked Michael.

The Father smirked. "All things are possible, but I'd suggest if you were to attempt something like that that you make sure Jesus is right there with you."

By November, Michael was broadly acknowledged as the best athlete at Shore. Daniel couldn't have been prouder of his son and sat next to him on the lowest bench of a row of bleachers.

"I believe you could stop competing altogether and still have a good enough rating to make it into the Commonwealth Games," said Daniel.

Michael beamed and was on the verge of replying when Campbell strutted by and gave him an evil leer. The lad climbed the bleachers and sat by his father, a few levels above and behind the Fomenkos.

Several minutes later, Campbell's father began lecturing him on how to improve his distance in the shot put competition, which would start shortly. And then this led to the man denigrating his son's main competitor—Michael.

The Fomenkos couldn't hear everything, but it was clear the man was speaking about Michael. Every other word was, "communists... refos... Russians..."

It wasn't worth pointing out that the Fomenkos were Australian citizens now. Michael losing and Campbell taking his place was the only thing that would appease him.

Daniel sat there with his head bowed slightly, pretending he hadn't heard a thing. It broke Michael's heart to see his father like that. Once he'd been so proud of his former homeland, Russia, but he did not endorse the communist government or the heavy toll it had taken on the Russian people. These days, with the Cold War in full swing, it was better not to draw attention to their Russian heritage at all.

When they announced the next round, Michael and Campbell made their way to the shot put ring. Not far from the bleachers, Campbell roughly bumped into Michael.

His smirk angered Michael so much that he stormed over to the ring and began warming up, determined to outperform his rude classmate.

When they announced the results for the shot put competition a half-hour later, Michael had won with 12.6 metres. Campbell wasn't even in the top three competitors.

By the edge of the field, Michael saw Campbell—red-faced—standing by his father, who was talking heatedly with the acting Headmaster, L.C. Robson.

Robson looked uncomfortable and cast a guilty glance at Michael and his father as they walked by.

One month later, Daniel Fomenko sat at his breakfast table again, reading an article in a Sydney newspaper called *The Truth*.

Suddenly he sat up straight and yelled out in a voice that grabbed everyone's attention.

"*Bozhe moi!*" he yelled (Goodness!) "Everyone, come here!"

Quickly, Michael was by his side, with several of his sisters crowding around as well. Nobody knew what had gotten into Daniel, but he was more excited than any of them could remember.

"It says here that the New South Wales State Amateur Athletics selectors have chosen twelve of the fourteen athletes to represent the State at the Australian track and field championships in Adelaide."

He stared proudly at his son and added, "And Michael is one of them!"

Everyone cheered, and Elizabeth hugged her son.

Daniel continued reading, now louder, "These athletes will have all expenses paid at the event and training camps."

Now all of them were hugging Michael. Daniel added, "Do you realise how monumental this is? This will cement your place in the Commonwealth Games — and two years after that is the Olympics!"

He hugged his son. "I'm so proud of you."

Chapter Nine

The Odyssey V – Princess Charlotte Bay
(February 1959)

*M*onths before, when the rains first began, Michael had hardly noticed them. The sky had been overcast for so long that he no longer sought out the sun or its golden rays. The misty precipitation that fell on his shoulders, so lightly, seemed like a gift from Calypso, the love-starved daughter of Poseidon.

Then, as the clouds thickened, the mist collected into droplets. First as tiny, delicate pearls of moisture, then later, as big pregnant drops that splattered when they hit the wooden deck.

Michael paddled along happily through these soakings, feeling mesmerised and connected to the sea and his sturdy canoe. The birds sang despite the moisture, and the days kept flowing into one another.

He was glad to be on the move again, to be journeying north, and the weather seemed of minor consequence.

Eventually, though, the heavens unleashed sheets of heavy rain that cascaded down in torrential downpours. That got his attention as he was forced to stop and bail out his canoe.

The rain murmured and hissed when it hit the water, whispering to him about dangers ahead. It grew so loud at times, roaring madly with the wind, that it absorbed all other sounds until he found himself voyaging through an otherworldly blue void.

He remembered Father Gilfeather stating in a lecture, "The Monsoon isn't fully in swing until the continuous rate of fall is greater than 7.5 mm per hour."

Facts and numbers! he scoffed, *I'd like to see Father Gilfeather ride out one of these storms.*

Hour after hour, he struggled north through the bad weather. Sometimes he couldn't see more than the bow of the boat. To calm his mind, he counted strokes—like when swimming—and stared at the deep water below the canoe.

And it was there, when he grew exhausted, that he saw things—impossible things—like shadowy sea deities and other aquatic creatures moving in the inky blackness below him. One day he thought he glimpsed a drowned heroine swimming in the depths. She leered up at him from her watery grave, and he was so distracted he almost capsized when a random wave came along.

He wondered if Jesus was by his side—a prerequisite for this adventure, according to Father Gilfeather.

For weeks on end, his efforts seemed futile. The rain poured on land and sea, swelling the rivers that flowed out to him. The great East Australian Current surged mightily, wrapping around the northeast corner of Cape York before plunging south.

He often had no idea how far he had travelled, the constant downpour obscuring the shore even when only a stone's throw away. The careless wind had taken his craft several times and blown it offshore where the current and gust grabbed it, requiring all of his strength simply to make it back to shore—losing days of progress each time.

He had always travelled slow, but now he dragged his feet—especially when he found a shelter. He would never stay long, just enough to get a fire going and find something to eat. But his fare was basic—raw shellfish and coconuts—and did little to raise his spirits.

Huddled under dripping vegetation, his mind shut down like a lizard on a cold night. He didn't think about his parents or siblings. He didn't plan repairs to his boat or guess where he might obtain more supplies. He didn't wonder if there were people out there who would help him or share his dream. Instead, his mind dwelt only on his destination—a shining beach in a far-off land. He imagined the islands in the Arafura Sea, serene and inviting, as a gentle tide lapped at them.

When on the water, he occasionally reflected on his former classmates and professors at North Shore. He had no regrets, but a patient voice in the back of his mind whispered that he wasn't through with that Sydney crowd yet.

At times, when the pounding rain and wind seemed on the verge of defeating him, he would lean forward and put his last effort into his strokes.

I'm not done, he told himself. *I haven't quit. I'll show them Old Boys a feat none of them would dare."*

On a quiet morning in February, Michael propelled his canoe along the southern end of Princess Charlotte Bay. He turned away from the sea at the mouth of the North Kennedy River, following the flow of the high tide as it swept inland.

He looked spent. And a little defeated by the knowledge that in two months since leaving his cave, he'd only travelled about 250 kilometres. *I would have sworn I covered more distance.*

With slow, methodical strokes, he continued up the river until he sighted a cattle barge — the *Myrenia* — anchored at the confluence of another river that spilled in from the west.

From its railing, several men watched him paddle slowly in their direction. The men noted his haggard appearance and that he'd been at sea for some bad weather. Around his waist, he'd looped a rope that had its other end tied to the thwart—a precaution against getting swept away.

His hair had grown unruly in the salt air, and long, despite being cut at Barrow Point less than two months prior. He wore only a pair of ragged shorts, had no shirt or shoes, and sported a thick beard. The exposure had roughed and darkened his skin.

He still carried the stabbing spear and wore a leather sheath around his waist with his old cane knife sticking out of it.

He had no possessions other than the spear and knife: no clothes, food, sails, or water jugs. There wasn't even a bailing bucket—something he desperately needed. A few coconut husks floated in the shin-deep water that sloshed around inside the canoe.

Michael's eyes contained an angry glare, as if he wanted to confront whoever had sent the monsoon rains. The men held back, observing him quietly. The only sound was of Michael's paddle strokes and the birds.

One of the men whispered, "Anybody know who that bloke is?"

Another commented, "He looks like a blackfella."

"Nah," answered a third man. "He's dark, but he's no Aboriginal—we should help him."

His words floated over the water, and Michael bristled when he heard them. *They can see I need help – would it really matter what race I am?*

A fourth man, Russel Jervis, said, "I saw that bloke down by Flattery Bay a few months ago when I was on the *Wewak*. Can't believe he's been battling the monsoon since then."

The canoe bumped against the bigger boat, and the men stared down at Michael until one of them asked, "Where you from, mate?"

A list of responses floated sluggishly through Michael's mind, which wasn't used to conversation. He didn't want to say Sydney. *Why give these blokes the satisfaction? Of course, they'd be more than happy to help me if they knew I was white – but that shouldn't matter.*

Instead, he answered, "Russia" and received blank stares all around.

Russel snapped to before his companions and said, "Come on, let's get him some tucker—he looks about ready to drop."

Over the next half hour, Michael waited while they scrounged up some supplies from their kitchen. They gave him water, flour, sugar, matches and rice. Russel passed down a three-pound fish dangling from a string and said, "You look hungry, mate, take it. I'll just catch me another one."

While handing down the supplies, one of the men asked where Michael was going.

"Thursday Island," he replied, and again received blank stares. He couldn't tell if it was because they'd never heard of the island or that they didn't think he could make it.

When they were done loading, he reached into his pocket and pulled out a tattered note.

He stood and held it up, but nobody moved to accept it.

"Fine," he said, pocketing the note. "Thank you."

He sat back down and began paddling further up the river when one of the men shouted out, "Hey, what's your name?"

He stared back, straight-faced, and said, "Nobody."

Before he was out of sight, the men began talking about him.

"Who d'ya think he is?" asked one man.

A crewman commented, "Don't know who he is, but he's doing it tough."

Russel Jervis said, "Boys, I reckon that's the bloke they call The King of the Coral Sea. That crazy bastard is trying to paddle all the way to Dutch New Guinea."

Michael continued up the smaller river that flowed behind the *Myrenia*. It was called the Annie, and he hoped he might find a suitable place to camp among the mangroves. He spent most of the day meandering along the twisting waterway, conscious of the pull of the river — and how it changed with the tides.

When suddenly he looked up and realised the sun had fallen, he knew he needed to stop. He'd been paddling mindlessly for hours. His exhaustion was beyond measure.

He tied off to a mangrove with the rope the old man had left him — the other end still tied to the thwart. His stomach had been rubbed raw from where he had wrapped himself with it. But the night was calm, and he no longer feared the weather.

In a few heartbeats, he was asleep, his head leaning against the inner hull.

Through the night, the river gently played with his boat. When the tide went out, the canoe slipped into the middle of the river. The rope looked like it might snap or become untied at any minute, but it never did. When the tide came back in, the canoe closed the distance to the bank and nudged against the verdant mangroves.

Through it all, Michael slept like the dead.

He never saw the moon make a rare appearance between the silver clouds or the light breeze that picked up just before dawn and shook the leaves free of dew and rain.

With a sack of flour underneath him, he hugged the side of the boat, the fingertips of his left hand dangling in the water. For most of the night, he embraced his exhaustion dreamlessly, but closer to dawn, his mind replayed the time in Manchuria when he had sensed a tiger.

The tide was at its midpoint, the water still, but Michael twisted and rolled in his attempt to wake from the dream in which something was watching him. Finally, just before dawn, when a soft pink light swept over the land, Michael opened his eyes.

And less than a foot from his head, he spied an enormous male crocodile staring right at him.

His heart stopped. *I'm done.*

The croc stared back coldly, and Michael slowly sat up.

"You're a big boy," he told the saltwater croc. "I'm surprised you didn't grab me already."

Scars and a bullet mark on his head indicated that more than one man had tried to grab his hide for the lucrative crocodile skin industry. Michael guessed he was about six metres. Because of poaching and unrestricted hunting, most of the big crocodiles had disappeared.

Michael looked over his possessions and spotted the fish. He pulled the string out of its gills and tossed it at the head of the crocodile. "Here you go," he said.

The croc didn't move as the fish floated in front of its snout.

"I think I'm gonna name you Poseidon," said Michael.

Suddenly, Poseidon snatched the fish in one lightning-fast motion and disappeared in a move that set the canoe rocking.

That's a fine welcome, thought Michael. *I hope he doesn't mind if I rest up here a few days.*

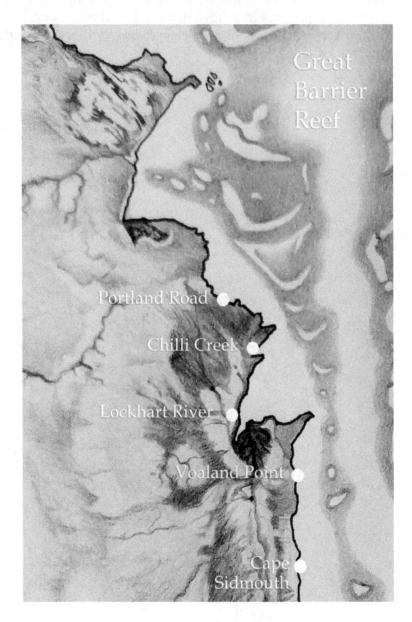

Map 4 – Cape Sidmouth to Portland Road.
Illustration by Tom Fish.

Chapter Ten

Michael's Story – Age Twenty
(Shore 1950)

Daniel Fomenko stood on the far end of a field, watching a group of boys run through rugby drills. Usually, being anywhere on the school grounds picked up his spirits, but not today.

Michael approached him from behind, noting how his shoulders sagged. *The Sydney Morning Herald* had run an article that morning which stated the athletes going to the championships in Adelaide would now have to pay their own way.

Michael didn't have to be told that his parents couldn't afford to do that, or that his father would accept that fact as a failure on his part.

"I just don't understand it," stammered Daniel. "*The Herald* said you were the best all-around athlete in the Northern Suburbs Club."

"I know, Pa," said Michael.

"And just last month, they printed that you were the leading athlete in the 100-metre swim, broad jump, shot put and 400-metre sprint. Surely, they must know if you don't attend, they will be losing one of their best athletes."

Michael stared at his father. He felt hollow inside. For nearly a decade, he'd chased the goal of representing his state in the Commonwealth Games, and now it was finished.

"They know, Pa," said Michael hollowly.

Daniel scanned around him as if there were someone he could ask for help or clarification. "I doubt that. I must talk to Master Robson—I can't believe he knows. I doubt more than a half-dozen students come from families who can afford to pay their way. Who would that leave them with?"

It broke Michael's heart to say the words, but he had to.

"That would be the kids from the richest families," he said.

Daniel shook his head. "I can't imagine they would go to that extreme."

Michael didn't reply. He remembered seeing Campbell and his father angrily talking with the acting Headmaster, L.C. Robson, after one of their last meets. Robson was an old man now… maybe he had given in to the pressure.

His father's eyes sank to the ground.

After a pause, he asked his son, "What are you going to do now?"

Michael took a deep breath and lifted his head, and then in the most confident voice he could summon, said, "I'm not sure, but I have to do something."

Daniel nodded and tried his best to shake the fog of depression that was overwhelming him. "Maybe it's just as important how you do it. I know through sports you hoped to gain pride by representing Australia in the games—and you gave it your all. But perhaps now it's more important that you do something for yourself, something you enjoy."

"I can't imagine what that would be," said Michael.

His father shrugged. "You may have to wait… but it will come to you."

Chapter Eleven

The Odyssey VI – Lockhart River
(March 1959)

*T*he Annie River made for a restless camp. The twisting watercourse ran back for at least ten kilometres, one bend looking just like the last. The tide coming and going, always pulling on the river, made the place feel in constant flux—like a yoyo barely working in low gravity.

Michael yearned to find a quiet spot where he could light a fire and cook a few meals, but two things prevented him.

First, the mangroves and shrubs along the bank were so thick and sprawling that he had difficulty reaching land. The few possible camps he'd found all but disappeared when the tide came surging in.

Secondly, and more importantly, Poseidon the crocodile was still around.

Poseidon was adept at keeping hidden for such a big croc, but a few times, Michael had spotted bubbles trailing under his canoe.

He knew he was close.

During the day, Poseidon would swim by and give Michael a good stare. At night, he glimpsed red eyes watching from the river.

Even when he couldn't locate the long reptilian body, Michael often sensed the croc's eyes on him.

Michael had seen plenty of crocs in his time in Queensland, but they had been small and skittish because of overhunting. He, too, had killed a few smaller crocs for their skins, but he had no intentions of fighting Poseidon. One look, and you could tell he was a crafty old beast.

Although estuarine crocodiles travel great distances, using the sea currents to get to remote islands that might have sea turtles or other delicacies, Poseidon stayed in the Annie River. Michael wished he knew if the beast watched him out of hunger or curiosity.

You're better off not knowing that one, mate, he told himself.

A few days later, Michael followed the Annie downstream into the North Kennedy River and, shortly after, flowed back into Princess Charlotte Bay. Over the next few weeks, he tried to force his way up the left-hand side of the Bay, continuing his efforts up the Cape York Peninsula.

He encountered blustery winds and vicious little storms that tossed his canoe about like a cork in the ocean. More than once, he pulled ashore only to realise the wind had blown him south, and he had lost ground despite a full day of paddling.

It seemed the rain never stopped, only occasionally it reduced to a dull drizzle.

He found no good camps either. Often the weather obscured visibility so severely that he couldn't see the shore, and he was sure he'd passed spots that might have offered shelter. He was concerned more with riding in the high tide and not hitting reefs, and as a result, spent most nights lying under his canoe in the sand.

I should have stayed longer on the Annie, he thought about a week later. Then he remembered the way Poseidon had eye-balled him, and he was glad he'd moved on.

Ironically, the next day some movement underwater caught his eye, and he glimpsed the massive croc swimming north with the current, easily outpacing his craft. To witness the saltwater beast using the water currents for his journey was a sight to behold.

Wonder where he's heading? thought Michael.

Several times Michael had sighted a 14-metre boat that ran with an Aboriginal captain and crew. The ship, *Yola*, had two masts and a 30-horsepower engine that allowed her to motor right through the bad weather.

The first time he'd seen them by Cape Sidmouth, a hundred kilometres north of Princess Charlotte Bay, both boats had been fighting a strong headwind. For a few moments, they had run parallel to each other, and between strokes, Michael had looked sideways and grinned.

The men of the *Yola* had been all smiles as they shouted back at him, encouraging his efforts. Although they were in a bigger boat, they had all at times battled the waves of the Coral Sea.

The second time they passed him, two weeks later, they were more sombre. They were just off Voaland Point, and when they were close, the men made gestures and offers to tow him.

"No, thanks," shouted Michael.

The wind had temporarily died down, so the captain of the *Yola*—a man named Jabiru—cut the engine and floated next to Michael's canoe. A crew member threw a line to Michael and secured him.

Jabiru ordered someone to bring Michael water, and then they talked casually about the weather for a few minutes. When Jabiru asked his destination, Michael just motioned north while swallowing a large gulp.

One of the crew members remembered reading about Michael in the paper. Soon word had spread to Jabiru, who stared long at Michael before speaking. "You're trying to get to Dutch New Guinea?"

Michael nodded.

Jabiru shook his head. "Not gonna happen the way you're goin'." Then he explained how little progress Michael had made over the last two weeks.

Michael let his head drop.

"No problem," said the captain, "we'll take you to Lockhart — to the Mission. Mr Warby will want to see you."

At this comment, the other men all nodded. Michael surrendered to their goodwill.

They welcomed Michael on board and arranged to tow *Tortoise* behind them. The crew were a ragged looking lot: barefoot, bare-legged and mostly bare-chested, in worn khaki shorts. Yet, they wore expressions that could only be described as pride as they helped him aboard. There was something about them that shouted their knowing that they were equal to any man.

"Lockhart River is less than fifty klicks away," said one of the men, "you'll be out of the rain by dinner."

Michael sat with his head down, trying to shake off his exhaustion. A part of him felt it was cheating to accept help, but he knew he'd done everything possible and still hadn't made progress. He sighed, and when he lifted his head, he realised a dozen men were watching him.

He nodded at them and said, "Thank you."

Several put their hands on his shoulders and squeezed. They were no strangers to fatigue.

It was late in the day, and the sun made a rare appearance, lighting up the water and the distant land. Michael stood and scanned the horizon, not used to riding this high above the water.

He looked over the boat, which appeared to be used for fishing. "Nice boat," he said. "I hope I don't get you in trouble for towing me."

Jabiru said, "She belongs to Lockhart Mission. The Mission owns three boats, employing sixty men, and we answer to nobody but Mr Warby."

Several men behind him nodded proudly. He heard someone mutter, "We help who we want."

The Lockhart River Mission Superintendent, John Warby, watched Michael as he entered his office and took a seat. The last article he'd read about the lad claimed he was "fined down by lack of food, and his legs were covered in boils," but the man that sat before him appeared to be in splendid health.

Yet, he still looked to be in the middle of an ordeal. Michael's gaze shifted around the room uneasily, and he had a hungry look in his eyes that Warby didn't think food would appease. Regardless, Warby had ordered a dinner of fried fish and spuds to be served, knowing the lad would have an appetite.

Michael's eyes bulged as they set the plate in front of him, but before he dug in, he said, "Please don't punish the crew of the *Yola*. I've heard that they're not supposed to assist Europeans — me in particular."

Warby shrugged graciously and motioned for Michael to begin eating. "We are a Christian organisation, so we will help who we see fit. And the boat is owned by The Lockhart River Aboriginal Christian Cooperative Society, so the men will stay out of it."

He stared down at Michael and added, "If someone needs to answer for you, it will be me."

Michael stopped mid-chomp, and Warby burst out laughing. "You are welcome here, my friend. The Diocese purchased the *Yola* — and two other boats — to be independent and make our own money. And now we have helped a fellow Christian."

Michael had never been very devout, and he found in times of need, he would look to nature before praying to the heavens for assistance. The profound awareness in nature that he perceived from time to time far outweighed any experience he ever had studying scripture or in a church.

Those few instances when he did shout out, it could just as easily have been to his father, or Zeus, before looking to the Christian God. But maybe he still had Jesus sitting by his side.

Father Gilfeather was convinced the Lord loved sailing, and perhaps that wasn't so far from Michael's inkling that God was to be found in nature.

Michael remembered his father's lecture on *The Odyssey* and said, "My father would have said the crew on the *Yola* exhibited good *xenia*."

Warby nodded, a raised eyebrow hinting that he got the reference. "Those men and the boats represent hope for all of us," he said. "I would only expect good conduct from them towards our neighbours. Working on that boat has done wonders for some of them."

The meal had ended, and Michael was preparing to leave when he uncomfortably broached the subject of supplies. "I'd like to pick up a few things before I continue with my journey, but…"

Warby cut him off with a gentle hand gesture.

"I'm not sure if you're aware," he began, "but your father has sent word all along the Queensland coast that if you need supplies, he will foot the bill."

Michael sensed some movement of the lonely, hollow place his soul had resided in throughout the rainy season. It had started with the understanding smiles of the crew of the *Yola*, warmed more during the meal with Warby, and now hearing of his father's support made him glow inside. He felt overwhelmed with *xenia*.

"Thank you," he said, "I'll make a list of what I need. I also plan on writing a letter to my folks that will need posting, but when you telegraph my father for the money, can you tell him I'm doing alright?"

"I can do that," said Warby.

Michael stayed at the Mission for a week. He washed and showered with soap and hot water, shaved off his beard, slept in a bed with clean sheets, and ate meals with the others in the community hall.

Warby had helped him with the supplies, too.

The bottom of his canoe was now packed with flour (23 kg), sugar (16 kg), rice (9 kg), salt (2 kg), tea (250 g) and other sundry items. All of it was wrapped in plastic and held in place by straps.

When he finished loading, he went to Warby's office to say goodbye—he'd be on the water at first light.

The man sat at his desk with an open newspaper — *The Sydney Morning Herald* — in front of him. "Says here that the Queensland Police are 'investigating' you, Michael. Police Commissioner Bischoff feels he should prevent you from going ahead with your plans because others might get killed trying to save you if things go wrong."

"Then tell 'em not to search for me—I don't need their help."

Warby nodded. "I'm not going to tell them anything," he said. "They can manage without our assistance on this one. But I want to warn you to lay low. I've seen their idea of 'investigating' and you don't want any part of it."

Michael nodded soberly. He shook the man's hand and gave him the letter to post to his family in Sydney.

"God be with you," said Warby as he shook his hand goodbye.

That night, while everyone at the Mission slept, Michael left silently. A sudden fear of being arrested kept him from sleep. He shoved off into the water, slowly following the coast north.

While he paddled, he thought of the letter he'd written to his family.

"Lonely for you after not seeing you for such a long time," it began. And he was lonely for them. Staying at the Mission had brought him out of the long stupor that had accompanied these past months during the wet.

The truth was he missed people. He yearned suddenly to be at Horn Island to see John Caldwell again. If it hadn't been so far away, he might have paddled back to Barrow Point to see Bill and Doreen.

Instead, he had only his journey. And he was still forcing his way through the miserable monsoon. *Although it should be tapering off soon,* he thought. *If I can hold out just a few more weeks, the easterlies will finally arrive.*

More lines from the letter accompanied each stroke, and he let them flow through his gentle thoughts, "Love to all... want you to come north and live with me... don't worry about me... newspaper cuttings are a bit exaggerated..."

With no moon or witness watching from the shore, Michael disappeared into the black night.

Chapter Twelve

Michael's Story – Age Twenty-Five
(Cairns 1955)

*M*ichael left Sydney feeling like a failure. For five years, he had tried his hand at various occupations, but nothing seemed to fit. His latest employment for the Adelaide Steamship Company had been fun, but he still sensed something was missing in his life.

To make matters worse, the Summer Olympics would be held in Melbourne the following year, and it was all anyone could talk about. Michael didn't mind walking away from sports; he just regretted that he hadn't found anything to take their place.

Shortly after his twenty-fifth birthday, he made his way to Cairns, in the northeast corner of the country. He would miss his family, but they were busy with their own lives. Inessa and Nina Oom, the older girls, were in their twenties and no longer lived at home. Renee, the baby, was now a teenager and suddenly had a social life.

Michael had lingered in the quiet home, nestled in the Northbridge suburb of Sydney. They lived only a short walk from the Shore grounds, and the buildings and young men strutting around in their uniforms were constant reminders of his past — *my failures.*

Daniel still taught at the school, but since his son had been unable to pursue his dream of being a professional athlete, a fire had gone out in him. He continued to lecture, but his bright vision of Australia had dimmed somewhat.

Michael had taken the train north from Sydney. He wanted to get as far away as he could and rode the line for nearly two thousand kilometres, following the Queensland coast to the train's northern terminus at Cairns.

Before he'd even disembarked, he knew he'd found his new home. When they stopped at Innisfail, he watched the Johnstone River flow by and yearned to get off and explore, but they were only thirty kilometres shy of Cairns, so he stayed put.

He loved Cairns at first sight. It was right on the water, and the orderly square blocks and shops painted white gave him a sense of order he hadn't expected.

The town was in a pitched battle against the perpetual growth of uncontrolled vegetation. In the middle of the road, trees shot up effortlessly, and others existed with houses seemingly built around them. Vines and the creeping tendrils of a million plants crept along the windows sills, over gates, and up posts, engulfing entire roofs.

There were patches of grasslands and eucalyptus, but mostly he sensed the encroaching jungle that crept in from all sides; it took his breath away.

A monsoonal downpour had just rolled through and cloaked everything in mist, and all around him, the hills were alive with birdsong. The dewdrops sparkled restlessly on leaves that appeared polished by the rain.

The thick, humid air seemed charged when Michael stepped out of the station with a bag thrown over his shoulder. He'd heard about the infamous weather in the north where they received over 650 mm of rain a year. More than one person had warned him it would drive him back to Sydney.

Not a chance, he thought. The heat and humidity were so intense; it was like he moved through a vapour. His shirt was soon soaked, but it didn't bother him. For some reason, he liked the warm mugginess. He sensed his body relaxing into it despite breathing the wet, steamy mist the Queenslanders called air.

It was the first affinity he felt with the place: the air.

Michael knew the dense rainforest canopy prevented moisture from escaping, in turn creating an extraordinary, cool microclimate that was ideal for plants. As a result, numerous epiphytes like ferns and orchids thrived in the constant high temperatures and rainfall.

Michael took a deep breath and filled his lungs, determined that he would thrive in the thick air as well.

The skies cleared, and white billowy clouds sailed by in a sea of rich, dense blue. Coconut palms waved, and in the sunshine, every colour of green imaginable filled his sight. Sparsely scattered amongst the jungle, like rare gems, were flowers of purple, orange, pink and white.

He paused at the end of one block when confronted by a wall of bamboo twelve metres high.

He stopped at a fish and chip shop and walked away with a newspaper-wrapped bundle of batter-dipped fried fish. The meal was greasy and still too hot. He burned his tongue, but it was the first warm meal he'd had in days, so he devoured it anyway.

While walking through town, he passed under a massive fig tree. He heard commotion above in the branches and glanced up to see hundreds of fox bats clinging upside down by their feet.

They squawked a chorus at him, and Michael knew: *This is where I must live.*

He drifted around the area, asking about work or places he should see, and it didn't take him long to realise he wanted to be in the countryside, not a city.

Before he left town, he decided to leave a few things in Cairns. He'd heard about a Russian guesthouse on Terminus Street behind the train station, and he made his way there.

The neighbourhood supported a few other boarding houses, some of which he understood doubled as brothels. The area abutted the railway freight shunning yard, where out-of-town Aboriginals met and stayed the night when passing through.

When Michael approached the guest house, a young girl of about ten eyed him from the porch.

"You need a room?" she asked.

Michael shook his head. "I only need to stow a bag."

She said, "My name is Losha — my parents own this place."

Then she looked around to make sure no adults were within earshot and added, "Normally, they charge for storage. It's what they do for the men who cut cane — but I'll do it for free."

"That would help a lot, Losha," said Michael. "I don't have much. I just don't want to lug it all around with me."

She smiled. "It's no big deal. I'll stick it in the storage room until you return."

Michael thanked her and continued on his way.

From Cairns south down to Innisfail, he followed the sugar cane country for seventy kilometres. Sometimes he enquired at the farms or mills for work, but mostly he just wanted to see it all. He slept in the open or bunkhouses, and there was plenty of fresh fruit he could eat, so he didn't need much money.

A change came over his appearance, too, although he was so enchanted with the world around him, he didn't notice. His hair became unruly, and he let a beard grow. He wore less and less clothing and went without shoes whenever possible.

The most significant change was in his eyes. When he first arrived, there had been a look of defeat in them, but the more time he spent in the countryside, the more that faded. Now, he began each day excited, wondering what adventure lay in store.

The foreman at the cane farm in Deeral didn't know what to think of Michael when he approached him for a job. One look in his eyes was enough for Michael to see the man didn't care about any sorrows he might have tagging along.

"You ever cut cane before?" he asked.

"Nope," replied Michael.

The man looked over Michael's frame, which was solid enough, but he paused after glancing at his hands.

"Those hands are gonna be raw after a couple days," he said.

Michael nodded. "I'll deal with it."

This job won't beat me, he thought.

The man sighed, "Alright. I'm short-handed, so you'll have to do." He introduced himself as Jack.

The cane fields grew along the Mulgrave River in a stretch of land about two kilometres wide and twenty kilometres long. Beyond the river, the land rose until it met vast, jungle-clad mountains. Here the cultivation ended abruptly. Other peaks reared into the purple distance.

Michael looked down at the earth, a bit uncertain of the bright scarlet colour. He remembered hearing that the soil here ran over thirty metres deep.

Looks like freshly spilled blood, he thought.

They discussed the wage, and Jack handed him two cane knives. "The bunkhouse is over there," he said, pointing. "Be up at first light."

Over the next few days, Michael cut cane with three other men. The work was brutal. Mosquitoes buzzed all around them, and the air was thick with the musty smell of the earth. The other men kept to themselves, as did Michael, the hours passing while they remained lost in the physical toil. Jack was surprised at how well Michael held up.

Michael thought the job exhilarating. It was good to swing the cane knives after not having worked for a while. Even the blisters on his hands felt like some form of penance.

At times he lost himself while gripping and hacking at the mighty stalks—some as thick as his arm—the long green blades shaking some six metres above him.

Twice he glimpsed large snakes, but the sense of fear only made him enjoy the experience more. He wrote to his parents, hoping to convince them to move to the area.

Near the end of his first week, he paused at the end of the field, staring at a great wall of tropical forest that rose before him. Bird calls and hoots came out of that dark paradise, accompanied by the screams of a million insects.

He longed to explore it.

He sighed and returned to work but stopped short as a large creature cautiously stepped out of the rainforest. It was a flightless bird called a cassowary, standing nearly two metres tall. Michael guessed it weighed almost sixty kilos. Its head was blue with a horny growth, called a casque, sitting on its forehead. It looked prehistoric as it eyed him, bobbing its head a few times.

Michael watched, fascinated, as the bird stepped closer.

The cassowary walked on three-toed feet, and one of the toes sported a claw that was almost twelve centimetres long.

Michael couldn't take his eyes off the beast and continued to watch even after he heard Jack whistle from across the field.

Michael looked Jack's way for a second, and when he glanced back at the forest, the cassowary had mysteriously disappeared. He yearned to follow it, but he had work to do, and the boss was watching.

He sensed he was at a crossroads. Over the last few months, he'd tried to get by with less; to renounce materialistic possessions and get away from the lifestyle he'd been raised in. When he'd arrived in Queensland, he knew he'd discovered something that he vitally needed, and he didn't think owning things would get him closer to whatever that was.

Then what is the best way to embrace it? he asked himself.

On the other side of the field, Jack talked to a fellow farmer who was passing by. They noticed Michael standing there gawking at the jungle, and after a moment, Jack whistled.

"What's up with your man?" asked the neighbour.

"Not sure," replied Jack. "I just took him on, and I've been waiting to see how he finishes the week."

They watched Michael glance their way and then back at the jungle. Then, a rumble of thunder announced a scattered storm was moving their way.

The men looked at the sky to the north, where the sound had come from. When they peered back across the field, Michael was gone.

"Looks like you're gonna need another field hand," said the neighbour.

Jack chuckled, "No sweat off my back — that kid hasn't been paid for the week."

The neighbour said, "Well, it's still gonna cost you the two cane knives he walked off with."

Jack chuckled. "I'll take that trade — besides, how far can he go with only a couple knives?"

Michael stood in the gloom of the jungle, staring out at the bright green cane field. It was just a few steps away, but what a difference. Out there was the world of man, with its schedules and deadlines, but under the jungle canopy, things ran by different rules.

Old rules, thought Michael. *This place is older than time.*

In a sense, it was that old — 180 million years! The Queensland rainforest he stood in was one of the last remnants of an ancient tropical forest that once covered the supercontinent of Gondwanaland.

There were two layers to the forest. The canopy high above was comprised of giant Kari pines, palms and eucalyptuses. The ground level plants included ground and tree ferns, orchids and lichen-covered tree trunks. All of it steamed in the heat of the day.

Much of the upper canopy lay obscured by a layer of leafy, sagging vines that endlessly stretched from treetop to treetop. The luxuriant growth filtered the light dimly to reveal marvellous glimpses of flowers and butterflies.

Birds streaked by, their iridescent tail feathers flashing red and yellow. Fungi and exotic mushrooms appeared intent on devouring any stumps or trunks on the shadowy ground level, chewing relentlessly on the moist wood.

Michael felt his inner soul being embraced. From the moment he stepped into the verdant forest, he sensed it was aware of him. The presence of this "Nature God" confirmed his belief that he'd made the right decision in walking away from man.

I will not be going back to the field, he thought. He looked at the knives in his hand, which he'd forgotten he was holding. He didn't fear the dangers of this place, although he knew he should. There were countless poisonous spiders and venomous snakes, plus lizards, boars, crocodiles, and who knew what else.

I feel like I've come home.

He wanted nothing more than to live harmoniously in the seemingly impenetrable jungle. A massive strangler fig rose before him, and he skirted around it, trying to find a trail that led deeper into the forest. But there were none. It was as if nobody before him had even dared.

Mysteries seemed to sprout up all around him in the giant trees, hanging ferns and tangled vines. Only a few metres away, he spotted a massive spider's web stretching between two trunks. He peered closer and saw it housed hundreds of huge, speckled arachnids that watched him motionlessly.

He stepped around an ancient palm, and suddenly a large creature was charging at him. He felt a searing pain where it brushed his leg, and then he was propelled backwards.

The animal grunted angrily and came at him again.

Michael got his feet under him and ran for his life.

Chapter Thirteen

The Odyssey VII – Portland Roads
(April 1959)

*T*he night remained calm and quiet, the waves suspiciously subdued. Michael took full advantage and paddled his canoe almost twenty kilometres up the coast. He sensed the coppers would be searching for him before long, and he wanted to put some distance between himself and them.

Shortly before the sky began to lighten, he glimpsed starlight reflecting off a small stream flowing out to sea.

There was nowhere to hide on the water. Even tucked back on a beach, he was exposed, and Michael knew he needed to lay low for a while, out of sight.

The stream seemed the perfect place to disappear.

He would later discover the watercourse was called Chili Creek, and it ran back about a kilometre, usually no more than thirty metres wide. Beyond the stream, the Iron Range caught the first rays of the sun when it poked up over the blue horizon.

The narrow mouth of Chili Creek was shallow, and for most of the year, didn't flow regularly into the sea. But with all the monsoon rain, it trickled out with just enough water to drag the canoe over it.

Michael grunted his way from the beach into the smaller flow of water, sometimes pushing, sometimes dragging, the craft. His extra supplies added to the weight, but he was glad for them and the knowledge that he wouldn't have to leave the creek for a while.

He would wait there, somewhere up that creek, until the monsoon ended and the southeasterlies began.

Once on the stream, the water deepened to about a metre. The creek widened after that, always with plenty of shrubs and tall palms to hide him from search planes.

He spent most of the day exploring Chili Creek after covering his tracks and those of the hull moving through the sand. In the early afternoon, he settled on a camp about three-quarters of the way in, on an elevated shelf with plenty of cover.

He pulled his boat ashore, climbed up onto the shelf, and within minutes fell into a deep sleep.

When he awoke, close to sunset, the sky was filled with thousands of giant fruit bats — flying foxes — as they moved north to some unknown destination. They glided in awesome, pulsating sheets, like harbingers of doom with the sky lit red behind them.

Over the coming weeks, he settled in at his new camp, which had all the essentials: privacy, shelter and freshwater. It was not visible from the air or the sea, the trees along the bank forming a perfect canopy, and because the tide didn't overflow into the creek, the freshwater remained untainted and drinkable.

A slower examination of the creek revealed that there were fresh fish in it. He set about making several basket traps for bait and finding a limb suitable for a fishing pole.

At the Lockhart Mission, he had purchased fishing line and hooks, and now he put them to use, catching trout and catfish at will. When he had more than he could eat, Michael broke into his stores and used some salt to preserve the fish.

The elevated shelf had an easterly view, so he could easily see any search planes following the coast. Since his first day at the new camp, he'd noticed an unusual number of them flying by, and he felt sure some were looking for him.

He worried that the people who had helped him might get in trouble. Even though John Warby didn't seem to care who he aided, the police might. He remembered the pride and courage of the crew members of the *Yola*.

Those men risked their lives whenever they went to sea. And they weren't going to get rich as fishermen — the bulk of their profit went to the Mission. But they were filled with pride, happily contributing whatever they could to help the boat return with a good catch.

It wasn't all about making money for the crew. That's why they understood his journey so much better than any of those Old Boys ever would. While he worked at creating his new camp, one thought echoed in his mind: *I hope someday I can be as happy as them.*

He had yet to encounter any crocodiles, but on the muddy banks, he glimpsed their tracks. The prints he saw were not from a large croc, but their hides would still be worth some money after he salted them down — if he dared show his face in a port where he might sell them.

Whenever he heard a plane's engine, he paused and watched the sky. As a teenager at Shore, he'd seen countless military planes leaving Sydney for the war against the Japanese empire. He could identify most by sight and sound. The boys had made a game of it, and whether it be a single-engine, single-seat fighter, a fighter bomber, or a transport aircraft, Michael knew its firepower capacity, engine and range.

He listened to the planes pass by, pretending to be unconcerned, as he went through his daily chores.

One afternoon, he came across a worn log near the creek's mouth. He considered turning it into a smaller canoe. Two boats gave him more options, and with the southeasterlies due soon, he wouldn't be limited to paddle power.

He towed it back to his camp, propped it up on a log, and proceeded to slowly hack away at the ends until it was about three metres long. The inside, he hollowed out by placing hot coals on the log and then gouging out the burned area.

He also created a trail that ran along the creek, so he didn't have to paddle the whole way when he wanted to take a peek to see if any boats were scanning the coast for him.

Thanks to these projects, the days passed smoothly.

After another month, however, he grew restless. He missed his family, and his supplies were beginning to dwindle. He'd given up on the new canoe after developing a deep crack that ran through the entire log, and he lacked a project.

What fueled his impatience was that the monsoon was now completely over, the skies clear and blue, and he could feel the weather changing.

And suddenly, he realised that when he'd been at Lockhart Mission, he had not purchased a sail. With the constant rain battering him, it had been the last thing on his mind.

But he would need one soon.

At first, he'd hoped he might collect enough crocodile hides to pay for it. The reptile's belly was very much sought after for handbags and shoes—the world's mad desire for it would come close to wiping out the crocs before the 1960s were through.

But a careful search led to finding only a couple of them in Chili Creek. He killed them with his cane knife, regardless, and used salt and sand to cure their hides. At night, he ate the flesh by his fire.

When the first traces of a breeze from the southeast passed along the sea, he knew it was time to move on.

He just had to make one stop first.

On a silvery night with a half-moon dangling over the water, Michael paddled to the settlement of Portland Roads, located about fifteen kilometres to the north. He pulled his canoe ashore and walked along the jetty quietly, not wanting to wake all of the residents in the location's three houses—just one of them.

He stopped outside the home of the postmaster, believing he'd be the person in a position to help, and knocked gently on his door.

Gone was the "I don't give a damn attitude" he'd worn at Barrow Point. Now, he didn't want anyone to remember him—and if he hadn't been so desperate for a sail, he wouldn't have come to the settlement at all.

Hector McDonald peered into the evening and made out a figure wearing only a laplap. The newspapers had been full of Michael's story and the search for him, so he knew who the stranger in front of him was.

"What can I do for you?" asked Hector.

"I need some canvas for a sail," replied Michael.

He then pointed at the jetty and added, "I've got a few croc skins I can trade."

Hector shook his head. "I don't need your hides—I know who you are."

Michael froze. Finally, he asked, "Do you intend to turn me in?"

"Heck, son," said Hector, laughing, "I don't let the police or that Sydney crowd tell me how to live my life. Why don't you come inside for a feed?"

Michael glanced down at his half-naked form and shook his head. His shorts had finally decayed off him.

"I'm not dressed properly," he said.

"I don't care about that," said Hector dismissively.

Michael shook his head, "No, I've got plenty of grub—I just need some sailcloth."

"Okay," he said, "hold on."

Michael waited in the shadows. He thought he saw one of the curtains of an upstairs window move.

Finally, Hector returned with a folded length of thick canvas.

"This should do," he said.

Michael squirmed as he accepted it and said, "If you call my father in Sydney, he'll pay for it."

Hector nodded. "I've heard that—but I don't need his money. I've been reading about you, and I want to help. I always wished I'd gone on an adventure when I was young."

A blush appeared on Michael's face, creeping around his beard. He nodded thanks, and Hector added, "Is there anything else you need? Anything? I want to help."

"Well, I could use some tomato sauce," said Michael hesitantly.

Hector seemed overjoyed to disappear back into his house and return with a large tin can of it.

"Here you go, son," said Hector when he returned. "Now get on your way before they throw you in the jail—there's a lot of people looking for you."

Michael thanked him and slipped back onto the water.

The following day, late in the morning, Michael was still on the sea, trying to make it back to Chili Creek. The weather had turned, and his progress was slow. He was about three-quarters of the way there when he heard the dull drone of an aircraft engine coming from the south.

There was nothing to do but keep paddling. He knew the plane would not be a boat plane that could land near him on the water, and there were no roads inland, so he did not fear immediate arrest.

But once they sighted him, they would come.

Before long, he spotted a bomber. It was an Avro Type 694 Lincoln, built by the British, now repurposed for non-war use by the Australian government. The four engines purred loudly as it got closer.

It was flying low to the water for such a big plane, and when it got closer, he glimpsed people in the cockpit.

Michael waved, indicating that he was okay. *I'm sure they won't be satisfied with that,* he laughed. *I better get out of here.*

The weather was changing, and he knew he could find the southeasterlies soon, but a local squall following the coast created more immediate problems.

Michael watched the storm move his way, and he got an idea.

When he reached Chili Creek, he left his canoe pulled up on the beach, tucked under the trees. The rain began to pelt down, but he ignored it as he used his trail to get back to his camp to retrieve his remaining gear and supplies.

It took a few trips. After it was all stowed in the canoe, Michael returned to his camp a final time, pushed the smaller canoe he'd been working on into the water, and floated it to the creek's mouth. It still had a crack in the hull that would cause a slow leak, but the canoe would work fine for what he needed.

Through the night, he added a makeshift outrigger and propped up a fake mast that had been broken in half. When he woke in the morning with the high tide, he pushed the smaller canoe over an incoming wave and paddled out to the deeper water.

He planned to move the boat into the offshore currents and send it floating south. With a bit of luck, from the air, it would look like his boat had been destroyed in the storm.

Maybe they'll think I drowned and leave me alone.

He had to go almost two kilometres offshore to reach the current, and halfway there, water began seeping in through the crack. Before long, the water had risen over his ankles and was creeping up his shins. *It doesn't matter, she won't sink.*

He had just reached his destination when he heard the aircraft engine again. His heart sank. *This will ruin everything,* he thought. *If they see me, they'll only search harder.*

Just as the plane was coming into view, he slipped over the edge of the canoe and into the water. He stayed on the far side of the craft until the plane got closer and then slipped underwater and wrapped his arms around the hull.

For what seemed an eternity, the plane passed overhead. Michael felt the vibration of its engine reach him underwater, shaking him as he clung to the hull like it was the belly of a giant beast.

When the plane had passed, he let go of the canoe and let it drift south. He swam to shore with his paddle in hand.

Within an hour of returning to *Tortoise*, he had turned the length of canvas into a rough sail. He was still short on rope and didn't want to sacrifice all of the one he used with the anchor. He settled for tying one corner of the sail to the top of the mast and the other two to the sides of the canoe near the stern.

He stayed with the boat, resting in the shade of a coconut tree by the river's mouth until later in the day. The last thing he wanted was to be spotted by another aeroplane.

In the late afternoon, with the final rays of the sun blocked by the jungle-clad hills to his west, he took to the water again. He paddled straight into the night, quietly passing Portland Roads around midnight when the only lights left on were the ones to guide sailors. He said a silent goodbye — and thank you — to Hector.

Over the next few weeks, the search for Michael Fomenko turned chaotic. *The Cairns Post* reported that an R.A.A.F. Lincoln Bomber crew had sighted an abandoned dugout canoe floating at sea about fifteen kilometres southeast of the Iron Range.

Numerous towns along the Queensland coast were now coming out with sightings and rumours of Michael Fomenko's whereabouts — almost all of them false.

Hector McDonald at Portland Roads had been pressured into commenting to reports that Michael had visited the location. His leads sent a dozen reporters and police scurrying south and turned out later to be incorrect information.

When Michael heard that, he thought, *Thanks for misleading them — I appreciate the head start.*

Finally, in early June, the Queensland police stated that Michael Fomenko was lost and most likely dead.

Chapter Fourteen

Michael's Story – Age Twenty-Six
(Gordonvale 1956)

*T*he scar didn't really bother him. He rubbed it, his mind drifting, as he remembered receiving the injury about a year prior. His first day of living on his own in this beautiful paradise had almost been his last... within minutes of entering the jungle, a feral pig had charged him.

Yet he had survived — albeit with a chunk of skin missing from his calf. He took pride in the fact that Odysseus had been injured by a boar when young and then carried the scar throughout his life.

By now, Michael had explored quite a bit of the area; from the coast of Cairns up to the Tablelands behind him. He'd seen his share of animals, too, from wallabies to platypus to ringtail possums. And more types of kangaroos than he knew existed including musky rat kangaroos and even tree-climbing kangaroos. He'd spent thousands of hours observing them.

He was currently at one of his favourite camps, located under the Mulgrave River bridge outside Gordonvale. It wasn't a bad camp if you stayed away from the slippery banks at night. Shine a light on the water after sunset, and you'd find a dozen red eyes flashing back at you.

Of course, there was always the smell of the cane mill; even the strongest breeze wouldn't clear that. It was an unbearable sweat stench, a bit like decay, and Michael hoped with time it would fade.

Most of the processing took place elsewhere. Here they only extracted the sugar. Down the line, it would be refined to liquid glucose, golden syrup, molasses, brown sugar and white sugar. The dry remnants of cane minus the sugar – bagasse – would be shipped off and made into fibrous building boards like Masonite. Nothing wasted.

A kookaburra was shouting at the rising sun, and Michael stomped around trying to get the circulation back in his feet.

He glanced at the scar again, remembering the huge boar. He'd never seen one before, so he had nothing to compare it with but guessed it was around 260 kilos. Michael had seen a lot of boars since then, but never one so big.

He thought about naming it Campbell after his old classmate but settled on Caly. In *The Iliad* – the prequel to *The Odyssey* – there was a great hunt for the Calydonian boar.

He was always on the lookout for him.

Today Michael planned to work on a dugout canoe. He often camped along the Mulgrave River and yearned to explore more of it. A boat would help. He had always admired the South Sea Islanders, who covered thousands of kilometres from island to island in dugout canoes. He hoped to imitate them.

He had located a fat log floating in the river, dragged it ashore, and had it propped up on two short parallel logs. The day before, he had trimmed the ends to what he reckoned was a suitable length: five metres.

Today's project would be hacking out the inside with an axe.

He had been at it for a few hours when he heard a voice over his shoulder say, "Be a lot quicker if you burned it out."

Michael looked up the bank to see a white man in his late twenties, with short-cut black hair, khaki shorts and a button-up short-sleeved shirt.

"Is that right?" asked Michael.

The man nodded and followed the path down the embankment to the ledge, where Michael had set the boat.

"G'day mate. My name is Jimmy—Jimmy Solomon—I'll show you how to do it."

Michael gave him his best smile and shook his hand.

The first thing they did was steal a few coals from Michael's fire and move them closer to the canoe. Then they added more wood until a good blaze was burning.

"While that fire burns down," said Jimmy, "let's dig out and outline the area we want to remove."

Together they prepared the canoe and then placed a layer of hot coals on the log. "Just let that burn for the rest of the day," said Jimmy. "I'll swing by tomorrow and check it out."

Later that day, Michael walked over to the Mulgrave sugar mill, about a kilometre away. The men there knew him and didn't mind filling his billycan with sugar from time to time.

He found he could get much of what he needed from the land. There was always cane and plenty of fruit trees—both wild and cultivated—that he could pick from. Any other items he purchased at the store in town.

Not many people knew about him in his first few years in the area. He kept a low profile and didn't mix much with folks. But he was always polite and helpful when he could be.

Michael also hunted. There were plenty of bush turkeys, and from time to time, he got a boar which put him in good standing with the cane farmers. Several times he sent a box containing tusks, feathers and other trophies home to his parents. Some residents might not have liked having a vagrant living by the river, but he did far less damage than a wild pig.

"Any sign of that big boar you're always askin' about?" enquired a man at the mill named Garry.

Michael shrugged. "Haven't seen any sign for a while."

"Well, something's been tearing up the paddocks lately," said Garry.

"I'll get onto it," replied Michael. Wild pigs had been a problem since the 1860s. The pigs damaged pastures, wrecked sugar cane fields, and ate cultivated tropical fruits like bananas, mangoes and pawpaws. They also polluted water sources and damaged fences.

A tree full of ripe mangoes caught Michael's eye, and Garry nodded at it. "Help yourself."

Michael felt quite pleased when he returned to the bridge, only to find his camp destroyed.

There was no doubt who the culprit was—large boar tracks were all over the place. And these were big tracks that could only belong to one animal.

"I'm gonna get you this time, Caly," said Michael out loud.

He grabbed his rifle and a sugar sack with some fruit and set off following the tracks up the Mulgrave River. Within an hour, he had lost the boar's prints but felt confident that he should continue.

But when he reached the town of Goldsborough, seven kilometres away, he admitted that he'd lost him.

He returned to the bridge camp, fuming mad.

The next day Jimmy returned and helped Michael chisel out the blackened inner wood of the canoe. They would repeat the process again and again with fresh coals until they'd hollowed out the log.

"I saw those tracks," said Jimmy. "That's one big boar."

"I know," said Michael. "I've been hearing more and more reports about him too. I'll be ready next time."

The next time though, the same thing happened. Caly destroyed the camp while Michael was away, and when he tracked him up the river, he mysteriously disappeared.

Jimmy said, "I bet you he goes over to Behana Gorge when he gives you the slip."

South of Michael's camp was a triangular mountain called Walsh's Pyramid. It stood at 922 metres and filled his southerly view. Behind the pyramid, a valley narrowed and eventually slanted up the plateau until it became a beautiful granite gorge.

The third time Caly attacked his camp, Michael skirted southeast around Walsh's Pyramid and headed straight into the gorge. Within a few minutes, he began to see signs of the big boar everywhere: the ground was all torn up, several small trees were uprooted, and large tracks punctured the earth.

Michael continued into the gorge, following a trail that ran along a pristine stream. Long shafts of sunlight streamed through the canopy, falling on the jungle floor in puddles of gold. The torrent tumbled and roared down from above at times, spilling into magnificent waterfalls. He stopped at one and swam to cool off.

For nearly five kilometres, he continued, constantly climbing higher past cascades and trickling lagoons. He saw no other people, only large goannas sunning themselves on the rocks.

He was about to turn around when he heard a noise.

He took the safety off his rifle.

A sudden crashing behind him made him spin, and he lost his footing. He glimpsed the boar charging at him as he fell.

He managed to get one shot off, blowing away half of the pig's left ear. The roar of the weapon sent the boar scurrying.

He looked for Caly the rest of the day but never sighted him again. On his way out of the gorge, the pig's grunts echoed off the walls as if he were laughing.

Over the next few weeks, Jimmy helped Michael finish the canoe. The log had not been a great choice, and he wished he had taken the time to find a better one, but they decided to complete the work anyway. They had all sorts of plans to add an outrigger and mast, but an event happened that changed all of that.

In March of 1956, Cyclone Agnes descended on the area causing damage from Mackay to Cairns. The storm brought little water but high winds that did heaps of damage. Most of the valley's cultivated vegetables were destroyed, and all of the fruit was knocked from the trees.

For the farmers in the area, it was a blow — for Michael, it was devastating. Now the only thing he could eat was cane. Even the animals seemed to have fled the area, and he had no luck hunting. The rivers were clogged with fallen trees, and he caught no fish.

Almost overnight, the farmers began to look at him differently. They were in strife now and not as generous. He began to fear being moved on or arrested and made a camp in the middle of the Eubenangee Swamp, located between Babinda and Innisfail.

He liked his swamp camp for its rugged beauty as much as the isolation. The moist soil conditions meant the palms and paperbark trees gave way to mangroves and screw pines. The pines had edible fruit, and he used their fibrous foliage for thatching on his simple hut.

Wherever a long shaft of sunlight managed to land on earth or water, the buzz of insects filled the air. Dragonflies, damselflies and mosquitoes congregated in thick clouds, churning amongst the moths and butterflies and the thousands of birds attracted by such a feast.

River turtles and small native fish scurried about in the water while skinks and water rats crept amongst the shoreline. In the branches above the water, snakes, in turn, hunted the birds, slithering around the climbing swamp ferns and spiky leaves.

One morning he spied a forest dragon. Michael didn't know what it was, but at sixty centimetres, it was bigger than any skink or gecko he'd seen.

He said, "I dub you the King of the Lizards."

He had a secret track into the swamp. A few curious locals tried to follow it to discover his camp, but none ever did. Sometimes he would venture over to Babinda to the sugar mill to fill his billy.

On one of his trips there, a young man of about fifteen watched him. Peter worked to help maintain the locomotives that hauled in the cane and took away the raw sugar and bagasse for processing.

He had plenty to do at the moment, but the sight of Michael walking by stopped him completely.

He'd never seen anyone like Michael. To him, Michael looked like he'd sprouted out of the wilderness — like something out of a movie.

"Where you from?" was the best question he could come up with when Michael got closer.

Michael seemed happy to be talked to, and his face lit up when he answered, "Oh, I live all over the place."

The boy introduced himself as Peter. "That sounds like a fun life," he said.

Michael grinned. Except for the cyclone, it hadn't been bad. "It's alright."

A month later, Michael was passing through Gordonvale when he spied Jimmy Solomon. The two walked to the bridge camp and found his old canoe, still sitting on the bank. They had abandoned the boat earlier because of a crack near the stern, but otherwise, it was still functional.

"I think this area is done for me for a while," said Michael. "Since the cyclone, it's become a tough place to live."

Jimmy nodded. "If I were you, I'd ride this canoe to the ocean — it's at least thirty-five kilometres, but at Russell Heads, you could have a nice camp by the sea."

Michael looked over his camp, sadly, not wanting to leave the area. Some pig tracks littered the ground, and he remembered Caly. *I'm not done with you,* he thought, *but our battle will have to wait for now.*

He took Solomon's advice, and over the next week, paddled to the coast.

His camp at Russell Heads was louder than the other camps. It took him a while to get used to the sound of the waves crashing. The wind was constant at times, too, driving and unrelenting.

But the rewards from beachcombing were rich. He could often find crabs in the mangroves, and he savoured their flesh after allowing them to steam in seaweed over hot coals. There were also oysters, some eight centimetres wide.

His only failure was in his attempts to make bread. Without yeast, it came out hard and unpalatable.

One afternoon he met a young Aboriginal girl of ten years named Cecilia Mow. She'd been observing him from a distance, watching him make flatbread on a heated rock by the fire.

Finally, after a few hesitant days, she came over and said, "Hi."

Michael had never been friends with an Aboriginal and was hesitant when she invited him to meet her parents. But the Mows were all smiles when he entered their small home.

Cecilia whispered something into her mother's ear, and soon she stood by Michael's side and said, "So I hear you're tryin' to make bread."

Michael blushed. "With horrible results."

She smiled and said, "You need to learn how to make damper."

The questioning look in Michael's eyes set her chuckling, and soon she had Cecilia fetching flour, salt, and a cup of water.

They moved to the kitchen, where she began to mix the flour and water. She added some salt and then began to fold and knead the dough.

"Normally," she said, "I would bake this in an oven, but because you're living on the land, I want to show you how we cook it in coals."

She picked up the dough and headed into their backyard.

"You're in luck because my husband had a fire going last night when he burned up some brush—and with a little luck, the coals will still be glowing."

Michael watched as she brushed away the soft, white ash on the top of what was left of the fire. She took a small handful of it and spread it over the outside of the dough.

Next, she dug a small hole with a stick. Soon she reached glowing coals that flickered red when exposed to fresh oxygen. She placed the dough in the cavity, covered it with another sprinkle of ash, and then buried everything with more coals.

"Let that sit for about forty minutes, and we'll see what we have," she said.

Later, when they dug it up, Michael was overjoyed with the results. It only took a minute to blow away the ash that clung to the outer crust, and when he bit into the hot bread, he knew he'd stumbled on a meal that could sustain him on his journey.

"Thanks so much," he told the Mows when he left for his camp.

The cyclone had knocked down quite a few trees, so there was a good selection of dugout making materials. He retired the canoe he'd paddled from Gordonvale and began to work on a new one.

Jimmy Solomon came by and helped him with it. They selected the log together, cut it to length, and got lucky when Cecilia's father came by and helped them haul it to his camp.

Next, they hacked and burned out the inside.

Eventually, they added an outrigger and mast, and Michael began to try his hand at sea — with disastrous results.

Within a month, he had almost wrecked his canoe several times. He even lost it once for a few days when a storm took it in the night. A few times, he was spotted by fishing boats, and eventually, his name appeared in the Cairns paper.

It wasn't long before too many people knew about his camp at Russell Heads, and so, it was time to move on. He wished he could have remained longer — he was beginning to make friends — but suddenly, he was seized with a compulsion.

Being near the sea had brought on a change in Michael. For two years, he had roamed the cane country, but now he yearned to see more of Queensland.

He longed to set forth like his hero Odysseus had done two thousand years ago, and he began to plan a great adventure.

When inland, Michael mostly watched the earth as he walked. It was the safest way to travel, and often he found things by having his eyes on the ground. But since arriving at Russell Heads, he found he looked more to the horizon. He watched the waves, and the ones further out, and then the distant horizon.

When he realised he had a new dream, Michael knew this journey would take some planning—he had work to do.

And he couldn't do that where he was. The beach camp was too exposed, and this area was still suffering from the cyclone. He needed to get north, to somewhere he could stay put while gathering supplies.

After a month, he set out, following the coast north. He passed Fitzroy Island on his right, near the end of his first week on the water. The next day a few locals spotted him going by Cairns, starting rumours of another "Kon-Tiki" voyage.

He tried his sail once and discovered he had not attached it properly, and the cloth nearly blew away. He'd been tying the corners of the sail to the bow and top and bottom of the mast, and it just wasn't a good system as it barely caught the wind.

The outrigger wasn't connected securely either and shifted severely, making the boat lean to the port side.

Somehow, he made it to the Daintree River, located about one hundred and fifty kilometres from Russell Heads. Unfortunately, the canoe was nearly destroyed by the time he got there, and he barely managed to make it a few kilometres up the river before pulling ashore.

You're officially retired, said Michael, his head filled with plans for the bigger, more secure boat he would soon begin building.

He loved his camp on the Daintree River. There seemed to be something magical about the area, and he felt accepted by the ancient forest. The banks of the river were thick with colourful butterflies and dragonflies that constantly fluttered around him.

The location was further away from people, so he only wore a laplap and didn't worry about offending anyone. He was grateful for the solitude—he could be alone with nature here.

He built a shelter using forked branches propped up against a few close-growing trees, with a roof of interwoven branches. The monsoon had ended a while ago, and he no longer worried about rain — most nights, he just slept in the open on a shelf above the river.

He kept busy with projects. He planned to head north once the next monsoon ended, but he had a lot to do before then. He decided he needed two boats for this venture, plus lots of coconuts, dried fish, and fruit, as well as sails, rope and a host of other items.

He also needed tools and other things like fishing line and hooks. He had converted one of the cane knives into a stabbing blade mounted at the end of a stick; the other he wore around his waist in a sheath.

Thankfully, food wasn't a problem. There were plenty of fish in the river and lots of animals to hunt in the bush.

Early one morning, Michael got up, grabbed his rifle, and headed into the jungle to look for bush turkeys. In the pre-dawn light, he quietly padded through the ferns and creepers.

The sun had just lit the uppermost branches in the canopy when he glimpsed a bird creeping out of the olive-green scrub that was still dripping with dew.

The bird spread its wings and began preening himself.

The sunlight glinted down from above, catching the dewdrops on the bird's wings, making them glitter like jewels.

The bird called around, maybe for a mate, and Michael thought the scene so beautiful he didn't want to kill the animal. But he was down on grub and needed food, so he took the shot.

He sent some of the feathers home to his parents.

Over the coming months, Michael selected two logs for his boats, cut them to size, and began chopping and burning out the interior. He also harvested coconuts and began catching and salting fish.

He didn't plan on leaving before the monsoon, which caused a slight problem because he needed to get everything ready before the rains began — and then just wait.

He wasn't good at waiting these days and knew he'd be restless through the long wet.

He was just about ready when the skies overhead began to darken. He had crafted an outrigger and mast for the larger of the two boats and purchased canvas for a sail. In addition, he had a crate of repair materials that included screws and spikes, an auger to drill holes, plus wire and several lengths of rope. Some of the items — like fishhooks and fishing line — he could only obtain by heading into town.

On those runs, he inevitably caught some news stories. They were all about the upcoming Olympics, which were soon to be held in Melbourne.

He didn't want to hear any of it, but it was unavoidable. Especially in November when the Olympic torch arrived in Cairns after being carried by an Australian-born Greek named Constantine Verevis. And then again in December when another runner named Anthony Mark did the final leg. Mark was a runner from North Queensland who was specially chosen to represent the Aboriginal people of Australia.

All of Queensland talked about that, making Michael want to set out on his adventure early. But he knew better than to try his hand against the monsoon this early in the season.

He hunkered down and waited.

When the games began, he sat in his hut, ignoring the dripping rain while he waited for the clouds to pass.

I'll be on my way soon enough, he thought. *Then I'll show the world a physical feat they won't soon forget. I just have to wait for March.*

Chapter Fifteen

The Odyssey VIII – On the Wind
(June 1959)

*A*fter the sighting of the storm-damaged canoe, there were no more verified accounts of anyone glimpsing Michael Fomenko. His father grew despondent. He called or wrote to any locations on the Queensland coast he hoped his son might reach and then made plans to fly up to Thursday Island to be there if he made it that far.

On the flight, the pilot followed the coast from Princess Charlotte Bay north. Daniel located the North Kennedy River and then the Annie branching off from that. The winding labyrinth of mangroves and billabongs took his breath away. He had known his son would travel through remote, wild land — but that place looked savage.

It was no better when they followed the coast further north. From the air, the coral reefs and jagged shoals appeared unavoidable. And he saw no towns or settlements where Michael might appeal for help. He truly was on his own.

The police had only made things worse by informing him that his son's chances of survival in such a hostile environment were slight. Furthermore, they had become more and more determined that Michael's actions were an embarrassment to "white society" and repeatedly tried to get Daniel to encourage his son to give up his epic journey.

Daniel would have none of it. In an interview in *The Mirror* in February, he had defended Michael: "I believe he is leading a man's life. Perhaps it is a waste. Perhaps it is selfish. But perhaps it is better than for Michael to take some insignificant job as a clerk and live an insignificant life in suburbia."

He had ended the interview by saying, "All I want is for him to be happy. I believe he is not doing anything bad... he is not committing any sin."

But now, as he stared down at the coast, he prayed he hadn't supported his son on a venture that may have claimed his life.

He tried to be positive as they passed over the Coral Sea, flying over Cape Sidmouth, then Portland Road and the small settlement of Shelburne. But by the time he reached Thursday Island, all the worrying had left him exhausted.

Michael, however, was having the time of his life. The southeasterlies had not arrived yet, but the storms had abated, and he found it much easier to make progress.

He had rigged a small sail to take advantage of what wind there was, but it required all of his attention — and a short burst of steady wind — to make it work at all. Because his sail had two ends tied to the hull, it was only as wide as *Tortoise*. As a result, he had to balance the wind directly from the stern. If he deviated much from that, the sail collapsed.

To prevent that, he had to control his direction by constantly paddling or using the paddle as a rudder.

It wasn't very effective, but for the short times that everything was working, it pushed him along almost as fast as he could paddle. He had plans to try out a rudder and improve the sail, but he wanted to get north before stopping again.

At Chili Creek, he had turned a rusted chunk of metal into an anchor, and he used it his first night to sleep in the canoe offshore rather than risk a landing in the dark.

He awoke to sea birds flocking around his boat.

He couldn't wait for the winds to arrive.

In *The Odyssey*, Aeolia gave Odysseus a bag containing all the winds to aid him in his quest to return home. *I wish I had the easterlies in a bag,* thought Michael.

Although in Homer's story, the bag of wind didn't help at all. When Odysseus was within sight of Ithaca, his shipmates tore the bag open, believing it was filled with gold and silver.

The result was almost ten more years of wandering.

In addition to the remnants of the supplies he'd picked up a few months earlier, at Lockhart River, he had dried lots of fish and collected plenty of coconuts. He lived off those resources for a while, not wanting to stop and make a camp with a fire.

But he craved a substantial meal.

One morning he bumped into a length of floating bamboo, and it gave him an idea. He hauled the bamboo out of the water and trimmed it down to a three-metre pole. Then he tied the middle of the pole to the thwart and used the two ends to hold both corners of the sail out away from the canoe's sides.

This provided more surface area for the wind to push and minimized the number of times the sail collapsed – although he still had to use the paddle to keep the wind at his back.

He continued to follow the coast, and whenever he saw a freshwater stream flowing out, he tried his luck at fishing. The monsoons had left the water murky, but he knew which fish lingered by the freshwater outlets. He had trapped freshwater minnows at Chili Creek and kept a plastic bucket of them in the canoe's bottom.

With a bit of luck, some live bait will do the trick.

He had a few good bites, and once, he got a barramundi, but it threw the hook. Barramundis are fierce fish that dominate tropical rivers. They can eat almost anything and grow up to 60 kg.

What I wouldn't give for a nice barra cooking over a fire, he thought, his mouth watering.

After the first one got away, Michael tried his luck at every freshwater stream he passed. When he fell into short naps, he dreamt about a fat barramundi sizzling over a fire.

And then, one day, everything changed. Suddenly there was a breeze at his back, and the water beneath him seemed to surge north. Through the morning it built, until by late afternoon that day, he could feel his boat make progress even without the sail.

With the pole extending the size of his sail, he was now cruising a bit faster than he could paddle. But only when the wind temporarily picked up a bit and he managed to keep the canoe pointed directly downwind.

The breeze threw his hair about, and a fine spray of saltwater kicked off the bow. Michael wished Father Gilfeather could see him now.

He felt so grateful that he thought he should thank someone. He wondered again if he had Jesus sitting by his side.

I do feel rather Godly, he chuckled to himself.

But oddly enough, he felt more of a kinship to Zeus at that moment. That was who Odysseus prayed to, and they'd had a fairly productive relationship: Odysseus obeyed and worshipped Zeus, and from time to time, the God helped him out — and without that help, Odysseus would surely have died.

Michael stood up and addressed the heavens above and shouted, "Thank you, Zeus, for blessing this journey and sending me a breeze!"

A sudden gust made him stagger, and he grabbed the mast. It felt like a reply, and he grinned. He heeded the message from the old God and took the rope — the same one the old man from Elim Beach had given him — and tied it around his waist. The other end was still connected to the thwart.

He felt exuberant and joyful and hollered at the wind as he cruised. He was enjoying the thrill of moving faster when he caught a glimpse of a large shape underwater.

It was Poseidon again, matching his speed even now as he swam with the current. From what Michael had read, the croc might cover hundreds of kilometres in a matter of weeks.

They were smart about how they did it as well. Estuarine crocodiles are not particularly good swimmers, so when the current doesn't flow the way they want, the crocs just hunker down and wait for it to change in their favour.

"Begone, Poseidon!" chided Michael. "I rule here."

Soon the massive croc was out of sight, leaving Michael alone.

About this time, Daniel Fomenko landed on Thursday Island. He was greeted by a host of reporters but by nobody who'd actually seen Michael.

He stayed a week and spent most of his time defending his son, arguing that he was still alive, to journalists who were anxious for some new news of Michael. Most left empty-handed and created far-fetched stories about what Michael had done while in Queensland.

These stories of killing crocodiles barehanded and other physical exploits angered Daniel. How far from the truth they are, he thought. My son is not running from anything — he's on a journey — he has a destination.

Daniel again let it be known that he would pay for any supplies Michael needed when he arrived, and then he reluctantly flew back to Sydney.

Michael was quickly learning that his current sail rigging was far from perfect. Unless *Tortoise* was constantly pointed directly downwind, the sail would collapse. There was almost no margin for error, and if the canoe wandered a bit or was suddenly pushed off course by a wave from the stern, the sail would collapse, and he'd find himself floundering.

But still, with the southeasterlies blowing and the currents flowing north, he seemed to make better time each day.

Because he was running low on freshwater and just about out of coconuts, he knew he'd have to stop and make camp soon.

He didn't want to; the new speeds he'd reached with *Tortoise* were addictive, and he just wanted to keep moving. He saw only a few aircraft and hoped he'd given the search planes the slip. Most likely, they were still focused further south, which was all the more reason to keep moving.

But his stomach growled constantly.

He decided he'd start putting more effort into fishing, and after he caught something substantial — either a barramundi or some other fish — he would stop and make camp.

When he passed the mouth of the Jardine River, he removed the bamboo pole and all but collapsed the sail until *Tortoise* maintained a steady speed of about one knot. The wind pushed his canoe north, the current flowing that way as well. It seemed impossible to go slower.

He dropped a line in the water with a large minnow impaled on the hook. He had no fishing pole, only a sixty-metre spool of fishing line.

He let about half of it out, holding the spool in his bare hands as the line trailed off behind the stern.

It was early morning, and the sun had not yet crested the horizon. *Tortoise* cruised along slowly under a slight breeze that seemed perfect for trolling.

Suddenly the line became taut, and the spool popped out of his hand to the bottom of the boat. The spool hissed and jumped as the line disappeared, and Michael picked it up only seconds before it ran out.

The line was as tight as a piano string, and Michael knew he was on the verge of losing whatever monster fish he had hooked. There was not much he could do other than hold on. The boat's motion kept tension on the line and would eventually exhaust the fish, but the line was rated at only 18 kg, and Michael suspected this fish was much larger than that.

He held tight, hoping the line didn't snap. When the fish yanked hard, Michael tried to use his arms as shock absorbers. The boat slowed slightly and straightened out; the fish was like a sea anchor.

Michael kept his feet planted on the stern of the canoe, and whenever he felt the line slacken, he slowly wound it in. The minutes seemed to last forever.

Eventually, he sensed the fish tire, but the fight still went on for over an hour before he got a glimpse of it. He had figured it was big, but when he saw it was a barra — one that had to weigh at least 50 kilos! — he redoubled his efforts.

For the next hour, Michael patiently played the fish until both of them were utterly depleted.

Eventually, the big barra lay exhausted by the outer hull.

Michael clubbed it with his cane knife but was too weak to pull it into the boat. He began to fear he might lose it until he looped a section of rope through its mouth and out the gills and then pulled it higher, out of the water.

It hung against the stern with only the tail dragging in the water, the mouth wide open as if trying to utter last words.

He stared at it proudly, wanting to brag to someone about the battle. He couldn't wait to sink his teeth into the barra.

Now, as he cruised along, all he wanted was to find a nice spot to camp and get a fire going. He smiled for the first time in days and began to imagine how he might add a few spices to the fish.

He looked to the heavens again and said, "Thank you, Zeus, you certainly know how to take care of your favourite sons."

Overcome with excitement, he stood again, and was about to shout more when he glimpsed an ominous shape trailing him in the water.

Poseidon was approaching, heading straight for the barramundi! The croc's eyes were fixated on the small wake the fish's tail left in the water, and with clear intent, he closed the distance. Michael stood, grabbed his paddle and began slapping the water in front of the tied fish.

"Go away!" he screamed at the croc. "You can't have it!"

He dropped the paddle and lifted his cane knife, and added, "I am the son of Zeus! You will obey me!"

Suddenly, the croc lunged for the fish and smashed into the back of the canoe, sending Michael flying through the air. He made a big splash as he plunged underwater.

When he opened his eyes, Poseidon stared at him from only a few paces away. The croc had its mouth around the barramundi, and while Michael watched, it jerked its head sideways, shredded the rope, and ripped the fish away from the boat.

Then the croc swam his way and slowly circled him, blood flowing out of the puncture wounds of the fish. A bullet hole scar on the croc's snout showed where someone had once shot it.

Michael realised that he had dropped his knife at the moment of impact, and he was now defenceless.

The reptile was so enormous that he made the fish in his mouth look small. Poseidon's eyes never left Michael, and finally, the croc stopped right in front of him and stared.

Suddenly Michael felt a tug around his waist as the rope reached its limit. The boat wasn't moving fast, but it was enough momentum that it slowly pulled Michael backwards.

Poseidon eyed him coldly until he was out of sight, and once Michael came to his senses, he turned and swam back to the boat, using the rope as an aid.

When he was seated inside once more, he decided to push on through the night. There wasn't any reason to stop now that Poseidon had eaten his dinner. Michael could almost taste the fish grilling over a fire.

He glanced behind him to make sure the croc wasn't following him. *That was close,* he thought. He wondered if the croc had considered trading in the barramundi for a human meal.

What a horrible way to die, he thought.

Up until that moment, he'd felt quite immortal, but now that he had freshly confronted death—a living breathing death at that!—he wanted only to get some distance from it.

I'm going to put up every bit of sail I can muster, he thought, *and I won't stop until I hit Horn Island.*

Saltwater Crocodile.
Photo courtesy of Robert DeMayo.

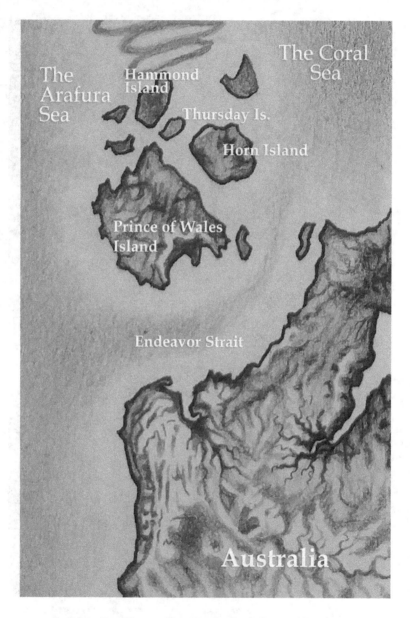

Map 5 – Torres Strait, the Southern Islands.
Illustration by Tom Fish.

Chapter Sixteen

The Odyssey IX – Horn Island
(July 1959)

*T*he Torres Strait sits in the gap between the tip of the York Peninsula and Dutch New Guinea. After passing through it, you leave the Coral Sea; the Gulf of Carpentaria sits to the south, and dead to the west is the Arafura Sea. Between are the Torres Strait Islands, a group of 274 islands scattered over 48,000 square kilometres.

Michael decided to head to Horn Island, about sixteen kilometres off the coast. But to get there, he had to cross the Endeavor Strait, one of the main routes used by the smaller international and interisland freighters.

He tried not to imagine his boat being pulverised by one of them when he anchored in an offshore reef and stopped at sunset to look over the channel.

He spotted his first ship coming in from the west. At first, the ominous bulky shape appeared not to move at all, and then it rushed by when it got closer.

The waves it created seemed to take forever to reach *Tortoise*, and Michael had just about forgotten them when suddenly a wall of water rushed over the breakers and nearly swamped him.

There was a lot of open water to cross, and he decided to wait until morning. The shore looked inhospitable, so he remained anchored in the reef for the night.

Sleep evaded him for a few hours, his mind constantly running through the dangers ahead.

He woke later that night to a roaring sound and blackness. He sat up, disoriented, feeling his boat tilting and moving fast. He felt sure he was about to flip or smash into something.

He'd expected to see a sharp-horned moon and a sky full of stars, not this nothingness.

What the hell is happening? he asked himself.

And then a line of stars came into view, and he realised a large object was blocking out the night sky.

It was a freighter. The large ship was charging past him, less than a hundred metres away.

After the initial waves passed, *Tortoise* and Michael's racing heart settled down. He looked around with no idea where he was. He tugged on the anchor and found it was dangling in deep water.

He figured it had gotten dislodged, and he had floated into the shipping lane.

He didn't know the stars well enough to navigate by them. And the moon was now high in the sky, not near the horizon.

He let his eyes sweep the seas until they rested on a dark shadow low in the sky.

That has to be the mainland, he thought.

An hour later, the eastern sky began to lighten, and soon he made out Horn Island to the northwest. It seemed closer, and he figured he got lucky with the wind and currents because he had drifted in that direction.

Over the following hours, a strong breeze blew him right at the island. His bamboo pole was back in place, widening the sail.

He experimented on the way by trying to find the best technique for steering by paddling on either side of the canoe and using the paddle as a rudder to keep pointing downwind. Using the results of these experiments, the sail collapsed less.

I might be making five knots! he thought excitedly.

He arrived late in the day and pulled ashore for the night, camping in a quiet cove with good shelter from the wind. He was tempted to stay for a while and carry out repairs on *Tortoise*, but he needed supplies — some of which had to be store-bought.

He also looked forward to seeing John Caldwell again. The only town on the island was Horn, located on the other side, and he figured *Outward Bound* would be anchored there. The round island was about eight kilometres wide, so the next day he paddled fifteen kilometres to get to the other side.

The small town had less than five hundred residents but still sported an impressive pier and boat dock. Michael would later learn the amenities were relics from the town's prosperous days as a base for the pearling industry.

Michael paddled in slowly, glancing at several sailboats anchored offshore. He recognised *Outward Bound* immediately. It didn't look like anyone was on board.

He turned his bow towards the beach and glimpsed a row of white houses behind a line of palms and shrubs. The buildings were visible because they were all set on four-metre pilings in the Queensland fashion. Michael found himself wishing fewer people were living in the area; it didn't look like he could camp nearby without drawing attention.

But he really couldn't keep going. He desperately needed to work on his boat; the outrigger had shifted and was about ready to fall off. He also knew that if he didn't figure out how to rig a sail properly, it would blow away — or shred.

His boat limped in, looking like the final runner in a marathon. Its tired condition grabbed the attention of an Islander wearing a solid blue short-sleeved button-up shirt. The man was in his sixties, with coarse black hair that had frosted with age. He looked like he'd once been a rugged bloke but had now softened.

What made him appear even mellower was his smile, which lit up his entire face. It warmed those who witnessed it and caught Michael's eye when he was barely within shouting distance.

Many years before, the man had been aptly nicknamed Smiley.

"What do we have here?" asked Smiley when the canoe got closer to shore. "You look like a character from some story."

"I need to come ashore for some repairs," said Michael, his thoughts on how much trouble Smiley might get in for helping him. What Michael hadn't realised was he had left the territory of the Aboriginals and was now in the realm of another indigenous group called the Torres Strait Islanders. And at present, they were not restricted by the same rules that governed the lives of the Aboriginals.

Michael reached the shore and began dragging his canoe out of the water. Without being asked, Smiley kicked off his sandals and stepped forward to help.

His eyes sparkled as he watched Michael, like a mischievous idea was waiting to sneak out. He glanced into the boat, expecting to see supplies and was surprised it was nearly empty.

Michael glanced up and down the beach.

"Do you think anyone will mind if I stay here for a while and complete some repairs?"

Smiley shook his head. "I don't think so—but why don't you come stay with me? My sons are gone, and I have an extra room. My wife won't mind none."

The offer took Michael by surprise. He'd maintained a distance from most of the Aboriginal people he'd met and hadn't expected it. He stared at Smiley for a minute, taking him in.

Smiley added, "I live right around the corner—you can walk over whenever you want to work or check on your boat."

"Sure," said Michael, reluctantly. "Thanks."

He glanced at *Tortoise* and asked, "But what about my canoe— will anyone mess with it here?"

Smiley grinned. "No, I'll put the word out. And if anyone asks, you just tell them your name is Tagai and not to touch your things while you're away."

Michael gave him a questioning stare as he coiled up his rope and threw it over one shoulder, but Smiley only shrugged. He then picked up his cane knives and said, "All set."

There was nothing left in the hull of the craft worth salvaging. Smiley chuckled as he led the man to his home.

About a block away from the surf, they came upon Smiley's house: a small Queenslander, with the main living space on the second level above the ground. There it could avoid flooding and achieve maximum air circulation.

The mailbox read "Paul" in hand-painted letters.

Beautiful, blooming hibiscus bushes surrounded a well-tended front lawn, and small palms with fans like the tails of strutting peacocks cast shade from the hedges lining the grass.

A woman in her sixties was collecting some of the beautiful red flowers, cutting them and then placing them in a wicker basket. She had gloves on her hands, wore a big straw hat and a cotton dress.

"Hello, Granny!" yelled Smiley. "We got company."

The woman stood and brushed her hands on her lap.

"*Niiyalang*," she said with a look that warmed Michael's heart.

She glanced at his laplap and the wind-burned skin on his face and shoulders. "And where did you wash in from?"

Michael nodded south. "The mainland, I was..."

He was about to say more when Smiley cut in, "His name is Tagai, and he is in the middle of an adventure. He's gonna stay with us while he repairs his boat."

Granny turned her eyes full on Smiley. "What are you up to, Daddy?"

His eyes glinted again. "Nothing you need worry about."

She shrugged. "We'll see about that."

When she glanced back at Michael, he extended his hand.

"My name is Michael," he said.

Granny shook his hand and nodded at the long staircase that led up to the house. "There's a bedroom in the back—you're welcome there as long as you need a place."

She grabbed her basket and hobbled up the stairs ahead of them. When she passed Smiley, she shook her head and mumbled, "Tagai?"

Over the coming days, Smiley brought Michael around town, introducing him to various shop owners and tradies. He always got a few chuckles when he presented Michael as Tagai, but several had been in correspondence with his father, Daniel, and were well aware of who he was. They were willing to extend him credit when he was ready but unfortunately, he would have to get much of what he needed — including permits — at nearby Thursday Island, which was more densely populated.

Smiley lent Michael a razor, and the beard quickly came off, though he still happily wore only the laplap. Nobody seemed to mind that his hair had grown long. Unlike when he'd drifted through Barrow Point, the people of Horn barely glanced at him.

Meanwhile, *Outward Bound* still floated at anchor with no sign of life. Michael enquired around and discovered John Caldwell had taken his family by ferry to Thursday Island and would be gone a few days yet. *It seems like everything is pulling me towards Thursday Island,* he thought.

Horn Island and Thursday Island had a very symbiotic relationship. Horn was almost ten times larger and mostly uninhabited, so that's where they placed the airport. But Port Kennedy, on Thursday Island, had been the administrative and commercial capital of Torres Strait since 1877.

A ferry ran daily between the two islands, and Horn residents regularly travelled there for work and school. But, for now, Michael was content with the slow pace of Horn. He wasn't quite ready to step into the government buildings or be around the police.

Horn had seen a lot of activity during WWII; it had been the second most bombed place in Australia after Darwin. Something about that fact connected with Michael, who felt somewhat battered and beaten himself.

In the cool mornings, Smiley would accompany Michael to the beach to work on the canoe. He always carried with him a plastic bucket filled with various tools. Only a few pieces of the former outrigger were salvageable, but the two men combed the shorelines for logs and found several that would work. Smiley broke out a rugged saw that made trimming them to length much easier. And with credit at the nearby shops, Michael purchased more rope and ordered new sailcloth.

One day they were joined by Smiley's nephew, a twenty-year-old kid named Tyler, who walked with a cane. When Smiley first spotted him slowly ambling his way along the beach, he said, "That lucky boy was grabbed by a big tiger shark when he was young, and his left leg never recovered."

Michael scratched his head. "Why would that be lucky?"

Smiley said, "Well, he was only ten when the shark attacked him, and his uncle claims that tiger had him by the thigh when he sank out of sight. But for some reason, he spit him out."

"I guess he's lucky he survived," said Michael.

"He is blessed," said Smiley. "The ancestors were watching over him—and that shark knew it."

When Tyler finally reached them, Smiley did the introductions.

After, he said to Michael, "It's good that you two meet—Tyler works in the Department of Territories office, and you'll need to go there if you intend to get a permit for your crossing of the strait. It doesn't hurt to have a man on the inside."

Tyler nodded politely, but it was clear he was a bit shy. He stayed an hour, watching the two men work from the shade of a palm. At one point, Michael and Smiley were focused on attaching the new outrigger, and when they looked up, he was gone.

Michael enjoyed spending time with Smiley. All the work they completed was done in a relaxed manner, out of the hot sun. Whenever they paused, Smiley talked about the myths and legends of the Torres Strait Islanders. Something about the way Michael had paddled in made the old stories pour out of him.

137

Michael was all ears. He'd been fascinated by the seafaring peoples of the world and felt an affinity with them when on the open water. Smiley told him how the Islanders were descended from Melanesians and that the men of Dutch New Guinea used dugouts very similar to *Tortoise*.

"Traditionally, we were hunters but also farmers," he said one morning. "We travelled far and wide visiting our brothers on the other islands—we were great seafarers!"

He then made a chopping motion at Michael's neck and grinned broadly as he added, "And we were also headhunters."

Michael smiled at the comment, then stared off to the north and said, "Following the coast was difficult during the wet, but I managed—but I don't know about crossing the strait. I may not be ready for that yet. Could you teach me a little about putting up a sail?"

Smiley stared at him but held his tongue for once. He lay back against a palm after that, closed his eyes, and fell asleep.

When Smiley woke, he saw Michael a few paces away, watching a few palm trees swaying in the breeze. His eyes were relaxed, and he swayed slightly as if he were one of them.

There's something special about this young man, he thought.

Michael made the Islander feel lucky to be around him. He was adventure, danger and tradition, all mixed into a dashing, fearless figure.

Michael noticed Smiley had come around, walked over, and crouched next to him. "Are you ready to tell me a little about sailing now?" he asked.

Smiley shook his head. "No, first we have to talk about a few other things."

He patted the ground by his side, indicating for Michael to sit.

"Like the Aboriginals, we Islanders believe in the Dreamtime," said Smiley. "We believe that there is a spirit world that lives alongside this physical one. Our ancestors are there, and when we pass away, we will go there too."

Michael's heart sank a little; he'd so hoped for advice on sailing. This next crossing scared him with its tricky currents, heavy international shipping traffic, and more significant seas. If he drowned, it would only confirm everyone's belief that he was on a suicide mission. It pulled at his heart to think of the burden it would place on his family.

He didn't want to focus on that, so he shifted his thoughts to the idea that there could be another world running parallel to the one he was in. It didn't seem too different from the Christian heaven in some senses, yet they were opposites in other ways.

Michael had heard about the Dreamtime but never connected it with the "Nature God" he worshipped. It had seemed disparate, like someone else's religion. But now he wondered about that. When he glimpsed an awareness in nature, was he witnessing the Dreamtime?

Smiley continued, "We choose to base our lives on the Dreaming. Our communities are divided into clans, and elders regulate the culture."

He paused when he saw a vacant look in Michael's eyes. "I think you want to know how these stories — or the Dreamtime — can help you sail. Is that correct?"

Michael grinned. "It's kinda tough to get it off my mind."

Smiley scratched his silver hair. "Try lookin' at it this way. Before the Dreaming, there was nothing. The land was empty. There were no mountains, no trees, no rivers — nothing. Imagine being on the water at night when there is no motion and no light."

Michael closed his eyes and pictured it, and Smiley continued.

"The Dreaming is the time when everything emerged. The Creator Spirits roamed the land, and in their travels, they created the rivers and lakes as well as the rocks, mountains and deserts."

Smiley paused, then added, "And the seas — they created the seas — and all that grew out of them."

Michael imagined the flat dark water as a slight ripple of a wave passed through it. Soon that was followed by another, and another. He imagined the dark world slowly lightening, and then he glimpsed an island on the horizon.

In his mind, he floated towards it, making out more and more detail as he got closer: The palm trees, the birds and their chatter, the wind—and suddenly a myriad of salty, green scents.

Smiley said, "And during their time, the spirits created the birds and the fish. They made dingoes and kangaroos and emus and wombats—and then they made us."

In Michael's mind, the beautiful island stood redolent with life—chirping, squawking, sighing—all of it conscious and aware of him. He saw the Dreamtime connect with his Nature God.

Suddenly, he saw that the sea was also alive and conscious.

And he knew he needed to understand it better before attempting the crossing.

One morning as the high tide began to ebb, Michael spotted a small dinghy heading his way. He'd been in the process of attaching a new mast, with Smiley's help, when they paused to watch the boat approach. "That's your mate, Caldwell," said Smiley.

Michael brushed his hands off, and when the dinghy reached the shore, he pulled it further out of the water.

Caldwell shook his hand. "Well, you made it," he said.

Michael glanced at *Tortoise* and laughed. "Barely."

Michael remembered Smiley and introduced him.

While shaking his hand, Caldwell said, "I was about to invite Michael over for breakfast—would you like to join us?"

Smiley flashed a mouth full of teeth before shaking his head, "Thank you, but no—I've promised Granny to take her to the market."

He sauntered off, and on the next wave, Michael and Caldwell were on the water heading towards *Outward Bound*.

From the below deck, Mary Caldwell watched them approach. She put the coffee on and prepared a tray with milk and sugar.

The young man riding with her husband had shaved but still looked a bit like a savage. His skin had been burned almost black from the sun, and he seemed like he might look more natural in a dense jungle than on the deck of a boat.

I suppose the grass skirt is in part responsible for that, she thought. She watched as he climbed on deck and looked around. He laughed easily when talking with John. He appeared younger with the whiskers gone, and when he smiled—which was often— he could be quite charming.

"Coffee is ready," she announced when she came up on deck.

Michael shook her hand, suddenly self-conscious of his laplap. Even under his sunbaked skin, she could see him blush.

"Why don't you boys sit at the table, and I'll bring out a few scones," she added.

"Thanks, Sweetie," said Caldwell, suddenly sounding very American. He kissed her cheek then took a seat. Michael sat opposite him. A dozen newspaper clippings were on the table in front of him. Michael had seen some of them, but not all.

And nothing in the last few months.

Scanning over them, he saw a few had claimed him dead, lost at sea. *My poor parents,* he thought.

Caldwell lifted one and said, "I never realised how lucky I was not to have the entire world watching my every move. Don't get me wrong, during my time adrift, I'd have done anything to get rescued—but the things they say about you are truly ridiculous. And I'm not even talking about them claiming you're dead."

"I know," said Michael. He took a sip of coffee and added, "They just don't understand me, so they make things up."

Caldwell scanned the articles with a scornful look. He picked out words and read them aloud as he went. "Reckless... Starving... In poor health... Emaciated... Thin... A recluse who will not communicate with the world—did any of these people even see you or talk with you?"

Michael shook his head. "Only a few—I avoid them when I can."

Mary came by, and Caldwell said, "Mary is a writer: describe Mr Fomenko here in one word."

Mary stared into Michael's face and saw a young man ready to take on the world. It didn't seem one could be healthier.

"Robust," she said.

"I like it," agreed Caldwell. "See, that wasn't so difficult."

Caldwell sighed. Then he brightened and said, "I did read one article here that quotes your father. Have you read it? It's lovely — I believe I would like your father."

He picked up a clipping and read an excerpt aloud, "Michael is obsessed with the character of the wanderer, warrior and athlete, Odysseus. Looking back, I believe he had been waiting years for that moment when he could walk out of the house wearing a flannel shirt, jeans and sandals, carrying a haversack and a tomahawk to begin his long journey."

Michael reached for his cane knife and remembered he'd left it with the rope in his room at Smiley's house.

"I'm not running away from anything," he said.

Caldwell held his eye. "No, I don't suppose you are."

Mary came back with a plate of scones and flipped on the radio. The BBC had a blues hour running, and she turned it up as Nina Simone sang *Little Girl Blue*. She sat down next to her husband and snuggled against him.

Michael continued, "All of these claims that I shun my fellow man are untrue — I like company. But life is never wholly what you want it to be."

Mary caught Michael's eye and asked, "But are you around people enough to feel your life is balanced?"

Michael stared off the bow at *Tortoise* on the far shore. He thought of his journey to Horn Island: losing his boats initially and then the long walk to Cape Flattery, living in the cave alone, then battling the monsoon up to Princess Charlotte Bay and beyond.

He thought of Poseidon, watching him underwater when he'd been knocked from the boat.

Then he remembered the thrill of riding under sail with the southeasterlies blowing, of the sky littered with countless stars and the beauty of the sun rising out of the water. He remembered the countless fish and birds along the reefs and the hum of insects from within the dense rainforest.

He recalled the awareness and being part of it.

Caldwell watched him with a knowing look.

I bet he understands me pretty well after his time adrift, thought Michael.

"You have to accept the balance of things," said Michael. "In finding solitude — and solace — I also found loneliness. Sometimes, in my canoe, I feel terribly lonely. But then again, on balance, I like to be on my own because then I can commune directly with nature."

Suddenly they were invaded by two young boys. The youngest was only three, wore a lifejacket, and had a rope tied to him.

"He wanders," said the older.

"This is John and Roger," said Caldwell, indicating Roger as the oldest. Michael guessed he was about eleven.

"Hello, boys," said Michael.

Roger glanced across the water to where *Tortoise* lay beached and asked, "Why did you make that boat?"

Michael smiled. "I wanted to go on an adventure."

The boy's eyes sparkled as he reached into his pocket and took out a small magnifying glass. He handed it to Michael and said, "For your adventure."

Michael glanced at Caldwell, not certain he should accept the gift.

Caldwell laughed and said, "It's his to give away — and not a bad gift at all. That'll come in handy when your matches are wet."

Roger beamed triumphantly and said, "We're going for a swim — want to join?"

Caldwell glanced at Michael's laplap. "I better lend you a swimsuit while you're on board."

Michael nodded sheepishly, and Caldwell added, "And you might want to borrow some of my clothes before you head over to Thursday Island — no reason to give the authorities or the reporters ammunition that they'll use against you."

The young man was on the verge of rejecting the offer when he realised that Caldwell was correct. Reluctantly he nodded and said, "As long as it's not an imposition."

Caldwell winked and said, "All part of showing good *xenia*."

Smiley enjoyed having a celebrity in his house. In the last few weeks, he'd collected quite a few articles about Michael from all over Australia, and—like John Caldwell—it became his habit to read off tidbits while he enjoyed a coffee with Michael and Granny.

Michael listened shyly, alternating between pride and embarrassment—especially when the articles exaggerated his physical battles with crocodiles or boars.

On this morning, Smiley had a clipping from *The Sydney Morning Herald*. The article had been published a few days before and then arrived by plane this morning.

Smiley said, "They got some white woman from Thursday Island to write this one—a Mrs Maloney."

"I remember her," said Michael.

"She said you were in remarkable health," said Smiley. He scanned ahead and read an excerpt: "Fomenko was handsome with charming manners, but also a very non-committal young man."

"What does that mean?" asked Granny.

Michael chuckled, "It means I didn't give her the time of day."

They all laughed at that until Smiley read some more.

"Oh, boy—I'm afraid she didn't like your boat," he said and then recited the following lines out loud:

"You wouldn't go two metres in it. The bottom of the dugout was filled with crocodile skins, rotting coconut meat, and several Aboriginal-type spears and a bailer—that's it."

"Well, maybe I should take her for a trip up the coast," suggested Michael. "A moonlit cruise, maybe?"

Smiley giggled about that comment all morning while they finished stepping the new mast to the boat. Next, they would need to rig a sail. When cruising up the coast, Michael had thrown up the most basic sail he could. Now he had to learn how to harness the wind.

John Caldwell had agreed to take him out sailing in the next few days and explain how the wind pulled *Outward Bound* along. Michael also wanted to learn how the Islanders did it.

But Smiley was evasive and always talked of other things. Today they wanted to put the canoe in the water and see how the outrigger held up—and make sure the mast didn't wobble.

"Do you think today we might talk about sailing?" Michael asked while they dragged *Tortoise* to the water.

Smiley looked him over, and something about that expression told Michael that any advice about sailing would be indirect.

"Are you afraid of death?" asked Smiley.

"No," replied Michael easily.

"But do you know where you go when you die?"

This time Michael was slower to reply. "Not exactly."

Smiley nodded and grabbed his bucket of tools, setting it in the canoe. He motioned for Michael to get in the boat while he pushed them off. Then, at the last minute, he hopped onto the stern. He placed his feet inside the canoe, grabbed the paddle and, as he took a deep stroke, said, "We Islanders believe when we die, we return to the sky and the land."

He pointed out beyond the surf and added, "To the water, too."

Michael began to paddle as well, glad the outrigger seemed to ride solidly. Smiley steered *Tortoise* to the northeast as if they were going to circle the island counterclockwise. A steady current was pulling that way, although a strong breeze kept trying to push them ashore.

Smiley continued talking as they both paddled to get clear of the rocks. "We return just as our ancestors did. And we will watch over creation just as they do."

Michael stared over the water, watching it sway, thinking of it as some primordial home out of which everything came and then returned. It seemed so endless and eternal.

"And do we come back?" he asked.

Smiley shrugged. "I've heard that you can come back as an animal."

Michael grinned. "Come on."

"No. Like the spirits, you can be reborn as an animal that watches over your family."

Michael let his thoughts drift, wondering what animal he would be. People often want to be an animal because they think it will make them enjoy nature more purely. Yet, Michael had a direct connection and instead pondered how nice it might be to leave behind the world of man and live only in the wild.

Suddenly he was pulled out of his reverie by a warning from Smiley. "Here's trouble," he said, nodding at the shore. "You're gonna need a sea anchor here."

Michael looked shoreward to see some exposed rocks, and suddenly he noticed how the wind had increased and now appeared ready to push them into harm's way.

Smiley set aside his paddle and grabbed his plastic bucket. He emptied his tools into the bottom of the boat and said, "Give me your rope."

Michael handed him the new rope he'd purchased, glad he didn't have to untie the old one from the anchor anymore.

"Tie one end to the bow," said Smiley, while he attached the bucket to the line near the middle. He then tossed the bucket into the water, ahead of the boat, and waited for the current to take it.

The line tightened, and the boat turned towards the choppy waves heading their way. Quickly, Smiley attached the other end to the hull on the windward side and took in slack until the waves hit between the bow and the centre of the canoe.

He stopped when the boat was about a forty-five-degree angle to the incoming waves and tied it off.

"Never take on the waves head-on, or they'll break over the bow and swamp your canoe."

Michael had a feeling that one day that two-word lesson — sea anchor — might save his life.

It was just the two of them, and Smiley seemed unwilling to offer up any more sailing advice, so Michael decided to pin him with the question that had been on his mind since first arriving.

"So, are you ever going to tell me who Tagai was?" he asked.

Smiley chuckled and then pulled a straight face as he began.

"Tagai is always the warrior in the stories of the Islanders. He is a great fisherman, too, and that day you paddled in, you reminded me of him."

Michael nodded. "Okay, but why do people give me such strange looks when I tell them my name is Tagai?"

Smiley's eyes lit up. "You told someone this?"

"Just a man on the beach who was checking out my stores in the canoe. When I told him my name was Tagai, the man's eyes went wide, and then he backed away, assuring me he hadn't taken anything."

Smiley started laughing so hard it took him some time before he could speak. He began, "In one story about Tagai, he was fishing with a crew of twelve. Tagai left the group for a nearby reef because they had no luck catching fish. It was a hot day, and before long, the others consumed all their supplies and water.

"Eventually, they became frustrated waiting and drank Tagai's water, and ate his food, too. When he returned and saw what they had done, he flew into a rage and killed them all."

Michael's eyes grew wide. "So now everyone thinks I'll kill them if they take my stuff?"

Smiley began chuckling again. "It was a major crime — for seafaring people, drinking another's water or taking their food were unforgivable offences."

"But did he have to kill them?"

Smiley shrugged. "Maybe he didn't kill them — the story also states that he cast six of the men into the sky where they still sit in the Pleiades star cluster, and he threw the other six at great Orion. He turned away from them then, after telling the men never to bother him again."

Michael reflected on the stories he used to guide his path and remembered that Odysseus had not been forgiving upon his return to Ithaca, killing the one-hundred-and-eight suitors who'd pestered his wife since he'd departed.

I suppose in both instances, the men had broken the rules of xenia, he thought.

Smiley interrupted his musings by describing some of the islands he would encounter in the Arafura Sea. "From water level, it's tough to tell much about the islands. At a distance, the hilly or mountainous islands are easy to spot, but true coral islands are flat and barely visible because they are not much higher than the water."

Michael stared to the north as if he could see the islands.

Smiley continued, "If they are only a lump of reef rising above the sea, they're called cays, and if they are ring-shaped or enclose a lagoon, they're called atolls. And even when you approach one of the bigger islands, you have to be careful because they are still surrounded by coral reefs."

The Islander was a wealth of information, and Michael absorbed as much of it as possible, especially when he talked about which islands were inhabited or had water.

But as much as he soaked up every bit of advice, he still didn't feel ready for the crossing.

Chapter Seventeen

The Odyssey X – Thursday Island
(September 1959)

*A*fter a month on Horn Island, Michael caught the ferry over to Thursday Island. His first stop was the Department of Territories to apply for a permit to enter the Territory of Dutch New Guinea.

John Caldwell had supplied him with a pair of white slacks and a short-sleeved, button-up shirt. The shirt had a flamboyant coral print with fish on it, and its garishness appealed to him. Michael had learned that there were no current orders for his arrest in the Torres Islands, and he tried to appear well-mannered and confident as he entered the building.

The Sub-Collector of Customs was a pale little man in his forties with thick glasses and a mumbling habit. His nametag read Mueller.

Mueller had also read the numerous articles about Michael Fomenko, and even though Michael was now dressed and clean-shaven, he didn't need to see him in a laplap to know who he was.

Michael glimpsed Smiley's nephew, Tyler, at a smaller desk on the other side of the room. The young man was typing and kept his head down.

"What can I do for you?" asked Mueller.

"I'm heading towards Dutch New Guinea and was told I need a permit."

Mueller murmured, "You're gonna need several permits..."

But then, in a louder voice, said, "Before you get a permit, you're going to need a taxation clearance, a customs clearance, and a health clearance."

Michael looked dumbfounded. "And where do I get those?"

"You could start at the Taxation Department."

Mueller stared at him without blinking.

He reminds me of a stork, thought Michael.

Almost in jest, Michael asked, "Anything else?"

Mueller nodded. "There is... you will be required to lodge a money bond of fifty pounds and also show proof that you have access to another one-hundred-and-fifty pounds."

Michael thought the bloke was kidding, but before he said a word, Mueller added, "You also have to provide proof of employment and accommodations when you get there."

It took considerable effort for Michael not to laugh in the man's face. *Is he really telling me I can't go there unless I have a job lined up?*

Initially, he'd intended simply to bypass the government regulations and go for it, and he'd only decided to fill out the necessary paperwork at Caldwell's urging.

"Don't you think this is all a little much?" he asked.

Mueller shook his head. "These regulations are in place to ensure that you are not a burden to the authorities there."

He continued to pretend he'd never heard of Fomenko and asked, "And what will be your mode of transportation?"

Michael grinned and said, "I will be paddling a dugout canoe called *Tortoise*."

A slight shudder swept over Mueller as if he'd suddenly been confronted with completing the voyage himself. All he could envision was clinging to a half-submerged log, up to his neck in water with darkness coming on—and no land in sight.

It was dangerous. Charter a decent boat if you had to make the crossing, but why risk your life in a craft that's barely seaworthy? It was uncivilised, fumed Mueller, and he would have no part in it.

Michael knew it was a lost cause. The man before him would never understand doing something for the sheer sense of a challenge. To want to do it *because* it is difficult and dangerous.

The look in Mueller's eyes tugged at Michael's sense of purpose. He wondered if the little man had ever been on an adventure. Had he ever risked anything?

I've had just about enough of this tosser, he thought, before adding, "It's a fine craft—although I doubt you could handle it."

Mueller's face began to contort, and it looked like his skin couldn't decide whether it should go whiter or bright red.

He appeared to be arguing with himself as he crossed the room and picked up a piece of paper.

He mumbled, "...nothing to do with my competence..." and handed it to Michael and said, "You can begin by filling out this form with general information. Hand it in before you leave."

Michael looked up and caught Tyler sneaking a glance at him. Then the young man quickly looked away, perhaps afraid that Mueller might see him fraternising.

Mueller snapped at Tyler anyway, impatiently requesting another form.

Soon Tyler had retrieved it, limping as quickly as his leg would allow. For some reason, the young man didn't use his cane in the office.

Mueller snatched the paper from him and handed it to Michael.

"And hand these in before you depart," he said curtly before leaving the room.

Tyler ambled past him, and with a shy grin, whispered, "Good luck, Tagai."

Michael stepped outside and sat on the steps while he looked over the papers. Inside, he could hear Mueller on the phone with his supervisor.

"That kid was here... Fomenko, right... He still intends to paddle his *log* to Dutch New Guinea."

On the steps, Michael snickered when he heard the word *log*.

Mueller seemed annoyed at whatever responses he was getting from his boss and ended the conversation by saying, "As soon as you get permission to arrest him, let me know. I've given him the paperwork — he'll be back."

Michael tried to put the man out of his mind. He had collected some of the money his father had left for him. Now he had to get supplies for his voyage.

When he boarded the ferry that night, he had to make several trips because of all the supplies. That day he purchased 48 kg of sugar, 14 kg of rice, 9 kg of flour, 450 g of tea, condensed milk, jam, tomato sauce, a new axe, fishing line and tackle. He also had two plastic containers that would hold almost twenty litres of water. He was determined not to be thirsty on this voyage.

The week before in Horn, he had purchased tyre tubes that he would use to pack the food to keep it dry. At night, Michael quietly stowed the sugar, rice and flour in them.

A few days later, he was sailing amongst the islands on Caldwell's yacht while the older man gave him a few pointers — and warnings. Caldwell had been deadly serious when he talked about one of the dangers Michael would encounter.

"You really have to keep a steady watch out for the freighters because the Torres Strait has a few major shipping lanes, and those big ships tear through regularly."

Michael burst out laughing and told Caldwell about his near-miss, closer to the mainland, on the Endeavour Strait. Several times since arriving on Horn, he'd had nightmares about the big ship that had come dangerously close.

"Well, that channel is one of the shipping routes, but the Prince of Wales Channel to the north of Hammond Island is the primary passage for large international ships, and you still have to watch for interisland vessels near Badu and beyond."

"I'll definitely keep my eyes open," said Michael.

"If you stand in your canoe," continued Caldwell, "the most you'll see is about five or six kilometres. Those big freighters are giant, so maybe you glimpse them at fifteen or twenty kilometres."

"And they're moving fast," he added, "twenty-five knots or more—which is five times faster than you can move even with a sail. And don't count on them veering or stopping for you regardless of your situation."

Michael looked across the water to where *Tortoise* lay beached and took the opportunity to ask Caldwell about how best to attach his new sail.

Caldwell shook his head. "From what I saw, you were tying your sail to the top of the mast and then near the stern on either side of the hull."

Michael nodded sheepishly and then told him about using the bamboo pole to extend the width of the sail and his steering experiments.

Caldwell nodded while listening but then shook his head again.

"Well, it's a miracle you made it this far," he said. "I suppose it worked because you had the wind at your back—but rigged like that, you would have had to constantly paddle hard to keep the boat pointed directly downwind, or the wind would hit the sail at the wrong angle, and it would collapse."

Michael grinned. "Yeah, that's pretty much what happened."

The American pointed north, in the direction of Dutch New Guinea, and said, "You'll hit some strong winds out there—and tied the way you had it, your sail will tear away."

Michael began to fidget uncomfortably.

"What would you suggest?" he asked.

Caldwell smiled. "First, I think you should get some brass grommets and sew them into the corners of your sails and along the mast. That will create a solid anchor point for the ropes."

Michael walked over to the mast of *Outward Bound* and examined the corner of one of the sails.

"To be safe, you're gonna need more speed and control of your canoe, too, and I think for that, you need a boom."

Michael knew a boom was a pole, or spar, that ran along the foot of a rigged sail, but not much else.

"A boom allows you to sail a boat in directions other than just downwind. By moving it in or out, you can adjust the angle between the sail and the wind whenever the boat is steered toward a new direction," said Caldwell. "It allows you to get the maximum power out of the sail and wind."

Michael's blank expression made the American burst out laughing. He set a friendly hand on Michael's shoulder and said, "Don't worry, we'll work on it together."

For the rest of that afternoon, Caldwell put his boat through several different scenarios where Michael could experiment with a boom.

A few days later, Michael lay awake in bed listening to the night when he heard a stranger approach the house. The evening was dead still, with little noise, so the footsteps echoed clearly as the man approached. Even more distinctive was the sharp sound of a cane on the pathway, ringing out with every other step.

He didn't hear a knock, but soon Smiley's voice whispered at the stranger. Michael couldn't tell what they were talking about but heard his name mentioned several times.

Soon after, Smiley came up to bed and crawled in next to Granny. The quiet night allowed Michael to hear Smiley's last words before he drifted off to sleep.

"I don't like being in the middle of these things — and I don't trust that white fella at the Department of Territories at all."

The following day at breakfast, Smiley said to Michael, "I think you should avoid Thursday Island for a few days. I've heard rumours that they're looking for a reason to haul you in."

Michael never returned to the Department of Territories, and that left Mueller fuming mad. It was bad enough that Fomenko was even attempting the crazy voyage, but now he was disrespecting the agencies in charge of the area.

Tyler sat at his desk, buried in paperwork. When Mueller spat out a request, the young man was on his feet, heading towards a filing cabinet near the back of the room.

He'd taken his cane, but after the third time it had tapped the wooden floor, he noticed Mueller glaring at him. He lifted the cane and limped the rest of the way quietly.

Mueller picked up the phone and called his superior.

"Fred," he said, "this Fomenko is making a mockery of my entire existence. You should see what he wrote on his initial application. Under the question: Where do you live? He wrote: The Reef - Australian coast. And that the purpose of his visit was: Seeing the place."

The man on the other end of the line must have chuckled because Mueller spat back, "I don't think it's funny at all."

He stared at the initial application that Michael had turned in and added, "When asked how long he intended to stay in Dutch New Guinea, he said, 'Until I decide to travel further.' Of all the gall! He's not taking us seriously at all."

Mueller's face flushed red at his superior's comment.

"Well, he should," he spat, "that boat he's in is worse than a primitive craft, and I'm of the opinion that he would not let a little matter like permits or clearances stand in the way of doing just what he pleases and that he will eventually attempt the crossing."

His boss then spoke for a full minute. Mueller's face changed as he listened, like a python that has suddenly sighted a possible meal.

"Yes," he said, "he is staying with a local called Smiley Paul."

After another pause, he added, "I think we could put a little pressure on him, at least enough to know when Michael departs and where he's heading."

Across the room, Tyler kept his head down and tried to be invisible.

Late that night, when most of Horn was sleeping, Michael listened to the gentle tapping of a cane as it grew closer. He knew now the late-night visitor was Tyler, and he feared the young man brought bad news.

Like the time before, Michael could not hear the conversation.

He supposed Smiley would say something in the morning, but he feared that might be too late. If it weren't urgent, Tyler wouldn't have limped all the way here in the dead of night.

Michael reflected that Tyler was his Hermes — the Greek God of travellers and athletes — who delivered his messages on winged feet.

A bit ironic considering the young man's limp, he thought.

In *The Odyssey*, Hermes helps Odysseus by warning him that the witch, Circe, intended to poison him. He gave him a herb called *Moly*, making him resistant to her potion and allowing him to escape.

In the dark, Michael yearned to hear the message that was on the young man's lips.

When Smiley crept into bed beside Granny, Michael strained his ears to hear the conversation. Perhaps the Islander wanted his words heard because his voice carried clearly through the night.

"I'm to go to the police station on Thursday Island in the morning," he said. "I guess the Queensland coppers are putting on the pressure. They want me to let them know before Michael leaves in case they get the go-ahead to nab him."

Granny sucked in her breath. "They want you to spy on him."

The long sigh that escaped Smiley's lungs was felt throughout the house, like a fog of despair that drifted from room to room.

"How can I invite a man into my own home and then turn him in?" he asked.

Granny didn't respond for a while, but before she drifted off, she said, "It would be better if we don't know."

Michael looked over the tidy bedroom he slept in. The bed was clean with soft sheets, and lace curtains fluttered in the window. He hadn't been this comfortable since the Lockhart Mission, but he knew he couldn't stay.

Dawn was still hours away when Michael crept through the house, determined not to wake a soul. It took several trips to transfer his supplies to *Tortoise*, but he was on the water before the sky began to lighten.

He wouldn't allow Smiley and Granny to be put in an uncomfortable situation. If they didn't know where he was going, all the better.

But he wasn't quite ready to try crossing the strait.

His sailcloth had finally arrived, but he still needed the grommets that Caldwell had suggested. The American had gone to Thursday Island for business a few days before, and while there, ordered the brass rings.

They were due soon, but for now, Michael had to get off Horn and lay low. He decided to make for Hammond Island, which was about a fifteen-kilometre paddle to the northwest of Horn. The island was on the other side of Thursday Island, and with a bit of luck, Michael could hide out there until he was ready.

Then he could duck over to Thursday Island, grab his grommets, and be gone before anyone was the wiser.

He felt terrible for Smiley and hoped there were no repercussions.

I'll never understand why they can't just let me be, he thought sadly.

At least he hadn't mentioned the island specifically to Smiley, so he wouldn't have to lie when he said he didn't know Michael's whereabouts.

As Michael paddled over the starlit water, he imagined Tyler limping through the night to warn him.

Thank you, my Hermes, he thought.

The following day, Smiley Paul woke to discover that his houseguest had mysteriously disappeared in the night. At first, he was discouraged that Michael had not said goodbye, but on reflection, he realised he'd been let off the hook.

Smiley didn't show up at the station first thing in the morning but instead took the day's last ferry to Thursday Island, dragging his feet. The officer marked down that Michael Fomenko had "Left Horn Island" but seemed sceptical that Smiley didn't know where he was going.

But Smiley stuck to his story. "He just disappeared — I don't know where," he said over and over.

When they pressed on, he gave them his biggest smile and said, "Tagai has gone back to the sea."

Eventually, the police let him go.

On the last ferry back to Horn, Smiley sat by his nephew.

"I've never seen Mueller so mad," said Tyler. "He was livid when he heard that Michael had moved on, and then later in the day, he received a phone call stating that there were no laws that prevented Michael from continuing on his journey while still in Australian waters. That made him even madder."

"So, Michael's done with them?" asked Smiley.

Tyler shook his head. "I wish. He never completed the paperwork, and down the line, that will catch up with him. They don't care if their list of demands is unrealistic."

Smiley sighed, "I'm just glad he's back on the water — I didn't want the blood of the mighty Tagai on my hands."

Tyler said, "His name is Michael."

Smiley shook his head. "He will always be Tagai to me."

On the far side of Hammond Island, Michael encountered a small stream flowing out through a thick stand of mangroves. After paddling upstream about a kilometre, he left the beach and tidal trees behind and entered a bushy forest.

They won't even see me from the air here.

Michael stopped near the centre of the six-kilometre-wide oblong-shaped island. About two hundred people lived there, but nearly all of them on the other side, in the only town — Keriri, the traditional name of the island.

Initially, Michael planned on making a camp near the end of the stream, but there was a stagnant smell in the air there. Instead, he camped about a third of the way back to the beach, where the water still had a freshness to it.

He'd seen several fish jump and others scatter from his paddle strokes and decided to try for some dinner. He had stowed most of his supplies in the tyre tubes and didn't intend to tap into them until he was on his way, but his fishing gear was handy.

Luck was on his side, and he caught two in his first few casts.

He gutted them, stuck a small twig through their gills, and then hung them from a branch.

Soon after, he had a fire going, careful not to burn anything that would cause heavy smoke. When the fire had diminished, he wrapped the fish in a big leaf and set them on the coals.

Later, he ate them with his fingers.

By the time the afternoon had heated up, he was napping peacefully with a full belly. Soon he would have to find a way across the island, to Keriri, where there were daily ferries to Thursday Island.

He worried about the coppers and nasty Mr Mueller, and then reflected on how much he had enjoyed living with Smiley and Granny. He hoped again he didn't get them in trouble.

Suddenly it seemed that being around people brought on nothing but complications, and that fact reminded him of how much more he liked the wild, uninhabited places.

Michael stretched out on the dry piece of land he'd picked for a camp. With his fire crackling nearby, birds singing in the trees around him, and the smell of the saltwater, he felt like he could stay for a while.

Over the next few days, Michael explored Hammond Island, drifting along the lonely coast. Although he had arrived in the dead of night and felt the shadow of the law on the horizon, he didn't try to hide from the locals.

It was the authorities he watched out for, and there were none on the island as far as he knew.

And as it turned out, he didn't see a soul.

He scoured the coast for shellfish and collected a few fragments of fishing nets and several drifting buoys. He explored as much as he could while keeping some distance from Keriri. In Queensland, he'd had stretches of river or rainforest to himself, but never an island.

He liked living on an island.

One day he was surprised to hear the metal ringing of a large bell, and when he looked up to the top of a hill, he glimpsed an old mission building.

Later he would learn it was St. Joseph's Roman Catholic Mission of the Sacred Heart, set up to help Asian immigrants. But on that day, his only thought was that the way the structure was perched on the top of the basaltic rocks made it look like a great dog.

He climbed the steep slope to the Mission and found it empty, having been abandoned for at least twenty years from the looks of it. Frangipani trees grew all around the buildings, and their blossoms filled the air with heady scents.

When Michael reached the entrance to the Mission, he glimpsed a person sitting on a bench that overlooked the beach far below. Michael was about to slip away when he realised he knew the man.

He approached him and stuck out his hand.

"I was hoping I'd see you from up here," said Tyler, "but it appears you found me first."

Michael scratched his head and asked, "How'd you even know to look on Hammond?"

Tyler laughed, and it was a happy, uncomplicated sound that he hadn't heard from him yet.

"I wasn't sure—but Caldwell thought it would be the best place for you to launch from if you were heading north."

"You know Caldwell?" asked Michael, becoming even more confused.

"He came searching for Smiley when your grommets came in," said Tyler, "and then Smiley found me."

Tyler reached for a small daypack by his feet, opened it, and took out a small paper bag containing the grommets, plus a sturdy needle and coarse thread.

Michael beamed when he saw it all, relieved that he wouldn't have to go back to Thursday Island.

He thanked Tyler and told him to extend thanks to Smiley and Caldwell.

"You should be getting back," said Michael, eventually, concerned the young man might get in trouble.

"All good," said Tyler, "Mueller thinks I'm at the Territories office comparing records."

"Won't you get in trouble if he discovers you're not?"

A confident grin spread over Tyler's face as he said, "No, my contact there is a second cousin—he'll cover for me."

Michael noted how different Tyler was when outside of the office. There was a confidence in his eyes that he didn't display around Mueller.

"I hope the next time I see you," said Michael, "that you don't have to put up with a loser boss like Mueller."

Tyler let his gaze settle over the distant surf and said, "The next time you see me, I'll be running that department."

Over the next few days, Michael kept busy. First, he found a straight and narrow sapling and turned it into a suitable boom that he lashed to the mast. Then he sewed the grommets into the corners of his sail. He spaced them about every thirty centimetres along the mast, and he did the same for the bottom edge that would be connected to the boom.

He also topped off his fresh water and smoked a few fish to add to his stores, but otherwise, he was ready to go.

He prepared his boat on a night overrun by stars, using his new rope to thread it all together. His final project was to tie a line to the end of the boom and fasten it near the canoe's stern where he could let it in or out to adjust the sail. Caldwell had told him that sailors call this line a 'sheet'.

When the tide pulled away the following day, he rode the little stream out into the surf and pointed his boat north. He was as ready as he'd ever be.

Michael Fomenko on the Horn Island. 1959.
Photo courtesy of the Cairns Post.

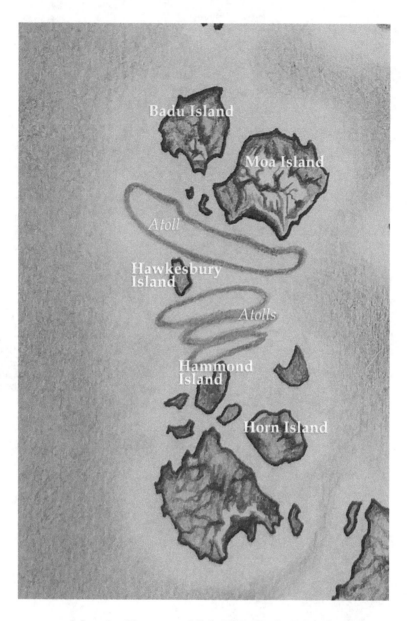

Map 6 – Hammond Island to Badu Island.
Illustration by Tom Fish.

Chapter Eighteen

The Odyssey XI – Nagi Island
(October 1959)

*T*he Torres Strait represented challenging new waters for Michael and *Tortoise*. A mere hundred and fifty kilometres separated Cape York from Dutch New Guinea, but he'd known all along that the stretch of open sea would be one of the most difficult segments of his voyage.

Michael floated on the water, his journey before him. To his left, the Arafura Sea rolled and threatened in darkness, while on his right, a ruddy sky was lightening over the Coral Sea.

Dutch New Guinea lay dead ahead. His immediate destination was Badu Island, forty kilometres away. Badu was in a Torres Island group called the Western Islands, and in sailing there, he would leave behind the Inner Islands like Horn, Thursday and Hammond.

Badu had shops and a dock and about six hundred residents. If he could get there and regroup, he had little doubt he could make the final crossing.

But in the gloom, his canoe felt small and insufficient.

A strong breeze blew in from the west, pushing his boat back towards the Coral Sea. He'd expected the wind to come from the other direction, and his outrigger was on the wrong side.

The southeasterlies should still be blowing now, he thought. But he knew the trade winds were unpredictable, and the Torres Strait was notorious for changing weather and currents.

He turned the boat around, which felt safer with the outrigger preventing him from flipping, but he couldn't use the sail for now.

He tried to dispel his nervousness by paddling hard. But the open water tossed his craft erratically, his strokes appearing to have little effect. His nerves were taut, ready to snap, like a stick in a crocodile's mouth.

And all the while, the wind pushed him eastward.

He tossed out a sea anchor bucket, rigging it the way Smiley had shown him. After their lesson, the Islander had insisted he keep the pail. In his mind, he heard Smiley warning him not to take the waves on directly.

He tied the bow end first and, after throwing the bucket ahead of them, used the stern line to tighten it until *Tortoise* faced northeast—not due north, where he really wanted to go.

Thank you, Smiley, he thought as he noticed the craft moving smoothly without taking on water.

About an hour after the sun had risen, the winds reversed, and Michael turned the boat around, pulled in the sea anchor, and put up his sail.

By taking in or releasing the sheet, he could now move the boom to catch more wind. He used his paddle off the stern as a rudder to keep them on course.

Over the next few hours, he continued to head north.

He sensed that he was out of the main shipping lanes, but he still couldn't shake his fear of being run down by a freighter. He constantly scanned to the east and west. The worry exhausted him. In his mind, he imagined them skimming over the water like a ghost.

Around mid-day, he noticed a stretch of breakers ahead of him. He tried to recall as much as he could of Smiley's lecture on islands and reefs. He remembered that lumps of coral rising above the sea were cays, and if they were ring-shaped or enclosed a lagoon, they were atolls.

This line of jagged coral extended as far east and west as he could see. He guessed he had reached the first of the massive atolls that lined the Torres Strait like tiger stripes.

From where he sat, it was nearly impossible to tell what lay underwater. Coral islands are flat and almost invisible. Much of the submerged landscape was created twelve thousand years earlier, at the end of the last ice age.

Before then, the Torres Strait was a land bridge that connected the present-day Australian continent with Dutch New Guinea. Today's islands are the remaining peaks that were not submerged when the ocean levels rose.

Michael collapsed his sail and held his breath as he steered his canoe between the visible coral outcroppings at the edge of the atoll. It was a tight fit, and the hull scraped over a submerged slab on the way in.

Only after he'd entered the atoll could he see that the tide was out and the water there shallower. Clumps of fantastic coral reefs sprawled all around him.

He dropped his anchor and exhaled. About five kilometres behind him, he could still see Hammond Island. It appeared pathetically close.

To the north lay only reef and water.

He ate one of his smoked fish, drank a cup of water, and then lay down in the bottom of his canoe. He needed to rest.

The sea was calmer over the atoll, and a soft swell rocked Michael to sleep, the pure hymn of the water his lullaby.

He awoke to a vibrant red sunset over the Arafura Sea. Only one outcropping of coral remained visible, and the dying sun painted it crimson. The tide had come in, and his anchor rope was stretched tight and nearly vertical.

Had he not seen the atoll at low tide, he wouldn't have believed he was over it.

The wind had died down, and he paddled for about an hour.

Darkness was coming on strong when he decided to stop again.

Suddenly, he realised his mistake. If he had paddled off the atoll, there would be no way for him to anchor. He would have to either paddle all night or take his chances drifting in the dark.

He let down his anchor and was relieved when he felt it hit bottom with a thud and take hold.

He lay on the bottom of the boat and stared at the rocking stars until sleep took him.

He woke the next day to a glassy sea that barely moved. The sun was well up, and he was surprised at how long he'd dozed.

I feel like I've slept for half of this crossing, he mused.

The only sounds were that of water lapping against the hull.

He could see only water in three directions. The aquamarine sea spread around him, feeling endless.

When he glanced over the side of *Tortoise*, Michael caught his breath. The still water was translucent, with no taint whatsoever, and he could see through it so clearly that the fathoms seemed to melt away.

The fragile world of coral was not only supported and bolstered by the water, but to Michael, it appeared that the life below was lovingly, intimately embraced by it.

Vibrant corals of blue, grey and pink waved in marvelous rainbows of colour. Fantastic tentacled anemones swayed next to giant fluted clams with feathery lips. Intricate laced fans and ribbons of twisting weeds danced to the currents.

Michael yearned to immerse himself in it, but he dared not leave his boat. He was still daunted by the remaining distance to the other side of the strait and wanted no mishaps.

Instead, he spent several hours watching, marvelling at the fish as they darted amongst the hidden grottoes below.

Some rushed by in schools of thousands, blinding him with identical silver flashes of light. Others were individually unique: flashy as precious jewels and gaudier than tropical birds.

He ate another smoked fish, drank some more water, and prepared himself mentally to start moving again.

He spent the next few hours meandering north, navigating through the coral outcroppings until he eventually approached the jagged edge of the massive atoll. He didn't use his sail for fear that more speed might cause an accident.

He paused there and dropped anchor.

Before he hit the open water again, he needed to assess. He realised it was easier to get on and off the atolls during the high tide. He'd be more aware of that now.

The wind was blowing from the southeast like it should be this time of year, so his outrigger was on the correct side.

No reason not to try the sail, he thought.

He made sure his supplies were tied down. Then he hauled up his anchor, and as a safety precaution, untied the end connected to the heavy piece of metal and wrapped it around his waist.

The tide was out, and it made for a dangerous passage past the breakers. He planned on approaching a gap slowly, but as soon as he let the sail out, it filled with air, and *Tortoise* shot forward.

They were heading straight for the rocks. Michael pulled the boom towards the centre of the canoe with his arms — not bothering with the sheet — to try to use the sail to point the canoe towards the wind and away from the rocks. In the middle of this action, he felt a surge of panic as he realised that this wouldn't turn the canoe enough to clear the rocks and that he should have used his paddle instead.

In the back of his mind, he heard Caldwell explaining that rudders steer a boat, not sails.

It appeared his mistake would cost him dearly as *Tortoise* was on course to collide with a slab of coral, but then suddenly, a big gust shifted their direction, and they were in the open water again, heading north.

It was only later that he discovered one of his plastic water jugs had been swept away in the confusion. It was only half-full, but the thought of lost water would eventually plague him.

It turned out that the next big atoll was only about a kilometre and a half away. With the wind pushing him steadily, Michael was there in less than an hour.

It came up suddenly, and Michael was in the process of taking down the sail when his momentum carried him right past the breakers and into the atoll.

That was lucky, he thought. He told himself that next time he would take down the sail sooner and paddle himself through the rocks with more caution.

You could've lost everything right there, he thought, his gut churning. He wondered how long he could survive clinging to one of the few clumps of coral that didn't get submerged.

That's pretty much how Mueller thought I'd die.

He paddled across the atoll until he reached the far side.

He stayed back far enough that any big waves would be diminished. And he dropped anchor as soon as he noticed the tide rising.

He was down to only a few smoked fish, and however much was left in the remaining plastic jug of water. He ate his dinner while the sky slowly filled with colour and fell asleep with his mind on the next open water crossing.

He woke the following day again to a peaceful sea. Behind him, to the south, he could still see the faint spectre of Hammond Island, and to the north, he could make out another island.

Caldwell had told him that you couldn't see more than fifteen or twenty kilometres at water level, even if the object was big, so he figured the island to the north couldn't be Badu.

Has to be Hawkesbury Island, he thought. That small island was about halfway to Badu.

This time, when he crossed the open water between atolls, he was better prepared. He waited until he'd maneuvered past the breakers before putting up his sail, and he took it down well before navigating his way past the breakers of the next atoll.

He couldn't tell how big the atoll's inner lagoon was, but it seemed endless. Finally, after spending several hours working his way across it, he guessed it to be three kilometres wide.

When he floated at the far end by the breakers, looking at distant Hawkesbury Island, he guessed he still had seven or eight kilometres to go.

It was late in the day, and the tide was retreating, so he decided to drop anchor there and stay put until morning. He ate his last smoked fish and lay down to sleep soon after sunset.

He paddled towards Hawkesbury Island early the following day and was close when the sun peeked over the horizon. He remembered Smiley warning that coral reefs still surrounded even the larger islands, so he waited until he could see better before trying to reach the shore.

When he did come in, the tide was high, and he glided right over the reef. He circled the island clockwise and found an idyllic beach on the western shore.

Michael had never been so happy to stand on solid ground. He walked along the brilliant white sand beach, glad to be exercising his legs. The beach grass tickled his feet. A grove of palm trees swayed inland with gulls and other birds singing from the canopy.

He hauled his boat up past the highwater mark and made a camp nearby, under the shade of a few palms.

Perched on a rock not too far from his camp, he came upon a Japanese helmet. It was a relic from the war, fourteen years old now, at least. The inner strappings were long gone and rotted away.

He washed it in the sea and then took it back to his camp.

Next, he collected dry branches and some withered beach grass and placed them in a depression he scooped out of the sand. He felt a rush of warmth when he got a small flame from the magnifying glass Caldwell's son, Roger, had given him.

And then another surge when the kindling took to flame.

Before long, he had a good fire going. He quickly added more fuel, his goal to get a bed of coals.

When he finally sat next to the flames, his stomach began to rumble incessantly. So far, he'd gotten by on a few smoked fish and water, but that wasn't enough, and his belly told him so.

He hauled out a few of the food-packed tyre tubes and broke into his supplies. His water was running low; he had less than half a plastic jug left.

That's five litres, tops, he thought.

He hoped he might find a freshwater spring on the island.

He took out the salt and flour and, using some of his precious remaining water, proceeded to mix the ingredients inside the helmet. Eventually, he made two large balls of dough.

When he'd kneaded them enough, he flattened them into big, thick pancakes and set them aside.

While he waited for the flames to settle, he scoured the area for coconuts. There were plenty in the trees, but Michael hadn't mastered the art of climbing up after them. He found a half-dozen on the ground; several were green and still full of juice.

He sat by the fire and ate one, savouring the milky liquid before devouring the soft meat inside. His skin had burned on the passage, and he massaged the coconut oil into the tender areas.

Finally, the fire had died down to coals, and Michael prepared the site the way the Mow family had shown him at Russell Heads. First, he scooped away the coals and made a small pit. Then he coated the flattened balls of dough with white ash and placed them inside the hole.

Lastly, he covered it all with coals.

He stared at the fire pit and wondered if he'd have the patience to wait. He remembered that Mrs Mow had let the damper cook for forty minutes, but the concept of measured time suddenly seemed funny.

He chuckled at the idea of wearing a watch and thought of lines of businessmen, all wearing expensive timepieces, as they headed off to work.

You're all prisoners, he chuckled.

His stomach was growling too loudly for him to stay put, so he searched the area for a while. Unfortunately, the beach had no oysters or other shellfish, although he thought he'd try his hand at fishing in the morning.

A careful search of his cove revealed no edible fruit other than the coconuts. He tried to climb one of the trees but deemed it too dangerous halfway.

But he did make one good discovery — water. Not much of it, just a small pool of rainwater in a depression of a rock. It wasn't enough to fill one of his jugs, but twice that day, he drank his fill.

Rinsing the helmet in the sea, he dug another hole in the coals. He set the helmet inside and half-filled it with water. While it heated, he dug into more of his supplies and took out the tea and sugar.

I'll be living large tonight, he thought.

Glancing at the helmet, he considered it a lucky break that the Japanese soldier had not been shot in the head. He wondered if the man had died here or how the helmet had come to rest on the island.

That night he ate one of the loaves of damper, overcome with how good a warm meal could be. He washed it all down with sugary tea, toasting the departed Japanese officer who'd contributed the pot.

He drifted off to sleep feeling sated and at ease.

The following day Michael tried to fish. He had no luck finding shellfish he might use as bait and had to settle for a few pieces of his remaining loaf of damper.

He had no bites and gave up by mid-day.

He walked up and down the coast but found nothing worth scavenging.

Later in the day, he returned to his puddle and drank what was left. *Not much sense in staying here any longer,* he thought. *I should get moving while I still have a few sips of water left in that jug.*

When he pushed *Tortoise* into the sea the next morning, the skies to the north were ominous. He had with him the Japanese helmet, a few coconuts, and what was left of his loaf of damper. He only had twenty kilometres to cover to reach Badu Island, but that was where the storm loomed.

An hour later, it became apparent that he should have stayed on Hawkesbury Island, but there was no turning back.

He reached a large atoll halfway to Badu Island and frantically searched for an outcropping of rock that would not disappear at high tide.

About halfway across the atoll, he found one with a small shelf and a pocket that offered shelter from two sides. He hauled the canoe out of the water with a huge effort and tied the bow end to the coral. His supplies were lashed down by the mast, and now he secured the two coconuts and the remaining water jug.

The tide returned, surging white before the gale, and the swells threatened to engulf him. Waves tugged at the bottom of the boat, trying to haul it away.

He clung to the rock and tried to creep higher, but nowhere could he escape the howling wind or the frenzied, unyielding sea.

For two days and two nights, he clung for his life. During that time, he prayed to — and cursed — all the forces that be. Jesus, Zeus, Father Gilfeather, and even his own father, Daniel, all felt the lash of his tongue.

The wind whipped him savagely, and the spray of waves soaked him to the bone. He ate the damper as the first rains hit, and by the time the storms ended, he was ravenous.

He was relieved to see blue sky when he woke, but a robust breeze from the west discouraged him. The current seemed to be pushing from that direction as well. He remembered Smiley telling him that this sometimes happened after a big blow.

My outrigger is on the wrong side again, he lamented.

He sensed the current was moving too fast, and he'd have no chance covering the remaining distance to Badu, regardless of how close it appeared. Moreover, he was emotionally drained, working with a sluggish mind.

But he had to try. And first, he had to move the outrigger to the other side.

His knuckles were sore and stiff from clinging to the rocks. It took some time for him to untie the rope connecting the canoe to the coral. He considered cutting it, but every bit of rope was precious now.

Eventually, he lowered *Tortoise* into the water, and over the next few hours, he moved the outrigger to the other side.

He worried about getting blown off course. If he got swept to the east, who knew where he would end up.

Somewhere deep in the Coral Sea, he thought.

Badu tantalised him. It appeared only seven or eight kilometres away. He threw caution to the wind and got back in the boat.

He downed a cup of water. Then, right before he took his first stroke, Michael looked at the heavens and said, "Do what you will."

The tide was in, and this edge of the atoll didn't have many visible rocks in his path, so Michael put up his sail. The moment he tightened the sheet, the canvas filled with air and the canoe ploughed forward.

He hit the open water with forward momentum, but instantly the wind and current grabbed the boat, and *Tortoise* shot to the right, heading east.

Michael paddled hard to point the craft towards the middle of the channel where he wanted to go, then untied the sheet from the stern. He let it out until the boom and sail moved leeward, enough to reach the best position to catch the wind and drive the boat in that direction.

But it was no use. Even though *Tortoise* was now pointed in the right direction with its sails filled and moving fast, the current swept the hull sideways towards the east at twice the speed generated by the sails.

He panicked as he realised at his present speed and angle, he would completely miss the island. There was no way he could cross the remaining kilometres before being swept away.

Then he noticed another landmass coming into view. This was Moa Island, and it sat southeast of Badu. For a brief moment, Michael thought he might make a landing there but then realised how strongly the current had him.

He was heading on a southeast track that would put him beyond all of the Western Islands. His first attempt at crossing the strait had failed.

When the wind blew itself out, and the erratic current let go of *Tortoise*, Michael found himself far from land. In all directions, he saw only water.

The endless struggle against the forces of wind and water had left him exhausted, and he didn't want to contemplate his fate.

The Torres Islands are spread over 48,000 square kilometres, and Michael knew only that he was in the middle of it. He was down to a couple of coconuts and three litres of water.

He'd drank only one litre during the storms, the constant rain giving him too much moisture at times. By morning he'd felt half-drowned but come noon, his lips were cracking.

He ate one of the coconuts that night, splitting it open with his cane knife just before sunset.

When he woke, he stared at his remaining water jug. He decided to ration himself to three cups of water a day: One at sunrise, one at noon, and one at sunset.

There's a little more than four cups in a litre, so that'll give me about four days, he calculated as he slowly downed his first cup of the day.

To each cup, he had the luxury of adding a handful of sugar. The salt, rice, flour and tea were useless to him now, but he could spare the sugar.

He kept his sail up, but there wasn't the slightest breeze in the air. It seemed they didn't move at all but instead waited for some unknown event.

In the quiet, pale void of the afternoon, he drank his second cup of sugar water and thought of others who had journeyed through the seas. Pedro Fernandes de Quieros had sailed through in 1606 on his voyage from Peru in search of *Terra Australis*. He'd named the strait after his Spanish navigator, Luis Vaez de Torres.

Captain James Cook was here in 1770 when he declared British sovereignty over the east coast of Australia; in one stroke claiming ownership of land that had been inhabited for tens of thousands of years.

Long before these white men came along, the islands' indigenous inhabitants travelled throughout the archipelago. In their time, they prospered, trading, growing crops on the islands, and sharing what they had.

Michael had learned that the contact wasn't always peaceful. A few tribes, like the Mer, were known to be fierce raiders. They waged constant war with their neighbours, the Darnley.

Michael remembered Smiley claiming descent from headhunters and grinned. The thought that there could be savage people out there, headhunters even, appealed to him greatly.

If only the world were still filled with monsters and gods, he thought sadly as he scanned the horizon.

That night he dreamt of a Kraken, the giant beast reaching up its long, tentacled arms from the dreary depths below.

They battled for hours in the watery underworld, and although he dreamt himself victorious, he still woke in the morning parched and barely able to swallow.

The eastern rim of the ocean lay colourless, unaware of the coming day until the sun rose above it like a delicate pink pearl. The glow hovered and grew for only a few moments until it burst forth, and suddenly the world existed only in flickers of vibrant gold.

Michael blinked at the blinding horizon, wondering what the day would have in store. *Will I strike land today?* he pondered.

It didn't seem like it. The sea looked perfectly flat and in no rush to go anywhere.

At one point, he glanced over the side of the canoe and realised that they were moving at about a knot. Mostly he only glimpsed deep blue water under the drifting canoe, but a few times, he saw dark stains where coral or weeds covered the ground.

They drifted ever so slowly, and it became difficult to distinguish minutes from hours.

Once, he spied a massive grouper lurking in the shadows of a grotto. But before he could grab his fishing gear, the bottom dropped away again, and the fish was gone.

Michael knew he needed to find land soon. He squinted at the horizon as he sipped his afternoon cup of sugar water. He winced while wetting his lips and tried his best to stay in the small puddle of shade cast by the limp sail.

He had less than two litres and one coconut—although he'd drained it of juice the night before. He planned on using some of the coconut meat as bait if they entered shallower waters or passed over coral reefs.

He turned away from the sun and tried to find shelter in the bottom of the canoe.

Michael woke to the sound of a motor chugging by. He sat up quickly and saw a pearling lugger heading towards him from about five hundred metres away.

The word *Sabatino* was painted on its side in black, italic letters.

On the deck, a dozen men leaned on the rails watching him.

Michael saw only Islanders, no white men, and wondered if the ship was owned by a mission—like the *Yola*.

He thought of those good men and smiled, which seemed to relax this crew because suddenly they were all grinning back.

"You look like you could use a tow, mate," said a tall man at the rail who spoke with an air of authority. "We're northbound, but we can drop you at Nagi Island when we pass it if you want."

Michael winced when he tried to talk, and his voice only came through as a whisper. "Yes," he said. "Thank you."

Another man tossed him a rope that he tied to the bow.

Soon he was on the deck of the bigger boat, wind in his hair and a group of men eyeing him curiously. He kept silent, in part because of his chapped lips and scratchy throat, but also because he'd been alone for some time now and didn't know what to say.

His thirst gripped him like a vice, and he wished he'd downed a cup of his precious water before leaving *Tortoise*. Had he not been overcome with shyness, he would have asked for something to drink. But, unfortunately, the men on this crew had been less observant of his condition.

He no longer noticed the sway of the ocean, and it was a thrill to be this high above the water again. From this vantage, he could see an island to the north, less than seven kilometres away. Had he woken in time, he might have spotted it, although he didn't know if the currents would have allowed him to reach it before sweeping him away.

How much easier to sail with a motor as a backup, he thought as he felt the engine's vibration through the deck.

"That's Nagi," said the tall man. "I can drop you at the Government station on the east side if you'd like."

Michael paused before replying. There were no arrest warrants that he knew about, but he still wanted to avoid the authorities.

The tall man picked up on his hesitation and added, "Or I could leave you on the other side — but there's a big reef there, so you'll have to paddle yourself in."

"Put me there," answered Michael decisively.

"Okay," he said, "It doesn't matter to me. Just watch the gusts — that windward side of the island blows hard."

Michael nodded, knowing if it were difficult to reach the shore, he'd most likely be left alone. He'd learned that lesson at Cape Flattery.

The bigger the reef, the better, he thought.

An hour later, Michael was back in his boat, untying the lead that connected *Tortoise* to the larger vessel. He gestured a thank you and used his paddle to shove off.

It was a relief to be back in his canoe. He floated offshore, not ready to tackle the coastal reef.

His fingers trembled when he grabbed the water jug and gulped down several long swallows.

When the sound of the motor completely faded, leaving only the lapping of waves, he relaxed again.

It seemed easier to face a shifting wall of coral reef than converse with his fellow man, but maybe that was natural. *There's nothing in this wilderness that's ever placed judgement on me,* he mused while surveying the coast.

Nagi Island was about two kilometres long and shaped like a giant scoop with the handle pointing to the northeast. The north shore had a wide reef that extended for nearly five hundred metres.

Michael scurried in at high tide and pulled up onto the white, sandy beach.

He saw no evidence of man anywhere. Instead, birds hooted and called from the trees while a light breeze swayed the palms along the shore. Further inland, the land rose to a peak — Mount Ernest — and Michael yearned to climb it.

This is what I've been looking for, he thought.

He pulled *Tortoise* further ashore and hid the canoe under the canopy of palms. He made a camp there, the view north a reminder that Dutch New Guinea still lay about a hundred kilometres away.

He wondered at the fate of his journey, but for now, he relaxed.

The beach he landed on was about a kilometre long. If he continued circling the island to the north, he would reach a wide coral bay filled with seagrass and countless fish.

In the other direction, the shoreline curved sharply until it pointed to the southwest. After a few days on the island, he explored that area but stopped when he noticed large crocodile tracks puncturing the ground.

I guess I've got enough space on my side of the island.

And he did. Michael enjoyed his camp and the surrounding bush. That first day he discovered a freshwater pool, located five minutes away, just before the land began to rise.

After drinking his fill of the sweet water, he plunged his head under and tried to rinse it free of salt. His beard and hair had grown long again, but with nobody else around, he forgot about his appearance.

Over the next week, he excelled at island life. He learned to climb the coconut trees and harvest their fruit. He visited the bay regularly and eventually figured out what bait the local fish preferred. He also had some success spearing fish using one of his old cane knives mounted to a pole.

He even climbed the mountain. Halfway up, he came across a trail and remembered that people lived on the other side of the isle.

181

And from the top, he spied several boats anchored off what he assumed was the government post.

He slunk away quietly and stayed on his side.

One day flowed into the next. The weather was perfect, with no rain and light breezes. He kept a fire going for cooking, although he no longer needed its warmth. The warm sand cradled him at night.

His supplies came in handy now, and he made plenty of damper to go along with the fried fish. In addition, he boiled rice in the Japanese helmet.

He washed it all down with sugary tea.

His favourite place was the coral bay. Often, he spied sea turtles there while fishing. He could not believe their numbers or the different species. He saw flatback and hawksbill turtles, as well as green and ridley turtles.

Often, he would swim with them, floating above the prehistoric-looking creatures, sometimes holding their shells while they cruised underwater among the seagrass.

One afternoon he surfaced after searching for shellfish and found himself face to face with a pale-skinned visitor with a warm, knowing gaze.

He blinked the saltwater out of his eyes and realised he was being confronted by a dugong—a herbivorous marine mammal related to the manatee.

The creature gazed at him, unafraid, through large eyes that seemed filled with curiosity.

"Hello," said Michael, feeling like he'd finally encountered a fabled creature. Throughout history, manatee-like animals have inspired legends of mermaids.

There was something maternal about the way the dugong watched him. He sensed that she was a female and unafraid of him.

That surprised Michael because one of the main threats to the species was hunting by man since they make easy targets.

In Queensland, he'd encountered a few poachers. They'd mostly been after crocodiles, but when paying clients were on board, almost anything was up for grabs.

He hoped the dugongs here were smart enough to hide if a boat came around.

On another day, he found a dead sea turtle washed up on the beach by a late afternoon tide. A cut on the neck suggested a boat propeller had hit it. He dragged it back to camp.

In the morning, he would clean out the meat and try to save the shell.

That night he fell asleep next to his fire while a nearly full moon glided across the sky.

In the morning, he woke to find the turtle carcass gone.

In the sand lay a line of crocodile tracks. The beast had crept to within a few paces of Michael, then grabbed the turtle carcass and hauled it away.

He decided after that that he had to see the giant croc. It felt too much like a mythical creature to ignore it—and the way the beast had stolen the turtle carcass seemed like a challenge.

Michael didn't like to leave tracks where others could see them. Maybe it was an old habit from 1956 when Cyclone Agnes had affected the generosity of the farmers in the Gordonvale area. He either skirted along the edge of the bush, or he stayed close enough to the surf that the tide ate his prints.

On this day, the tide was coming in, so he walked along the water. His feet were as hard as bone, but still, he watched out for urchins or stonefish.

One wrong step and you might be limping for a week, he thought, remembering the injury he'd had at Cape Flattery.

The north coast of Nagi Island took the brunt of the seasonal winds, and when he rounded the corner and turned southwest, it was much quieter.

He'd grown so used to the constant breeze that he barely noticed it. Like the smashing of waves, it felt like an inescapable force.

An image arose in his mind that he'd been living on the lungs of the island, and here he was closer to the heart. The silence on the leeward beach was enchanting, and he yearned to go into the rainforest that skirted the shore.

These days on the island, in solitude, had brought him back to that more profound connection with nature.

He sensed that the island was aware. It knew of him. He didn't know if this stemmed from his own Nature God or if he now also detected the world of the Aboriginals and Islanders.

Am I sensing the Dreamtime? he asked himself.

Michael didn't know. He didn't overthink things. And on that day, he silently followed the beach, moving at times to the edge of the bush that crept down to the water.

The palm fronds above rustled and whispered despite there being no wind.

Behind a fallen palm, the shoreline had eroded enough for the incoming tide to flow inland a short way. The crevasse stretched back a few paces before disappearing under the foliage.

Michael felt drawn to it, like a deep-sea creature to luminous bait.

He peeked through the foliage and saw the tunnel continued some distance — at least a dozen paces.

Hidden like that, it might make a good camp.

He entered the watery trail and found himself in a long, narrow ravine, about two metres wide with puddles of water covering his ankles. It was dark and musty there, and a scent reminded him of those ancient rainforests in Queensland.

He turned deeper into the labyrinth, and a warning bell went off in his head.

He suddenly recognised the smell!

Before he could move, the water appeared to explode in front of him. In the turbulence, he glimpsed scales and claws, and when it settled, a huge croc lay facing him.

It snapped aggressively, lunging its head.

I'm finished, thought Michael.

In the confined space, the roar was defining. Then, the croc snapped again while the sinuous tail smashed against the wall of the tunnel.

Yet, it didn't charge after him.

Time froze, the seconds entangled with eternity. Michael's racing heart only sounded off now and then with a loud *boom*.

He didn't need to breathe—he didn't blink. Michael just stood there, locking eyes with the giant reptile.

And suddenly, his perspective changed, and he was the jungle watching this scene play out... staring down at the scrawny man confronting the massive croc, observing curiously without judgement.

When the next heartbeat sounded off, *boom*, he was the croc, watching a foolish intruder. He felt the anger and fear locked inside that powerful body. He sensed himself.

And then, *boom*, he was back in his body...

Whether he heard seconds, or it was the beating of his own heart, he didn't know. The incident had been fleeting and eternal at the same time.

When the next *boom* sounded off, he moved back a half-step.

He sensed he had no control of his body, and yet he slowly began to back away. He crept back, expecting death with each step.

And when his heels found the surf, he still couldn't believe he had been spared. It was only later that he realised the croc had been the same size as Poseidon.

Could that have been him? he wondered.

He returned to his camp in a daze and only pulled out of it when he saw someone standing by his fire.

The man was an Islander, around forty, and wore matching khaki shorts and a short-sleeved shirt with black socks and boots. His nametag read *Dale*, and Michael wondered if that was a first or last name. Despite wearing a uniform, he still looked relaxed.

"G'day," he said. "I work for the Department of Native Affairs, and I'm sorry to say you can't camp here."

Michael tried to contain his anger. A part of him felt the man had no right on his beach. He'd become possessive of the island even though he knew he had no actual claim to it.

"And where am I supposed to go?" asked Michael.

Dale tightened his lips, then said, "I can't tell you that."

Michael was confused. "Are you telling me I can't camp on any of the islands?"

The ranger shrugged and gave a weak smile. "All I can say is there are more than two hundred and seventy-four islands in the Torres Strait, and only eighteen are inhabited," he said. "You just picked one that's a nature reserve with a ranger living on it."

Michael understood his drift. "So, you can't give me advice," he said with a nod, "but you're telling me I have to move on."

Dale appeared relieved. He looked to the north, where about seven kilometres away, another island lay barely visible. "There are plenty of islands within striking distance," he said.

Michael nodded somberly.

"I don't like chasing you off," said Dale as he looked over Michael's simple camp. "I'm here to watch out for poachers because this island is protected."

"I would never kill anything endangered," said Michael defensively. And he meant it. In Queensland, he hunted wild pigs and bush turkeys—he would never have shot a cassowary.

The man shook his head. "I don't think you get it. I can't even allow you to fish or collect shellfish. Nagheer Island is a reserve under the Torres Strait Islanders Act. The only non-native persons allowed on it are department staff, medical personnel and missionaries."

Dale extended his hand to Michael. "I'll give you a few days," he said. "And stop by our station before you move on, and I'll set you up with supplies."

That surprised Michael, and he suddenly warmed. He shook hands. *This bloke is just doing his job,* he thought.

"I might," he said with a nod.

That night Michael built a big fire and cooked several loaves of damper in the ashes. He didn't mind moving on, but he wished it had been his own decision.

A full moon lit up the sky, and under its glow, he packed his supplies in the hull of his canoe.

He still had a fair amount of flour, sugar and salt, but no tea or rice. The food was packed again in the tyre tubes, ready for another sea journey. He'd collected as many coconuts as he could find, maybe eight, and filled his one remaining water jug.

He was ready to go but would wait for the sun to rise.

Later that night, he heard the purr of a boat engine. It came from up the beach in the direction of the grassy coral bay.

Michael stood and then jogged that way. It wasn't long before he saw a sportfishing boat cruising along the moonlit shoreline. The tide was in, and they took advantage of the easy access to the inner reef.

That's risky, he thought, knowing there were coral outcroppings throughout the lagoon.

There was an enormous spotlight on the boat's bow, and a man with a rifle slung over his shoulder used it to scan the water. The man wore a wide brim hat and a thick black belt loaded with cartridges.

Michael's heart skipped a beat as he realised they were scanning for animals.

He hoped the dugongs were far away but knew the boat drove through the middle of the seagrass that the manatee-like creatures — as well as the turtles — loved. So, even if they weren't hunting them, their propeller might kill a few.

An Islander steered the boat, and a white man gave him directions. "Get 'er in closer to shore," he said.

"Sure thing, boss," said the Islander at the wheel. He navigated them to within fifteen metres of the shore, and from that distance, Michael could see the pilot was rightfully nervous.

A few tourists were on board as well. They wore gaudy shirts and staggered around the deck, unused to the motion. A dozen poles projected off the back of the boat, but there were no lines in the water.

"You're sure this's okay?" asked one of them.

"Sure," said the boss, showing missing teeth, "I just wanted to see if there are any croc tracks…"

He didn't say anything more because suddenly Michael shouted, "Hey!" and the spotlight swivelled to centre on him.

The moonlight was powerful and the light unnecessary, but the man kept it on Michael to blind him.

"What do we have here?" asked the boss, who now also had a rifle he levelled at Michael.

"You shouldn't be here," said Michael. "You're gonna kill a turtle with your propeller."

The man laughed. "We're not after turtles — seen any crocs?"

Michael shook his head. "You should leave."

The driver cut the engine. In the silence that followed, the hiss of the surf suddenly became audible. The boat sat about five paces away, perilously close to shore.

"I don't think you're in a position to tell me to do anything," said the boss. "We're just making a little extra cash — you know the game."

Michael stared back silently while the boat swayed.

Finally, he said, "I'm not playing your game."

The man glared at Michael for a full minute before nodding for the Islander to restart the engine. The roar of it silenced the insects.

When they pulled away, Michael was left in a cloud of exhaust.

The next morning Michael paddled around the island to the ranger station. Dale came out and welcomed him. By the water were several trees filled with ripe wongai plums, and Michael remembered Smiley claiming that those who eat the plums are destined to return to the islands.

Michael asked, "Do you mind if I collect some?"

"Take all you want—most of it will go to the birds."

It took Michael only five minutes to pick all he could carry. He filled the Japanese helmet and set the rest in the corner of the bow.

He let himself be led into the building because Dale offered to give him two large water containers.

"If you allow me to treat your wounds," said Dale, "I can also give you aid in the form of supplies."

Michael didn't understand all of the restrictions the man was under but grasped enough to do what was asked of him. He even let the ranger treat his numerous injuries with antiseptic and bandages.

Michael scoffed at the attention but otherwise sat there quietly.

Before he left the ranger station, he spent considerable time in front of a map on the wall, trying to memorise the location of as many islands as he could.

When it was time for him to go, Michael hesitated and then told Dale about the boat that visited in the night.

"We've been looking for that fella. I'll keep a night watch on that bay," said Dale. "Thanks for your help."

Michael shook his head. "I want no part of any of it—that poacher, the government, even you—I just want to be alone. I'm done with so-called civilisation."

Dale chuckled, "I bet the animals feel the same way."

Michael looked over at Dale again and said, "There's a big croc on the south shore—I sure hope those poachers leave him alone."

Dale looked up at the sky. "Well, the monsoons will be back soon, and he'll clear out then."

Michael nodded and turned away.

They walked back to the canoe, each one carrying a plastic jug holding ten litres. Dale also brought a bundle of tea and a larger one with flour.

Dale eyed Michael before saying, "I wish you luck."

Michael gave him a rare grin as he pushed off and pointed his bow to the northeast. Getullia Island lay less than seven kilometres away, but there were so many other islands out there stretching north. He couldn't wait to find his next—one without other people.

He would find his paradise of peace and solitude.

And then, before the weather turned and the monsoons arrived, he would reach Dutch New Guinea.

It was finally in his grasp.

This journey that had begun over a thousand kilometres back would end soon, and as he headed north, that thought filled him with both dread and excitement.

An easy breeze came at him from the south, and he knew he could harness some of it. He let down his sail, adjusted the sheet, and began the final leg of his journey.

Chapter Nineteen

Michael's Story – Age Thirty
(Sydney 1960)

*T*wo months after receiving a telegram informing him that Michael was alive in Dutch New Guinea, Daniel Fomenko rushed through the Sydney Airport to meet his son.

On 3 December 1959, Michael had walked into the village of Tomerau, on the Dutch New Guinea south coast, where he luckily found a few natives who spoke English. They welcomed him into their small town, and for a few days, he enjoyed being a celebrity.

But it was short-lived. Before long, the Dutch authorities sent the police to take him into custody. At the station, a round of interrogations revealed that he had no money, identification papers or landing permits.

What made things even more confusing was Michael didn't want to go home—not at all—but intended to continue to the Solomon Islands.

The officers questioning him said that was impossible; clearly, Michael didn't realise how much more hostile this coast was when compared to Queensland. He would have to paddle nearly a thousand kilometres along marshy uninhabited coastline simply to reach the first village, Fak Fak.

Michael wouldn't relent. He said, "I've proven I can travel safely here. I've covered over two-hundred-and-fifty kilometres of your coastline already!"

The Dutch authorities didn't care. Michael's status as a former immigrant, and Dutch New Guinea being a Dutch colony within Australian territory, complicated things immeasurably.

Daniel had tried to intervene and wrote to the Australian Department of Territories to encourage them to approach the Dutch government over the issue. He received a sarcastic reply from a bureaucrat named Mueller that sent his blood pressure soaring.

'That little twit doesn't know anything,' thought Daniel. 'My son surmounted all the problems he faced from Cooktown to New Guinea. If he wanted to reach the Solomons, he would have.'

But it did no good. In the end, they sent him home.

Ahead, Daniel saw a security barrier before the arrival gate where Michael's plane would disembark. On this side of the barricade, at least forty reporters crowded around, waiting for Michael's arrival. Somebody recognised Daniel, and suddenly everyone was rushing his way.

Daniel didn't understand the condemnation the newspapers threw at his son. Day after day, the editorials published angry comments about him. Why they hated his choice of lifestyle so much, he would never understand. Did the fact that he wanted to live in the wild, or befriend Aboriginals and Islanders, truly make him a traitor to white civilisation? How was learning from indigenous people letting "his side" down or "sliding back"?

All this nonsense about the superiority of the white race made him nauseous — and angry. In the last few weeks, he'd made a few statements about Michael being discriminated against, and that seemed only to fuel the flames.

When the first reporter stuck a microphone in his face, even though he knew he should hold his tongue, Daniel launched right into a speech.

"My son epitomises a tragedy of modern Australian life. I understand his quest, although I doubt many of you do—or ever will!"

The reporters crowded closer. A dozen cameras flashed.

He continued, "He never sought publicity—his fame stems entirely from his feats in the wild. To you, his existence may be unfathomable. How many of you have an undying love for the Australian bush that would match his? How many would show even a fraction of the effort he has in pursuit of his dreams?"

For a few heartbeats, the reporters stared back. But they were there to ask questions, not answer them, and suddenly they were all shouting at once.

One man jumped in front of Daniel, microphone in hand, and asked, "Do you think Michael was passed over for the Commonwealth Games because he was an immigrant?"

Daniel's face flushed red. He was about to comment when, thankfully, airport security arrived and forced the reporters aside so Daniel could show the KLM attendant his identification.

When a reporter stepped to follow, the attendant put up a hand and politely said, "Family only."

There was nobody else at the gate, and suddenly Daniel was left alone. The reporters faded into the distance as he thought of his son.

Before long, a KLM airliner touched down, and he waited while it taxied closer. Eventually, passengers began to disembark.

The words on the telegram, "Your son is alive," rang in his head over and over.

The first thought to pass through Michael's mind when he saw his father was that the man had aged. Daniel's grey hair had receded in the last few years, and his eyes were now lined with worry.

Probably fretting about me, thought Michael.

It took a few more moments for Michael to realise that he could see concern in his father's eyes over his own physical condition.

They embraced, and Michael unsuccessfully fought back his tears. It had been so long since he'd cried that the emotion confused him. There had been no room for tears on his journey — or over the last few years, for that matter.

They flowed now.

"I can't believe it's you," said Daniel, also crying, as he stared at Michael's tattered khaki slacks and shirt. Daniel wondered if this one set of clothes was all Michael had worn for the last few months.

He wore a talisman shell on a leather cord around his neck.

"For the longest time, we received no news — and then we were overwhelmed with conflicting reports. A month after you landed, I received a telegram stating that you escaped. And then, a few days later, another stated you were caught again. What happened to you?"

The barest of chuckles escaped Michael's lips.

He said, "At Merauke, I was put up in the police barracks while the authorities decided what to do with me. They treated me fine — but I was restless. I knew they weren't going to let me continue, and I couldn't just give up, so I hit the road."

A flicker of a smile crossed Daniel's lips as he said, "So you did escape! Good for you."

Michael nodded. "It did feel good for a few days. I tried to make my way to Port Moresby, and at first, I made good time. But eventually, I met some natives who sat me down and explained how impossible it would be to reach Port Moresby on foot. There were more than a few substantial rivers to cross, including the Fly River, which they described as massive."

"If it scared you away," said Daniel, "I bet it was big."

Michael sighed.

"I had no idea how much trouble I would stir up," said Michael. "The moment I left the barracks, the police called the Dutch government — which in turn called the Australian government. Everyone involved found my escape to be an embarrassment. And the reporters followed me there just like here, so in no time, my little interlude had made international headlines."

Daniel put his hand on his son's shoulder and said, "Well, you were never an embarrassment to me — I've never been prouder."

Michael nodded weakly. "They moved me to the capital, Hollandia, and kept a better eye on me. A month later, they put me on this KLM flight."

"You're home now, that's what's important," said Daniel, hoping to steer Michael to the parking lot. "But we're not done with the reporters. We'll have to run the gauntlet to get by them, and there are just as many camped on our doorstep."

Michael thought of a few of the editorials he'd read on the plane. A great wave of tiredness swept over him, and Daniel had to suppress a shudder as he watched his son. The constant sun and exertion, combined with a poor diet, had whittled him away to nothing—and something was troubling him.

Daniel sensed maybe dealing with the police and politics over the last few months had worn his nerves down.

Michael slowly filled his chest with the stagnant airport air while his gaze rose to meet his father's. Finally, he asked, "What happened to Odysseus after he finally returned home?"

Daniel almost burst into tears at the question. He knew Michael was well aware of what happened. He had eventually taken his class at Shore, where they studied it.

But the look in Michael's eyes suggested he had either forgotten or wanted to hear it again. Upon first seeing Michael, Daniel had noticed his gaunt physical condition, but now he glimpsed an entirely different look in his eyes. They were creased and burned by the sun, but there was also cautionary alertness.

Daniel said, "Well, he slew the suitors."

Michael gave a weak chuckle. "That's right, he killed them all."

Suddenly Daniel was the professor again, defending Odysseus.

"His wife, Penelope, had held the suitors at bay for years. She'd sent her son away, fearful for his life. And then poor Odysseus returns, with all of his crew dead. What else was he supposed to do?"

Michael leaned against the wall, unaware of all the reporters still watching his every move. "Odysseus had been away at war for ten years when he finally tried to return, and after angering

Poseidon, it took another decade to get back to Ithaca. That's twenty years!"

Daniel nodded, waiting for his son to continue.

"And when he finally got home, he found one-hundred-and-eight boisterous young men all attempting to swoon his wife. So, he kills them all. Right? Every last one. And he doesn't stop there, does he?"

Daniel blanched because he knew the answer, but he didn't understand why Michael was so worked up about it.

Michael spoke before Daniel could respond, "No, they hang a dozen housemaids who either betrayed Penelope or had sex with the suitors."

An uncomfortable silence lingered until Daniel said, "That's just about it as far as I remember."

Michael's eyes dropped. There was a sadness in his voice as he asked, "No final chapters about gardening or playing with grandchildren? No last hunting trip after another Calydonian boar? Or smaller voyages across the Mediterranean?"

"What's this all about, Michael?" asked Daniel.

"I learned a lot about myself out on the water, and one thing I know for sure is I didn't paddle all the way to Asia for vengeance."

Daniel glanced at the reporters and then, in a quiet voice, whispered, "I never said you seek revenge."

Michael's eyes simmered. "No, but you said I was slighted from the Commonwealth Games because I was an immigrant—and others have said it's because my skin is dark. The papers are full of it, and where does that leave me? Am I supposed to come back now and kill all the Old Boys? Enact my vengeance on the Masters?"

Daniel was speechless.

Michael paced in a tight circle and said, "No, I don't think so. Maybe I *was* slighted because I was an immigrant or not wealthy — maybe not. But that isn't important to me anymore. If you want me to learn a lesson from *The Odyssey*, you better find another one."

Daniel took a breath, and after a moment, asked, "How about *nostos*—Homecoming?"

Michael nodded. "That will work—but you might not be ready for what I now consider home."

The words floated in the air, stretched between them like a spiderweb.

They turned and faced the reporters. Michael kept his head down while Daniel forced their way through the crowd. Suddenly Michael wanted only to be surrounded by his family.

His father shouted out, "Michael is not well. We are taking him home to bed."

The reporters followed them to their car, constantly pestering Michael with questions. He ignored them. He didn't care.

Michael opened his eyes and saw an empty room painted a flat white. There were no pictures on the walls or decorations of any kind. Two plain white curtains covered the solitary window.

Suddenly he thought he was back in Dutch New Guinea, in the police barracks. His mind raced as he dreaded that the final, long-awaited return home had only been a dream.

He sat upright and must have uttered a cry because a young woman rushed into the room to his side.

"You're alright," she said.

"Where am I?" he asked desperately.

She laughed lightly, "You're in Sydney—you're home."

He stared at her, wild-eyed, as she slowly coaxed him back.

"I know you," he croaked.

She grinned and gave his arm a soft punch.

"Course you do, halfwit, I'm your sister."

It took Michael a few moments to process the revelation. The last time he'd seen his youngest sister had been almost three years ago. She'd been a sixteen-year-old tomboy with braces then. During his absence, she had blossomed into a beautiful young woman.

He would later learn that she'd lost none of her toughness.

"Renee," said Michael.

"Welcome, home, brother," she said as she opened the window.

As she exited the room, she added, "And I threw your smelly sack in the closet."

The next few days passed in a blur. Now that he knew he was home, he allowed his exhaustion to unfold. He had lost a lot of weight and could barely make it down the flight of stairs, so his mother brought him his meals on a tray.

She entered with a bowl of soup and a couple of slices of buttered bread. Glancing at the bare walls, she said, "We just painted. If you'd only been away a few more days, we'd have had a few photos back up."

She set down the tray.

The curtains fluttered on a breeze that carried the sound of two young women singing along to a new Elvis Presley song.

It's now or never...

Elizabeth nervously organised the spoon and napkin while throwing a disapproving stare in the direction of the singers.

Kiss me, my darling, be mine tonight...

The women giggled after that line but still sang the next.

Tomorrow will be too late...

His mother closed the window.

"Those Collins girls are a couple of Sirens." She looked flustered as she added, "If you were a young boy, I'd fill your ears with wax rather than let you listen to some of their music."

When Michael finally made it down the stairs to take a meal with the family, he saw the street lined with reporters. His father sat at the table with his coffee, and Renee was there too.

Michael pulled out a chair and sat, trying to look casual.

He nodded at the street, "How long has it been like this?"

"Months," said Daniel, "although it's been more since they announced you made it to Dutch New Guinea."

"We've called the police on them a few times," said Renee. "They were stomping all over our lawn—and one idiot was standing on mom's tulips!"

Elizabeth looked nervous when Renee raised her voice and mumbled, "Now now."

Daniel held up *The Sunday Mail*, which had just arrived, "Here's today's special—typical rubbish: After four years of 'going native', Michael Fomenko has been reduced from a polished schoolboy and a nationally-famed athlete to a lonely wanderer whose only possessions are a pair of shorts, two hunting knives, and a six-metre canoe hollowed out of a cedar tree."

Michael gave a weak grin, "That sounds pretty accurate."

"Don't trust any of them," spat Renee. "They'll take whatever you say and twist it."

A few days later, the four Fomenkos sat outside at a picnic table. For once, the reporters were gone—drawn away by some chaos—and they enjoyed a morning coffee with a few scones.

Renee had retrieved Michael's sugar sack from the closet, and now he was pulling out some items. He gave a few colourful feathers to his mother and a beautiful shell to Renee.

"I didn't dare reach my arm into that thing," said Renee as she accepted the shell.

Next, Michael produced a set of boar tusks and handed them to his father. "I got this fella near Gordonvale," said Michael. "He was tearing up the cane fields near my camp."

Michael thought of the big pig that had attacked him and wrecked his base camp and added, "And there's an even bigger one up north that I'm gonna get one day."

His father gave him a strange stare when he mentioned going north again but kept quiet.

Then Michael pulled out a large conch shell. He held it to his lips and blew a loud call that echoed through the neighbourhood.

Across the street, one of the Collins girls was walking to her car when she heard the note. She looked in their direction and smiled.

Daniel and Elizabeth took in the coffee cups and tray, leaving Michael alone with Renee. She took advantage of the moment and asked, "What did you find out there?"

Michael was quiet for a long moment, and Renee felt he was looking out over the water as he spoke.

"I wish I could tell you a story that would encompass everything, but I can't. It's all mixed together — the sun dropping down into the silent sea, the countless dazzling fish, the surf beating among the rocks, the yawning black mouths of sea caves, beaches strewn with singular shells, shining sand and coral, birds wheeling and diving among the sea cliffs, the quietness of the lee side of an island... I wouldn't know where to start."

Renee's eyes glittered as she challenged him.

"Then tell me with one word."

Michael creased his brows and, after a moment, said, "Magical."

The next day the yard was filled with reporters again. Michael wanted to go out and confront them, but he was still light on his feet and prone to dizzy spells.

Renee kept glancing out the window, glaring at them.

"Those jerks are on the lawn again — and they're playing with my rugby ball!" she shouted.

Michael gave her a questioning look. "You have a rugby ball?"

Elizabeth looked like she needed to sit down, but Daniel grabbed the phone. "I'm gonna call the police again."

When Renee saw that another reporter was trampling her mom's tulips, she'd had enough. "That's it!" she said and stormed outside.

She ran a few steps and intercepted the ball mid-flight, then turned and threw it hard right into the back of the man standing in the tulips. He coughed and dropped his microphone.

"Get out of there!" shouted Renee, and the man moved quickly, too stunned to confront her.

She charged towards the rest of them, continuing to shout until they were all off the grass and in the street.

And then she tore into them again.

"Michael is a real man," she yelled, "not a mouse like so many of you! You're all here because of the ludicrous situation of an Australian citizen being arrested for entering the Australian territory of Dutch New Guinea without a permit. Michael may have been an immigrant once, but he's a citizen now — and you all know that. What a mockery of the rights of Australian citizens."

They stared at her, nobody daring to speak.

She continued, "Show some mettle and write about the real story: Most Australian Aboriginals live their lives under similar restrictive laws that control their every movement. They can't travel about freely like you or me — let alone vote or order a drink in a bar. The government controls them just like they did my brother. What's next, I ask you?"

She must have made an impact because the next week, there was an article in *The Sydney Morning Herald* on that very subject.

Michael couldn't contain himself any longer, but when he stood and rushed to the door, he collapsed.

Elizabeth screamed, and Renee rushed back inside.

Michael was rushed to Sydney Hospital, where it was determined that malnutrition and exhaustion had caused anaemia.

After a night in the hospital, he was sent home to rest.

Late one night, a week later, Daniel passed by Michael's room and saw him sitting by the open window. He entered and asked, "Mind if I join you?"

Michael nodded, and Daniel quietly closed the door and pulled up a chair. A light breeze floated through the window, carrying with it the funky smell of the bay.

Daniel knew the odour would cause a yearning in his son and said, "You tempt yourself just like Odysseus. Remember when he passed the Sirens? Odysseus was tied to the mast, no wax in his ears, as he listened to their sweet song, knowing it might drive him mad."

"And you think smelling the sea will have the same effect on me?" asked Michael.

Daniel raised an eyebrow.

Michael shook his head. "It does, but that Elvis song affects me more. There's a clock ticking in my head, saying it's time to move on, and I wake every night hearing those lyrics..."

It's now or never. Tomorrow will be too late...

Daniel said, "You're still not well enough—you have to be patient. Remember it took Odysseus twenty years to get home."

Michael looked directly into Daniel's eyes and asked, "Why do you relate everything between us to *The Odyssey*?"

Daniel fidgeted for a moment while he considered the question, but when he answered, he looked confident.

"It's because it is some of the only common ground we share. I don't understand what it would be like to live in a jungle or on the open water—but I do appreciate the motives that drove Odysseus."

Michael nodded somberly but remained silent.

Daniel said, "Perhaps it was a mistake. I just want to understand you. Please, forget *The Odyssey*. Tell me what you love so much about the Queensland jungles."

Michael smiled weakly. "I wish it were that easy. All I can say is when I'm in that vast, ancient rainforest, I feel accepted. I sense an awareness there, and I want to be near it."

"What about the voyages?" asked Daniel.

"I did them for a challenge," replied Michael, "but I don't need to keep proving myself. If I can just be allowed to live in peace up there, that'll be enough."

"Was it worth the effort?" asked Daniel.

Michael paused for a moment and stared into his father's eyes. It seemed he was trying to decide if he should tell him something.

"It was. And I experienced things I'll never tell another soul—but I'll tell you."

With that, he leaned forward and whispered a story into Daniel's ear. After a moment, his father's eyes widened.

Daniel shook his head, smiling, and asked, "A Painted Man?"

Michael smiled but said no more.

Daniel nodded, "I support you, Michael, and it's my sincerest wish that you get back to your Queensland jungle. I just don't think you're strong enough right now."

"I'm stronger than you could ever imagine," said Michael.

The next day at breakfast, Renee argued with her father about how much longer Michael needed to recover. The conversation had started when Elizabeth suggested checking Michael into some sort of rehabilitation clinic.

"I'm not sending him there!" shouted Daniel.

"But how long will he stay here?" asked Renee. "He's not happy in Sydney. We've all heard him a hundred times saying, 'I have renounced what you call civilisation'… blah, blah, blah."

"I know, I know," said Daniel. "But he's not ready. And how would we get him past the reporters, anyway?"

Renee smiled dramatically. "We can dress him as an elderly beggar, and then you sneak him off while I cause a distraction."

"You'll cause a scene," said Elizabeth, looking shocked.

Renee grinned mischievously. "Well, anyway, I could distract the men, and you could sneak away with Michael."

Daniel shook his head. "He's not ready."

A week later, Michael slipped away on an afternoon when the others were either at work or running errands. The night before, he'd mumbled something about going away for a few days at dinner but wouldn't elaborate.

The first they knew about it was when Daniel received a call from a policeman friend who'd recognised Michael. The man had been a student of Daniel's and did him a double service by getting his son a warm meal.

Daniel hung up the receiver and turned to Elizabeth.

"Michael hopped a freight and made it to Armidale. A policeman brought him to the station and gave him a good feed."

Daniel paused and scratched his head. He looked worried.

"They said he didn't look well," he continued. "And also, Police Commissioner Bischoff up in Cairns said if Michael came to Queensland, the police would be watching his movements closely."

"What should we do?" asked Elizabeth while wringing her hands.

Daniel shrugged. "Well, I arranged to have his fare paid up to Tenterfield. That's less than six hundred kilometres away. Maybe I should drive there and meet him—just in case the police try to nab him at the station."

"I do so wish we'd put him in one of those nice facilities," said Elizabeth. "They seemed so confident they could help."

"They won't—they'd be the death of him," said Daniel. "I'm packing for Tenterfield."

Michael never made it to Tenterfield. Halfway there, at Glen Innes, he got off the train. He left the station and was walking down the small main street when a young man approached him.

"Are you Michael Fomenko?" asked the man.

Michael looked up from a daze, unsure of where he was.

"Do I know you?" he asked.

The man blushed and said, "Well, not exactly. My name is Jim, Jim Ryall. I went to Shore a few years after you—but everyone at Shore knows you now."

"Do they?" asked Michael, coming around slightly.

"Sure," said Jim. "We all followed along on your voyage to Dutch New Guinea—that was some rugged stuff."

Michael was eating up the comments, but he felt weak standing by the side of the road. He had a dizzy spell, and Jim noticed it.

"Why don't you come home with me," he said. "I don't live far, and I'd like to help you out—it's the least I can do for an Old Boy."

Michael let himself be led along, wondering at this strange turn of events.

He stayed with Jim and his wife for the night. When it became apparent that he wasn't any better in the morning, Jim called Michael's parents and discovered Daniel had already departed for Tenterfield.

Soon after, they made contact with Daniel. He arrived the next day and drove Michael back to Sydney.

The next time Michael went north was a month later. This time, he didn't rush his departure or try to hide it. Instead, the night before he left, he walked onto the lawn and told a few of the reporters his plan.

"Are you going to complete another dugout journey?" asked one of them.

"At the moment, I have no specific plans for making another canoe," he replied.

"So, you plan on returning to Queensland to be a vagrant?"

Michael stared at the man for a moment. There were a lot of things he would like to say but knew better.

Instead, he said, "If I want money, I can get a job on the land cutting cane or something like that. I have some other ideas, but I don't want to mention them—they're my own."

The reporters seemed anxious to find something Michael planned that might land him in trouble. Another man asked, "What about getting to Cairns—are you going to hop freights all the way there?"

Michael shook his head. "No, I've purchased a ticket—although I only had nine shillings left after I bought it."

"So, you'll be arriving in Cairns broke?" asked a reporter.

Michael ignored the man and went back inside; he'd said his bit.

This time when Michael went north, his reputation preceded him. When he passed through Gladstone on a goods train, word went straight to Police Commissioner Bischoff.

And then, at Rockhampton and Mackay, word was sent again.

"Michael Fomenko is returning to Cairns," was on every police officer's lips.

But before he got there, things had simmered. Police Commissioner Bischoff appeared to have changed his mind and issued a statement that said, "In view of the fact that earlier steps taken in the interests of this man's welfare were in some instances misplaced, he will be allowed to go merrily on his way."

Michael was being welcomed back into Queensland with open arms.

Chapter Twenty

Michael's Story – Age Thirty
(Daintree 1960-1964)

Michael tried not to draw any attention to himself upon returning to Queensland, but everywhere he went, people recognised him. On the streets of Cairns, folks shouted out as he passed.

"Where you goin' next, Michael?" they asked, or "Are you ready to begin making another canoe?"

He smiled and waved but held his tongue.

Michael drifted around the town, unsure of where to start.

He thought of heading over to Gordonvale but was warned there was currently a lot of commotion there. A few years before, two cane farmers started a bet regarding which could run up Walsh's Pyramid in the fastest time. That endurance race grew into a national event and drew visitors from all over Australia.

Michael remembered his battle with Caly up Behanna Gorge, in that area. It had been serene and beautiful and he yearned to return, but then he thought of the tourists milling about now, and the dozens of runners tearing through. He decided he needed something quieter.

He passed the old Russian guest house on Terminus Street and saw young Losha on the porch talking to a boy. She was maybe fifteen now and so engrossed in her conversation that she only glimpsed him at the last minute.

"Welcome back, Michael!" she yelled with a wave.

Michael gave her his best smile, wondering what it would be like to date a pretty girl like that.

Too young for you, he thought. *And a bit too normal.*

He wondered if there was a woman out there that could match his unconventional lifestyle. He had scrounged together a little money before leaving Sydney, and he bought what supplies he thought he'd need before leaving town.

He made his way back to the Daintree rainforest, setting up camp along Hutchinson Creek. It felt good to be home again — more than good — he finally felt alive again. His time at the police barracks in Dutch New Guinea and the long recovery in Sydney slowly faded.

He found it hard to believe he'd only been gone two years.

He found an old, abandoned hut on a shelf above the creek and fixed it up. Then he hacked a series of steps out of the rich earth and made the descent from the high bank easier — and safer. He knew the bank would be slippery during the wet, and the last thing he wanted was to slip down into the murky water.

Never know what might be there waiting, he thought.

He dug two deep holes into the bank where he stored snakes, bandicoots, and other animals he either ate or used for bait. The holes were thirty centimetres wide, half a metre deep, and covered with gates made from thick sticks.

A fat log lay propped up by the water, although he had yet to start transforming it into a canoe.

He sat on the bank for hours, watching butterflies, dragonflies and other bugs circle over the water. Now and then, a fish grabbed one. The chorus of insects was deafening at times, but to Michael, it sounded like a lullaby.

It seemed everyone he talked to wanted to know what he would do next, and he doubted any of them would understand that this was it. He simply wanted to be alone in nature.

Susan and Rhondda were seven and ten when they first dared to go spy on the camp. They lived at Bailey's Creek, a few kilometres away. When their father was gone for work for a few days, they decided to go on their mission.

Their father would have been furious if he had found out. He always referred to Michael as a "Hatter" – as in Mad Hatter – and they were strictly forbidden to go near his camp.

"Do you see him?" asked Susan as they peeked out from beneath a bush at the top of the bank.

"Shhhh," hissed Rhondda, and then she whispered, "Yes, he's down by the water."

Michael was stowing something in his sugar sack, and after dousing his fire, he walked off in the opposite direction.

Ten minutes later, the girls crept down to inspect the camp. They were jittery and passed right by his hut, not daring to go inside.

Susan lifted the gate to one of the pits, and when a snake poked its head through, she screamed and slammed it shut. The loud noise temporarily silenced the cicadas.

They grew fearful that Michael may have heard and fled.

After a few months of living by the creek, Michael woke one day to the sound of a stick snapping near the top of the bank. He grabbed his cane knife and walked up the steps to investigate.

At the top of the stairway, he found a woman sitting with her head in her hands. She'd obviously been crying for a while and was still sobbing.

He was out of his element and didn't know what to do, so he returned to the creek and left the woman alone.

A short while later, he returned with some water in a half coconut shell.

She looked up, accepted it, and took a sip.

She nodded a thank you, and he returned to the creek.

She stayed there for the remainder of the afternoon. Michael went about his chores like it was a typical day, but she was always on his mind. Near sunset, he wrapped several fish in a banana leaf and cooked them on a bed of coals.

He presented one to her.

Night fell quickly as it does in the tropics, and Michael added some fuel to his fire. About an hour after darkness had settled in fully, she walked down to the fire and stared at him.

She looked ready to flee at the slightest provocation.

She glanced at the fire and then back at Michael, with an expression that said, "Can I sit by your fire?"

Michael nodded, and while she looked over his camp, he examined her in the flickering light. The woman looked to be in her late twenties, of European descent. Her eyes had dark circles, and there was bruising on her forearms.

She kept glancing up the hill as if she feared someone might show up. Michael wanted to ask her questions but held back.

She'll talk when she's ready, he assumed.

But she didn't. The young woman stayed there for the coming days, never offering if she was on the run from the coppers, fleeing from some bad husband, or maybe just lost.

She didn't even offer up her name.

Michael understood a person's desire for privacy and let her be.

He shared his meals with her, pointed out the dangers in the water at night, and eventually made a sleeping place for her by the fire.

When he left to forage or hunt, he told her roughly how long he'd be gone, to which she only nodded.

He was always surprised that she was still there when he returned.

She had shown up with no luggage or even a purse, and before long, her one outfit was filthy and tattered. Michael only wore a laplap now, and soon the woman was also scantily clad. She'd arrived in a blouse and long skirt. The blouse had deteriorated to filthy rags, and the skirt was now reduced to a mini.

She wore only panties and a bra for a while, but before long, she went topless.

She looked at Michael questioningly the first time she discarded the bra. He shrugged. There was nobody around to offend.

"It's how we were created. Why not?" he said.

She uttered a short, almost inaudible, chuckle.

It was the first sound he'd heard from her.

They lived like that for a few more weeks, not talking, barely interacting, but seemingly at peace with each other. Winter was approaching, and although it never got freezing, the nights could be chilly at times.

One evening Michael heard a rustle in the dark and soon felt her body next to his. She was as tense as a piece of cold steel, and it was several hours before he felt her relax into sleep.

When he woke in the morning, she sat on the other side of the fire watching him. He nodded hello, and she nodded back.

Each night after that, she slept beside him.

One day melted into the next, and then there came a morning when she spoke. The sound took him by surprise.

A beautiful butterfly had fluttered down to land on her knee, and as she stared at it, she asked, "What kind of butterfly is this?"

Michael's voice was rusty as he answered, "That's a Ulysses."

She stared back but, maybe out of habit, remained quiet.

In the silence, Michael added, "Some call them the Blue Emperor, but I like Ulysses."

In a barely audible voice, she said, "That's right—you love *The Odyssey*. And Ulysses is the Latin variant of Odysseus."

Not sure how he felt about the fact that she knew who he was and had read about him, Michael sensed himself pull away.

I might have liked it better when she was quiet, he thought. But once the floodgates were opened, she began talking all the time. She still never gave her name or background, but now she asked about the

211

plants and animals all around them—what could she eat, what was poisonous, what should be avoided.

They camped beside a massive, red-leafed strangler fig, and often they lay on their backs and watched the blossom bats and pygmy possums climb through the branches.

She began accompanying him on his excursions, too, and suddenly Michael wasn't alone anymore. He liked having her with him, but he found it more challenging to be one with nature.

Soon after that, they became lovers.
"If you are Odysseus reborn, doesn't that make me Calypso?" she asked one morning as they sat sipping sweet tea on the riverbank.

Michael chuckled. "Not exactly. Calypso was a nymph who lived on the island of Ogygia, where she detained Odysseus for seven years."

"I rather like the sound of being a nymph," she said. "But did they love each other?"

Michael shook his head. "Calypso enchanted Odysseus and made him think he was in love—but his heart was always set on Penelope, his wife."

The woman stared at Michael for a moment.

"So, she kept him from his love," she said.

Michael nodded, and she added, "Well, it's a good thing I'm not keeping you from anything."

Over the coming days, Michael wondered about that. Since living with a woman, things had changed for him, and he speculated about what he might do if she weren't there.

She never did tell him her name, but after that—at least in his mind—he thought of her as Calypso.

One afternoon, when they returned to camp, they discovered a wild pig had been there and trashed it. Michael was furious when he examined the tracks and saw how big they were.

"That's Caly," he said.

He then told Calypso about the big boar that had attacked him when he first arrived in Queensland. He showed her his scar and told her how he had vowed to one day kill it.

"How can you be certain it's Caly?" she asked.

"I just know," he replied dryly.

She shook her head. "I don't see why you have to kill it. Besides, Gordonvale is pretty far away — it can't be the same boar. I doubt those pigs roam that far."

Michael furrowed his brows and busied himself collecting wood for the night's fire.

When he set out to follow the tracks the next day, Calypso stood to accompany him, but he stopped her. "I have to do this alone," he said. She watched him walk off with a cold stare.

Michael never sighted the big pig that had wrecked his camp. He was gone most of the day, and when he got close to camp, he heard shouting.

On the bank above camp, several local men stood staring down at Calypso, who screamed obscenities at them.

They seemed too engrossed in her near-naked form to be offended by her and appeared in no rush to leave.

Until they saw Michael.

When they glimpsed him charging up the steps with a cane knife in his hand, they hightailed it out of there.

Michael returned to camp and tried to console Calypso, but she wouldn't stop looking up the embankment. She appeared convinced the men would return.

Even later, when darkness had fully set in, she kept glancing in that direction.

"Don't let those perverts bother you," he said.

When Michael woke the following day, he was alone.

Later that day, he heard footsteps approach and thought she had come back. But instead, he found a white man who approached and said, "I'm sorry to be the one to inform you that your father has died."

News of his father's death hit Michael like a sledgehammer. Daniel Fomenko had been his biggest supporter and one of his anchors. Without him, he found any care he still had for the world of man seemed to disappear instantly.

The newspaper reporters pestered him for a quote, but he avoided them like they carried the plague. He read one article about his dad in which they found an old quotation from Daniel that read, "My son retreated further into a hermit-like existence as a result of misunderstanding and persecution."

That was enough. He no longer cared what they wrote — he'd had enough of being a celebrity.

Michael left the camp in the Daintree area after that and roamed far and wide. Under the hot, tropical sun, his skin turned almost black. And whenever he heard there was a reporter in the area looking for him, he moved on.

The journalists made stuff up regardless, stating, "Michael Fomenko has finally gone native."

For a year or so, nothing appeared in the papers. Then in 1962, it was reported that he was living in a cave at Cedar Bay, about fifty kilometres south of Cooktown.

George Konrat, a tourist from Germany, said he'd seen the recluse when diving in the area. Michael had become friendly with Cedar Bay Bill, an old man who lived in a hut there.

It didn't take long for the press to descend on Michael.

When he disappeared, Cedar Bay Bill gave them no new information. Whether Michael was working on a new canoe or planning another voyage, nobody knew. Again, the newspapers seemed only concerned with his laplap and the cane knife he always wore.

Out of desperation, one reporter dressed in ragged shorts and had blurry images taken of himself running down the beach. The public didn't buy it, and their complaints fuelled an even greater desire to learn what Michael Fomenko was doing.

Michael moved on and managed to avoid the press until the following year, when he appeared about eighty kilometres north of Cooktown, this time, at the mouth of the McIvor River.

Peter Clark sat in his sailboat, enjoying a morning cup of tea.

He was on his way north, taking advantage of the last of the southeasterlies when he stopped for a few days.

His wife, Joan, noticed an Aboriginal man limping down the beach and pointed him out.

"Look at that poor chap," she said. "We should see if he needs assistance."

Peter gave her a sceptical glance. The man was armed with a long spear and several knives and looked unruly — almost feral.

"I'm sure his own people are around somewhere."

She gave him a stare, and soon he was in his dinghy rowing for the river's bank. When he encountered the man, he saw that he was indeed sick. Despite his better judgement, he invited the man to his boat so he could examine his injuries.

It was only after they began asking about his health that the Clarks realised he was a white man.

"My stomach hurts," said Michael. "I believe I may have food poisoning."

"My goodness," said Joan, "You're European."

Michael chuckled at that but did not comment.

Joan fidgeted, not sure of what to do, but eventually, her maternal instincts took over, and she said, "I believe the best treatment for food poisoning is to keep hydrated. I've heard ginger tea helps — and I have some — would you like a cuppa?"

Michael nodded and noticed a mirror attached to the wall. He walked to it and stared at his reflection.

"I barely recognise myself," he said, and there was a note of pride in his voice, hinting that he liked the changes he saw.

"Where you heading?" asked Peter.

Michael nodded up the coast. "North, towards the Marina Plains Station near Princess Charlotte Bay."

While they sipped tea, he stared off at the mouth of the bay, watching the incoming waves battle the exiting river. He looked up at the sky for a minute and said, "Is it true that bloke Glenn really circled the earth in a tiny capsule?"

"Yes, it is," said Peter, a bit amazed that Michael had heard of John Glenn Jr.'s historic flight. The Clarks wondered what other current events Michael followed.

"Did you know that Marilyn Monroe committed suicide?" asked Joan.

Michael gave her a blank stare and asked, "Who?"

And then Peter got another empty look when he asked if Michael had heard about the Cuban Missile Crisis.

After several hours and a half-dozen cups of tea — which he loaded with sugar — Michael was on his way.

Michael headed inland to the Laura Basin. Here, three major river systems – the North Kennedy, Normanby and Morehead Rivers – all drained northwards into Princess Charlotte Bay.

The geological depression featured open woodlands of eucalypts and paperbarks, extensive grasslands and spectacular wetlands. Michael thought it a paradise and marvelled at how different it was from the Daintree rainforests or the coastal areas he'd explored.

It was teeming with wildlife. Wallabies grazed and slept in large numbers on the plains, wild pigs foraged along the riverbanks, and estuarine and freshwater crocodiles cruised the rivers.

And there were more birds than he'd ever seen. Along the shore, bustards, cranes and egrets patiently searched for a meal; geese and ducks filled the lagoons while the trees were overflowing with parrots, finches, and goshawks.

He camped by the lagoons, fishing and occasionally killing a wild pig. For a while, he did quite well in the Eden-like environment.

In October, he showed up at the Laura Station asking for food. The station once housed over eight thousand cattle, and a small town had grown next to it.

He'd misplaced his sugar sack and knives, and until he found them — or replaced the gear — he was having a hard time getting by.

Mrs Watkins, whose husband managed the station, gave him curry and rice and a few pawpaws. Michael came back several times asking for more, and one time in the dead of night, he arrived when Mr Watkins was away.

The experience scared Mrs Watkins, and when her husband Stan returned, she asked him to go into town and complain to the police.

Soon after, Michael learned that the authorities were looking for him, hoping to find him with no money so they could arrest him on charges of vagrancy.

Police Constable Ron Pocock was assigned the case of tracking down Michael. In early 1964 he stopped at the Lakefield Station — located about sixty kilometres north of the Laura Station — to talk with Rob Whelan, the manager.

"I hear that Fomenko fella has been stealing from the stations in the area," said Pocock.

Whelan shook his head and said, "To the best of my knowledge, he never stole anything — and he's always polite."

Pocock frowned. "Well, he's become a nuisance."

Whelan sighed. "I reckon I don't mind him stopping by when I'm here, but when I'm gone, it's a bit unnerving to have a fellow wandering around in the dark, barely clad, with a big hunk of steel in his hand. I've got family here that are alone when I'm away."

Whelan could not stop a shudder when he remembered seeing Michael step out of the shadow of the post of an electric light. The man had a way of remaining almost invisible until he wanted to be seen.

"I don't doubt it," said Pocock, "he gave Mrs Watkins down at Laura a good scare. Anyway, I'm gonna find him and bring him in. You feel up to helping me?"

The station manager shook his head. "I got enough going on here—but good luck."

Late one night, Whelan heard a soft knock on his back door and answered it to find Michael standing in the dark.

"I've heard the police plan to arrest me for vagrancy, and I could use a hand connecting with some money my mother has wired."

"Okay," said Whelan, "what can I do to help?"

Michael then explained that his mother had sent twenty pounds to the Laura Post Office, and he needed to claim it.

"I have some money on me—but not enough," he said. "I guess I need thirty pounds not to be considered a vagrant."

Whelan called the post office the next day.

"Michael Fomenko is staying here at Lakefield Station," he said, "and I'd like to collect some money his mother sent for him. How 'bout I give him twenty pounds, and next time I'm in Laura, I can collect it?"

After a slight pause, the post office official said, "I'm sorry, but his mother's instructions are he has to collect it in person."

When he relayed that to Michael, he said, "It's a trap. My mother thinks I'd do better in a hospital, and she's helping the police bring me in."

Whelan chuckled. "Don't you think that's a bit paranoid?"

Michael shrugged and walked off into the night.

After that, Michael avoided the stations for a while. Instead, he moved deep into the remote wilderness, where people wouldn't see him. The rainy season began, and soon the rivers overflowed their banks and spilled out onto the floodplains.

The brown vegetation returned to life, and Michael found himself in the middle of extensive wetlands comprised of swamps, lagoons, billabongs and lakes.

He starved at first. The birds and other smaller animals were too quick for him to kill without a gun. *It'd be so easy to get a wallaby if I only still had the rifle,* he thought sadly.

His hunger drove him to hunt wild pigs with a spear.

Over the coming months, he developed a style of hunting the wild pigs. Unfortunately, although his method was effective, it was also dangerous.

He would follow the pigs from a distance until they went into the water to feed on the water lily bulbs. And when they put their heads underwater, he would attack, jumping on them and striking with his cane knife.

Often, he saw the tracks of a large boar that he was convinced — beyond all logic — belonged to Caly. He was now nearly two-hundred-and-fifty kilometres from Gordonvale, well beyond the range of any wild pig. He remembered Calypso pointing out the same fact. "That can't be the same pig," she had said.

Still, he was convinced.

And then, one day, while napping by the base of a paperbark, he saw the massive wild pig walking by. The old beast had big tusks — at least thirteen centimetres long — and a hide marked by scars. But what took Michael's breath away was the left ear, of which half was missing.

I did that, thought Michael proudly.

He spent the morning tailing Caly quietly from a distance.

When the boar went into the water, Michael crept closer. He lost sight of him for a moment, and when he stood on the bank, Caly was nowhere in sight.

Michael stepped into the water and stood silently for five minutes but heard nothing. He turned to leave, and suddenly the boar charged at him from behind, knocking his legs out from under him. He scrambled to the shore and tried to flee again but got hit by another charge.

Luckily, there was a palm next to him, and he scrambled up it.

He stayed in the tree the remainder of the day, climbing down after sunset.

A week later, Michael staggered onto the Kalpowar Station. The station manager, Jim Rollinson, had made it clear he didn't want him around on his last visit, but Michael was desperate.

When he got close to the house, he heard Rollinson loading his rifle and tried to flee, but he could barely walk.

Rollinson lifted his .303 rifle and fired three quick shots at him, the first over his head as a warning, but the next two nearly hit him.

When he saw that Fomenko still hadn't got the hint, he sooled the dogs after him. They charged across the paddock, hackles raised, and Rollinson felt certain it was the last he'd see of the vagrant. When they stopped barking, he investigated.

Five minutes later, he reached Michael and was surprised to find the dogs licking him and wagging their tails as he talked soothingly to them.

"Well, I'll be damned," said Rollinson. "Can't you take a hint, son?"

Michael shook his head and nodded at his legs which were in a horrible state, covered in dried blood and scabs.

"I really had no choice," he said.

Suddenly Rollinson felt bad about his actions and said, "Okay, come with me — we'll get you fixed up."

He treated his wounds with iodine and supplied him with some tucker. Over the coming weeks, Rollinson allowed Michael to camp near the station, on the banks of the Normanby River.

When Michael was sufficiently healed, he left and disappeared again into the wetlands.

For the first time in his life, Michael experienced insomnia when he returned to the bush. He usually slept like a rock, unaware of the living creatures that crept and crawled through the night.

But now, he fidgeted, only realising he'd slept when he awoke from a nightmare.

He camped along the Normanby River, not too far from the Kalpowar Station. The monsoon was in full swing, and it seemed the entire world lay flooded.

He woke one morning, trying to shake a dream in which people were laughing and taunting him. One moment it was the police in the barracks in Merauke, the next, looking up at the locals jeering at Calypso by Hutchinson Creek.

In the dream, he was unable to shout or chase after the men who mocked him. He just had to take it.

With the rising sun glinting from the horizon, he squinted his sleepy eyes and watched an egret stalking the river's edge. The bird searched for small fish, frogs and shrimp, moving with admirable patience.

Suddenly its head darted down and then rose with a baby crocodile wiggling in its beak. Michael grinned and thought, *Get 'em when they're small, or they'll grow and turn the tables on you.*

Many of these bad dreams had been about Caly. He didn't know why he was obsessed with the big pig, but it was all he could think about since the last attack.

It seemed more than vengeance—he felt it was his destiny to kill the beast. *I'll get you yet, Caly*, he thought.

In some of the nightmares, Calypso questioned him softly, asking, "Why do you have to kill it?"

He tried to shake the dreams off while he enjoyed the brief burst of sunshine. The thin bark of the paperback trees fluttered in a gentle breeze, whispering to him, as the soft morning light lit up the large pink flowers of the lotus lilies.

On an old log, a cormorant perched next to several small turtles.

A flock of ducks grazed on the sedges and grasses under the water, popping up like corks after they had their fill.

And then Michael heard a pig grunting, and he sat up straight and looked in that direction. He didn't know if it was Caly, but he headed that way to investigate.

Over the coming weeks, he spent the better part of each day searching for the boar. He had never found his lost sugar bag and cane knives, but one of the hands at Kalpowar Station had given him a knife that he now wore at his waist.

He had also carved a sturdy spear that he gripped tightly whenever he found a set of large pig tracks.

But with so much of the land flooded, the tracks soon disappeared.

Aboriginals lived on the land for tens of thousands of years, and their trails followed the higher ground. Michael stuck to them when he could and often came across their traditional gathering sites.

One day he pursued a set of tracks that he was convinced belonged to Caly. They disappeared under a fallen paperbark, and Michael got on his hands and knees to crawl under the tree in pursuit.

When he emerged on the other side, he found Caly standing there facing him. Before he could get to his feet, the boar charged.

Michael took a hit to the chest, feeling one of the tusks rake his side. He screamed and tried to get clear of the tree. When Caly attacked again, Michael managed to grab his knife and bury it in the side of the beast.

Caly's screams echoed over the quiet countryside. When first struck, the pig had twisted, ripping the knife out of Michael's grasp, and it now protruded from behind the right shoulder.

But he didn't run off. Instead, the big pig charged again and again. Each time, Michael fought it fiercely, smashing the pig with a big rock he had managed to grab. He saw his spear on the ground, and when he crawled to it, the pig struck from behind, gouging his legs in a dozen places.

Michael didn't remember the battle ending or Caly finally leaving. He simply woke later, alone, covered in blood.

One look at his body, and he knew he would die without medical attention. His meagre knowledge of bush medicine was no match to the damage the pig had done.

He stood and stumbled his way to Kalpowar Station, empty-handed. But when he got there, he found the place vacant and figured Whelan had taken his family away for a few days.

With no other option, he started for Laura Station, more than sixty kilometres away.

The population of the small town of Laura were appalled as Michael staggered into town. He had no idea how many days he'd been walking or how badly he looked — only that he was starving.

He passed a bakery, grabbed a small loaf of bread, and devoured it while the shop owner stared at him, horrified. Michael's body was covered with wounds that had become infected, the back flap of his laplap was missing, and he had a wild look in his eyes.

Michael continued, looking for a doctor.

When he passed a small store with fruit on display out front, he grabbed an apple and sank his teeth into it. In three big bites, he just about devoured it.

Eventually, the police were notified. An officer approached him and said, "Come on, Michael, I gotta take you to the station."

Michael gave him a blank stare like he spoke in a foreign language. The officer shrugged, nodded to another officer, and together they wrestled him to the ground before forcibly escorting him to a cell.

While in custody, Michael was fed, and a doctor tended to his wounds. An officer informed he was being charged with vagrancy, stealing food, and behaving in public in an indecent manner.

Michael pleaded guilty to all counts.

A reporter from *The Sunday Mail* had caught wind of the incident. He was allowed to talk to Michael through the bars of his cell. The man said, "They're gonna fine you 38 pounds — and possibly sentence you to six months in jail."

Michael nodded soberly. "I'm a peaceful man," he said, "why couldn't they just give me some medical attention instead of imprisoning me for vagrancy?"

The journalist shrugged. "They can't keep you in that cell until they hear from the Cooktown courthouse. They'll let you out soon."

"Then that's the last they're gonna see of me," he said. "When I get out of here, I'll go so far away that they'll never find me again."

Upon his release, Michael made his way back to Kalpowar Station. He figured if he could get that far, he'd follow the Normanby River to its mouth on Princess Charlotte Bay. From there, he'd continue north until he was well beyond the reach of the Queensland police.

But the return journey seemed eternal, and he had little energy. He didn't hunt or forage on the way, and his body grew weaker with every step.

When he was once again on the banks of the river, he fished for a few days and attempted to regain his strength. He figured after a few weeks, he'd be strong enough to strike out.

Ron Pocock took his job seriously. He was fed up with Michael Fomenko and believed it was up to him to bring him in. What would this land be like if others were allowed to roam about like Fomenko? he asked himself. Soon Queensland would be filled with vagrants, loafers and other hippie-types.

His biggest obstacle so far had been finding someone to help him. Whether it was because people sympathised with Michael or were intimidated by his large size, he didn't know — but he couldn't find volunteers to help him capture the vagrant.

The captain had supplied him with an Aboriginal tracker named Jerry Musgrave. He was competent and had no choice in the affair, but Pocock knew he needed at least one other man.

When he reached Laura, he looked up a long-time resident of the area named Sam Elliot. Sam was a prospector, respected the law, and, more importantly, owned a .45 automatic pistol.

Pocock knocked on the man's door, and when he answered, said, "The brass in Cairns told me I've got to pick up that bastard

Fomenko. His last camp was near Kalpowar Station, and I'm headin' that way and could use another hand."

Sam hesitated for a moment, and Pocock added, "There's nobody else in Laura who'll help – all I have is an old tracker – I'd appreciate it if you came along."

Reluctantly, Sam agreed. "Let me grab my gear."

Soon the three men were on horseback, riding the sixty-odd kilometres to Kalpowar Station. A steady mist accompanied them, and they talked little.

When they passed Lakefield Station, Pocock sent Jerry to scout around. He returned thirty minutes later.

"Nobody here, Boss, except for a couple of blackfellas. But one of them said Fomenko is camped down by the river."

They approached slowly, and when they were close, Pocock turned to his tracker and said, "Jerry, you go down to the river and tell him Mrs Whelan has a letter from his mother. Tell him it feels like there's some money in it."

A crocodile-like grin spread over Pocock's face as he watched him depart.

Before long, Jerry found Michael resting by his camp. He approached quietly and gave Michael a jolt when he suddenly appeared by his side.

"What do you want?" asked Michael.

Jerry sighed. "I was told to tell you that Mrs Whelan has a letter for you – and maybe there's money in it."

Michael stared at the man for a minute, trying to read him. He'd asked the woman's husband, Rob, to help him connect with some money – but something about this felt fishy.

Finally, he asked, "And what do you think?"

Jerry looked over the simple camp and the surrounding beauty. It seemed Michael was living a life not too different from the one his grandfather always reminisced about.

He said, "I'd trust a croc before I put my faith in anything that Pocock says. I'd hightail it out of here if I were you."

Michael nodded. "Can you buy me some time?"

Jerry shrugged. "I'll do what I can."

Jerry kept his eyes down when he faced Pocock again. He didn't trust the man and was afraid he'd know he was lying when he said, "He's sleeping at his camp by the river — we should approach slow and quiet."

Pocock followed the tracker for a few kilometres before tying the horses to a tree and continuing on foot. They were within eyesight of the campsite when they heard a loud splash about a kilometre away.

Michael had been following the riverbank north but had slipped on a muddy patch and tumbled into the water.

"Jesus!" shouted Pocock, "He's runnin' for it."

The men raced back to their mounts and were soon in hot pursuit. At one point, Sam got a glimpse of Michael ahead and yelled, "He's heading for the scrub like a bloody wallaby."

Pocock took a shot at him, but Michael doubled his efforts and disappeared.

By the time they caught up with him again, he'd covered about six kilometres. Michael must have realised he'd never lose them while following the river and turned into a dense swamp.

It would be tougher to track him there, but he'd have to lose them first. So he charged through it, mindless of the crocs that slithered out of his way.

A flock of sulphur-tipped cockatoos took to the sky, alerting the men of his direction.

The area was usually a dried out plain, and there was little cover. Ahead, Michael saw a dense patch of forest.

If I can make it there, I might shake them, thought Michael.

He limped along frantically in water that was up to his knees — and sometimes rose to his waist.

Pocock caught up with him in a deep stretch where there was no cover. He fired several shots at Michael, the bullets hitting the water on either side of him. When Pocock stopped to reload, Sam picked up the chase.

Sam got within a few paces of Michael and said, "Where you goin'? I'm not going to harm you. We only want to talk."

Michael dove under the man's horse and tried to make for the forest again. But with the horse, it was easy for Sam to head him off. Still, Michael kept diving underwater, trying to swim for it.

By this time, Pocock had caught up, and when Michael surfaced, he smacked him in the head with the butt of his rifle.

Again and again, Michael went underwater, but each time he surfaced, one of the men was there waiting. And each time, they struck his head.

Eventually, Pocock jumped off his horse onto the stunned man.

He was just about drowned, coughing up a lungful of water, when they dragged him to shore.

Still, he fought like a tiger while they attempted to handcuff him. "This bloke is a mad Micky!" shouted Sam.

Suddenly, Michael bit Sam's hand, and in his anger, the man hit him again, striking his head with the pistol butt. Blood shot everywhere, and Pocock shouted, "Hey, not too hard — I'll be in deep shit if you kill the bastard."

When he was finally cuffed, they paused on the shore to catch their breath. Pocock also carried a whip, and he tied it around Michael's wrist as extra security — although he doubted the crazed man would ever get out of the handcuffs.

They threw Michael over the saddle of Jerry's horse and made the Aboriginal walk.

"Let's spend the night at Kalpowar Station," said Pocock.

About halfway there, Michael jumped off the horse and fled again. He'd somehow untied the whip with his teeth but still wore the handcuffs.

It wasn't difficult to recapture him with the men on horseback, although Michael managed to travel almost two kilometres before they nabbed him. Pocock was cursing everything in sight.

"By Christ! I'd have some explaining to do if I lost him," said Pocock, "especially with the cuffs on."

Whelan greeted them when they arrived at the Kalpowar Station. He eyed Michael sadly as they secured him to a tree. In addition to the handcuffs, they had also wrapped wire around his wrists.

"Don't you think that's all a bit much?" he asked.

Pocock was indignant. "This man is a dangerous fugitive."

Whelan scoffed. "He's a vagrant—that's all. If you'd have allowed him to collect the money his mother sent, you'd have had no excuse to bring him in."

Shaking his head, Pocock said, "He stole from a couple of vendors in Laura—that makes him a thief, too."

"Everybody knows his family will pay any debts he has," said Whelan, becoming more and more disgusted with the affair.

He walked off, feeling he wanted no part in the arrest.

Later that night, Whelan approached the tree where Michael was held. The other men were sleeping, but not Michael. Whelan watched as Michael stretched out his foot, trying to get a rock that was just beyond his reach.

The station owner never met Michael's eyes as he walked by, but his foot kicked the rock a little closer.

Several hours later, Pocock woke to a light tapping.

He walked over to Michael and discovered he'd almost smashed his way free of the handcuffs.

He smacked him across the face and said, "Not on my watch."

Michael stared back angrily. "You'll never keep me."

Pocock grinned. "We'll see about that."

The next morning, Jerry, the tracker, was nowhere in sight. Pocock fumed about it but tried to play it off.

"No matter," he said. "He did his part."

They put Michael on a horse, cuffing him and then tying his wrists with wire on top of that.

It took a few days to reach Dingo Yards, where they put him in the back of a Land Cruiser. Michael's eyes had taken on a wild, furtive look, and he constantly searched for a way to escape.

Pocock must have sensed it because now he added a dog chain to his wrists on top of the wire and handcuffs.

When they finally got him to the town of Laura, it took several officers to force him into a cell. The men saw his bruised and battered body and were reluctant. Some had known Fomenko for years and didn't think he was a threat.

But Pocock was adamant.

He said, "If he gets away, it'll be on you."

Still, they felt terrible, and after they locked his cell, they took off the cuffs and wire.

They gave him two good meals — dinner and breakfast — but both were untouched when he was taken away the next day. The Laura police commented that the wire and dog chains were inhumane, but Pocock only relented taking them off when they threw a set of leg irons on him.

"Let's see you run with those on, boy," said Pocock while leering at his captive.

When they finally brought Michael before the magistrate in Cooktown, he was a shell of a man. He barely spoke, resigned that his fate was out of his hands. In later years, the magistrate would comment that Michael Fomenko was the last person brought before him in leg irons.

They made another stop on the way to Brisbane at the Cairns police station. None of the men there would meet Michael's eyes, and they glared at Pocock, who suddenly found himself being weighed up as the bad one.

"We can't have people like Fomenko just roaming about," he said defensively.

Keith Barnes, the watch-house keeper, replied, "The poor bastard thought he was living in a free country."

On 20 April, *The Mirror* ran an article on Michael's treatment.

"The non-conformist in Australia does not have an easy time. Take the case of Michael Fomenko, a misfit in society. Years ago, Fomenko fled Sydney for the bush. He became a nature boy, living off the land and going without clothes. A harmless freak, one would have said. But society likes its members to toe the line, and this weekend society snapped back at Fomenko. We can't help thinking that what Fomenko is actually in jail for is the crime of being different."

Chapter Twenty-One

Michael's Story – Age Thirty-Five
(Ipswich Mental Hospital 1964-1966)

*B*y the time he reached the Stuart Creek Jail in Townsville, Michael's physical condition had deteriorated so much that he was seen immediately by both medical doctors and a team of psychiatrists.

The doctors concluded that he suffered from injuries inflicted during his capture as well as wounds from a prior encounter with a wild boar. The battle with Caly had left him scarred from head to toe, and now, as a result of not being treated, the lacerations were septic and infested with bacteria.

His head wounds from repeatedly being bashed with the butts of rifle and pistol were equally infected. His wrists were raw and bleeding from being cuffed and wrapped in wire.

The psychiatrists stated that he was in no shape to serve time and instead recommended placing him in a secure mental health facility. Dr Halberstater, the Government Medical Officer, said he could not understand why Michael—if he were sane—would choose to live such a life and hoped further medical evaluations might reveal what drove him to it.

He was allowed a few days in Townsville while he recuperated.

His transfer from Townsville to Brisbane made national headlines, and reporters and townsfolk crowded the stations along the way, trying to get a glimpse of him.

Two police accompanied him in a special van attached to a goods train, and when they arrived at Mayne Station in Brisbane, they were met with six well-armed officers.

The public that awaited his arrival were a bit let down when the "wild man of the north" arrived, smiling and waving. He shook hands and exchanged a few kind words with the two men who'd accompanied him.

The next day he was evaluated by one of the psychiatrists at the Ipswich Mental Hospital, first known as Sandy Gallop asylum when it was established in 1878.

A middle-aged doctor wearing glasses and a white lab coat approached Michael and stuck out his hand.

"I'm Doctor Meadon, but you can call me Aury."

Michael smiled, weary of the man's too friendly demeanour.

He asked, "Aury Meadon? Like Eurymedon?"

"I suppose," said the doctor, looking slightly confused.

Michael chuckled at the thought that the doctor had the same name as the King of the cannibalistic giants in *The Odyssey*.

"Of course, it is," said Michael, his laughter building.

"I don't understand what's so funny," he said.

When Michael refused to explain and kept chuckling, the doctor moved on. "We're going to run some tests and see how we might help you. The nurses will address your wounds, but I'm more concerned with how living in the wild may have damaged your mind."

Suddenly Michael had had enough for the day.

This bloke is never going to understand me, he thought.

"My mind is fine, Doc," he said, "why don't we wait a few days before we continue—I could use a break."

Doctor Meadon shook his head and said, "That's unacceptable. Sooner or later, you'll realise that we are no longer on your schedule."

Michael sat up to leave when suddenly a male nurse forced him back. When Michael tried to resist, the nurse called for help.

Suddenly, a half-dozen burly men were leaning over him like some six-headed monster. They pinned his arms, lashed them to the table, and then did the same with his legs.

"I'll get you for this Eurymedon!" screamed Michael.

The doctor looked confused — and a bit frightened — as he backed out of the room. "Sedate him for now," he said, "I'll talk to him later when he's more reasonable."

When Michael saw a man walking towards him with a syringe, he fought even harder, but it was no use. He could barely move.

Eventually, he gave in. Fighting was pointless and only brought on more pain. Instead, he lost himself in his memories, trying to flee down the hole like a pursued rabbit.

He remembered the birds squabbling and screeching along the coast, always accompanied by the crashing of waves; the sound of the ocean so constant he felt he'd never lose it. Then came the crack of lightning and its sad echo.

Often, he'd imagined Zeus talking to him through those rumbles, urging him on, coaxing him to take risks and not fear consequences.

The days on end of paddling up that coast merged into one epic struggle, and although at times exhausting, it was also mesmerising. He saw waters filled with countless fish, coral, and aquatic creatures, then found himself exploring the ancient rainforests, immersing himself in the thick growth.

And then he was back on the water with the wind, which was so constant at times that he thought he'd go mad. He remembered the other occasions, too, when he would have given anything to feel the slightest of breezes.

He lay there thinking of that lack of wind until the drugs kicked in and swept him away.

He woke later, strapped to a table. The IV was no longer in his right arm, but now there was a metal ring on his head—ironically, it felt like a crown, and not one he wanted. He was desperate to be anywhere but here. He would have pled for help, but he knew his cries would be pointless.

"I'm the King of the Coral Sea," he said to no one.

Dr Meadon returned and said, "It appears that your escapades in the wild have damaged your psyche. It's my opinion—and the other docs here agree with me—that you are clinically insane. Luckily for you, we've had great success with electric shock therapy—and you're a perfect candidate."

When they first applied voltage, Michael screamed, "Noooo!!!"

He tried desperately to wrench his arms free as the room spun around him. He glimpsed an orderly grinning at him.

After that, he retreated into his mind again. This was a battle he could not win. So instead, he drifted through his recollections.

He went back to his first days on the water, following along on that adventure, casually, reminiscing.

Not rushing at all, he remembered everything, beginning with that opening day he exited the Daintree River. He thought of that first stop when he trimmed the big canoe down because it was too bulky. Then he relived the loss of both his boats—one after another—and ending up in the cave in Flattery Bay. Finally, an image of himself drifting around that haunted cavern came to him, and he chuckled as he saw himself as the cyclops.

Caldwell had rightly named him Polyphemus. He'd been both Odysseus and the cyclops for nearly eight months until he continued on his journey. He remembered fighting the monsoon as he struggled north up that coast, and the good men of the *Yola* and the various people that had helped him.

He recalled the searches that had pursued him up the shoreline. He had hidden under the decoy canoe like it was the belly of a beast, listening to the bomber rumbling above. It had been a narrow escape, but one that bought him time.

When the weather finally turned, he rode the winds north, fishing as he went until he hooked the big barramundi that Poseidon stole from him.

He recalled the big croc slithering by his canoe while camped up the Annie River and then later when he followed the currents north. In the end, the great reptile had been a boon companion after all.

But still, he wished he'd managed to keep that barra.

In the seemingly endless rivers of time that unfolded before him, he missed his family and also the people who'd helped him on his journey—despite the government threats. In the Torres Islands, he'd encountered friends. Some, like Caldwell, showed great *xenia*.

He remembered Smiley and his words of wisdom, including his talks of the Dreamtime. And Tyler, the young man he thought of as Hermes, his winged messenger, who showed up in the dead of night with warnings.

Then there was his great crossing. The one they said he'd never complete. It should have taken weeks but took months.

During that period, he became master of the winds— eventually. It was there that he officially dubbed himself King.

He had found his place of peace and paradise. And would have stayed longer had the monsoon not chased him off.

For days on end, he pondered Smiley's belief that sometimes people come back as an animal. He thought of that now, and after more contemplation, he decided he'd come back as a crocodile, like Poseidon.

He remembered their encounter on Nagi Island when he'd stumbled into the crocodile's den. He'd experienced a change of perspective then and somehow seen himself through the mighty croc's eyes. Could a part of his spirit already live in him?

And there was so much more: His return and all the reporters; his family welcoming him back to Sydney; and his failed attempt to return to the wild.

Thankfully, he did get back to Queensland and resumed life in the jungle. He found that awareness, again — the one he so yearned for now — although it faded somewhat when he lived with Calypso.

He thought of her and wondered if things might have changed if they'd stayed together longer. Suppose he'd not become obsessed with Caly?

And what did that get me? he asked the darkness. More battles that eventually ended with me near dead. He thought of that mighty boar and wondered if he might, somehow, still be alive.

He imagined him up on the Laura plains, left ear half-gone and the knife still protruding from his shoulder.

He remembered finally reaching Dutch New Guinea… and the Painted Man.

In one sense, the time passed ever so slowly, but in another, it flew by. In reality, he was there for several brutal years.

Dr Meadon stood in a private room with Michael's extended family. His mother, Elizabeth, was there, looking nervous and out of place. She was in her seventies now and was seated. His sisters were there too, all three of them — Inessa, Nina Oom and Renee — and Renee's husband as well.

"Before Michael arrives," said Dr Meadon, "I'd like to address his case. We had hoped we might make him stop acting like a barbarian and convert him back to his roots as a civilised human, but I'm afraid we have not been entirely successful in that. Instead, he seems to exist between conventional reality and a world of his own making — an imagined one. He thinks we're all something called Laestrygonians, whatever that means."

Dr Meadon received cold looks when he scanned their faces. They'd all read the article in *The Truth* in which the institute claimed to have cured Michael.

The article headline read: "He's Tamed!" And the first sentence stated: "In a remarkable medical feat, doctors at Sandy Gallop Special Hospital, Ipswich, have civilised the 'Tarzan' of the North Queensland jungle, Michael Fomenko."

Inessa, now forty-one, was the first to speak.

"Your claims are false, Doctor. You have not cured him," she said. "And he's no sinister figure. He has merely taken a schoolboy dream and run with it."

The doctor shook his head sadly, "I'm afraid it has gone well past that. In my opinion, we should be discussing a lobotomy, not his release."

Renee, now twenty-five, stepped forward and appeared so angry that her husband put a restricting hand on her shoulder as she shouted, "So you're saying that anyone who dares to deviate from the norm and live an alternative lifestyle is mentally disturbed?"

Dr Meadon stammered a reply, but she cut him off.

"Because it seems to me that you consider placing electrodes on the head of someone that doesn't conform to society to be a *civilising* act—and I find that quite disturbing! Isn't it ironic that our government is led by a party that claims to believe in the freedom of the individual?"

The young woman was fuming mad, and the doctor didn't dare confront her, so instead, he turned to Elizabeth.

"I think we should consult Mrs Fomenko," he said. "After all, it was at her urging that he was captured and brought here."

Elizabeth appeared to shrink back into her chair as everyone looked at her. She said in a timid voice, "Yes, initially I thought it would be for the best—but I don't know anymore."

Now Nina said, "My father and I always understood what Michael was doing—but mother never did. He's not insane, just different, and nothing you've done here has made him any better. He's just more frightened—more of a recluse than ever."

"We still have options," said Dr Meadon. "I suggested earlier…"

Renee spat, "If you even say the word lobotomy again, I'm gonna smack you." The doctor looked at her, shocked.

She added, "And we're not leaving this place until you release him to us."

The other two sisters nodded in agreement.

"I find this all very inappropriate," said Dr Meadon.

Renee put her face centimetres from his and said, "We don't care—now you better go get him, or I'll really make a scene."

An hour later, they escorted Michael back to their car. His time in the institution was finally over.

Chapter Twenty-Two

Michael's Story – Age Sixty-Eight
(Gordonvale 1998)

Nobody knows when Michael Fomenko returned to Queensland. He was away for some time, and then suddenly, it seemed he'd never left.

There was little talk regarding what had happened to him during his absence. Few knew of his brutal capture in the Laura Basin, or the traumatic time spent in the Ipswich Mental Hospital. These were the most terrible incidents of his life, and yet without the right witnesses, how can the public consider something a tragic event? Michael's only witnesses were the arresting officers and medical staff, and they told a different story.

And so, there would be no collective gasps, cries or outrage.

Following his release, several newspapers ran headlines claiming he'd returned to his "barbaric" ways in his beloved jungles, and then for a while, he faded from the public eye altogether. He stayed with his Nature God, comforted by that awareness that had never abandoned him.

During those years, Michael frequented the places he knew and loved along the cane belt, keeping a low profile while prowling the rainforest that skirted the small towns. He stayed out of sight, perhaps afraid of being arrested again.

He resurfaced slowly, and by the 1980s, he was well established in the Bloomfield River area, frequenting places like Cedar Bay and Whalebone Beach. He also had friends in the small settlement of Ayton, located about fifty kilometres south of Cooktown, near the Wujal Wujal Aboriginal community.

The locals from that area accepted Michael and didn't complain about his eccentricities, like exercising and jogging up and down the beach or working on a canoe. Whether he ever put the canoe in the water, nobody knew, but plenty of people watched him hollow it out. To burn out the inside of the log, he used cooking oil that left his body—which was already dark from exposure to the sun—covered in oily smoke.

Several friends helped him organise a pension and offered him places to sleep when the rains blew in. Bill Smith ran the Ayton store and kept an eye on him, and Col Burns maintained a lean-to shed on his property that Michael could use at will. Another friend, Gordon Hickling, assisted him with shelter and helped with one of his canoes.

When Bill sold the store to Pearl Kendrick, she watched after Michael as well. Unfortunately, several ruffians occasionally preyed on Michael, caging him to hand over his food when his pension money came in. Because Pearl also ran the post office, she began to deposit his cheque for him when it arrived.

Michael still fished, ate palm-hearts, and hunted an occasional wild pig, but he consumed more store-bought food as he got older. One of his favourite meals was a T-bone steak grilled on fire with potatoes and onions. He also developed a sweet tooth.

In 1984 his sister Nina tried to visit him, but he fled, fearing she was a reporter.

"I swear that man can smell a journalist a kilometre away," said Pearl.

The two left a sign on the beach, signed by Nina, and a few days later, Michael returned and had a reunion with his sister.

When it was over, Nina said, "Michael was just born ahead of his time. If a man today decided to live with Aboriginals or paddle a canoe to Asia, nobody would take notice — they wouldn't even bat an eye."

Cedar Bay had a mixed population of alternatives and straights, but they all welcomed Michael. They didn't make a fuss about his presence and didn't alert the authorities or the press. Instead, they let him be, perhaps hoping the world would forget about him.

In 1985, the *Sunday Sun* reported that the fifty-five-year-old man had been seen jogging along the Bruce Highway. Soon after that, he appeared regularly in the newspapers. A journalist tracked Michael down and described him as "elegant and fit-looking in leopard skin jockettes and plastic sandals."

Over the years, the reporters had tagged him with numerous nicknames like Odysseus II and The Wildman of the North, but now one surfaced above the others — Tarzan.

The papers recycled the outlandish old claims from previous articles, many of which had Michael wrestling pythons, battling crocodiles, and narrowly escaping piranhas.

The facts of his life slowly faded away, with only the occasional mention of his Olympic hopes or his great sea voyage. At the same time, the journalists portrayed him as a trickster who hid behind tree trunks, or swung from branches, to creep up on unsuspecting vehicles as they passed through the forest.

They turned him into a character, maybe hoping that the doctors at Sandy Gallop had not truly shocked the savage out of him. After all, outrageous stories sold papers.

The residents that lived between Bloomfield and Cooktown saw him often and thought nothing of it. Queensland had its share of quirky, elusive characters, and they knew he was just making one of his sporadic trips to town to restock his supplies. Once he'd grabbed what food and other necessities he needed, he'd return to the rainforest again.

But over time, even they began to refer to Michael as Tarzan.

In 1998, Steve Douglas worked on his property on Terminus Street in Cairns, repairing a fence along the street. He'd first arrived in the area in 1985 when he was twenty, and like Michael Fomenko, had fallen in love with it.

He returned in 1990 with his wife, Sally, and their one-year-old daughter, Sorcha. The family immigrated from Europe – Steve from Northern Ireland, Sally from England – and in the next few years, they had two more children, Shay and Kiera.

Steve was wrestling with a fence post when he looked up to see Sorcha—now age nine—standing there with a glass of cold water.

"Thanks, Luv," he said as he paused his work and took a sip.

While they stood in the cool shadows, they noticed a woman walking down the street in their direction. She looked to be in her mid-fifties and seemed interested in the building behind the fence.

She glanced at the sign which read: *Dreamtime Travellers Rest.*

"Need a room?" asked Steve, joking, because the woman looked like a local, not a tourist.

She smiled. "I used to live here."

"Really?" asked Steve, anxious to hear her connection to the place.

"In the fifties," she said, "this was a guest house that catered to Russian immigrants—my parents owned it then."

"I would love to see a photo of it if you have one," he said. And then, "We immigrated here eight years ago, so I guess it's still for immigrants."

The woman introduced herself as Losha, glanced at Sorcha, and said, "I was just about your age when I met Cairns' most famous immigrant: Michael Fomenko."

Steve gave her a blank look, and she added, "Well, maybe not the most famous to everyone, but my family were Russians also, so we always followed his exploits in the papers."

She stared at Steve, and in a voice tinged with sadness, asked, "You never heard of Michael Fomenko?"

Steve shook his head, and she added, "You see him from time to time jogging along the Bruce Highway with an old sugar sack thrown over his shoulder."

Now Steve brightened. "Yes! I have seen him. Is that the bloke everyone calls Tarzan?"

She bristled slightly at the name. "That's him. His real name is Michael, and, in his day, he was quite a man."

They chatted for a few more minutes, and then Steve continued with his task. But for the rest of the day, Fomenko was on his mind.

Over the coming months, Steve learned how the various towns up and down the sugar belt had supported Michael. The Mirriwinni Hotel in Babinda always had a room available for him. Rusty's Backpacker Lodge and the Woree Caravan Park in Cairns also put him up. And there were many others.

It seemed that despite being a loner, Michael had a lot of friends. He'd frequented the area for over forty years, often living in the wild, and everyone had a story about their encounters with Tarzan.

One day Steve learned that Michael was frequenting an old camp on the outskirts of Gordonvale, only twenty-three kilometres south of Cairns. He'd moved the camp slightly upriver, under a bridge that crossed the Mulgrave River, but the locals saw him often.

When an old travel acquaintance and his wife came to Cairns to visit, Steve decided to show his friends what was special about Queensland. He'd begin in Cairns, move on up to the Tablelands, and maybe on the way get a glimpse of Tarzan. What better way to show someone a place than to introduce them to a local legend?

Rob and Dee were Americans on the tail end of a year of travel through Africa and Asia. In a month, they would continue down the coast to Sydney and then fly to New Zealand, but for now, they wanted to explore Queensland's rainforest.

Steve had been friends with Rob since they'd met in Eilat, Israel, in the mid-eighties. They'd both been young then, and it seemed every day had been an adventure as they explored the Sinai desert and the Red Sea. Now he wanted to show his friend exactly why he had settled here.

With Sally and the three kids in tow, Steve loaded everyone into his Kombi and headed to Yungaburra, up on the Tablelands. On the way, they stopped at the Greenpatch rest area on the outskirts of Gordonvale.

Steve parked the car, and while Sally set out a blanket, he showed Rob and Dee where they could access a nature trail that ran along the Mulgrave River.

"Why don't you two take a walk along the river," he said. "You might see something interesting."

"Sounds lovely," said Dee as they set off.

"Careful not to slip in," he warned. "There are crocs."

He was about to give further directions when nine-year-old Sorcha cut in, "I'll just go along and show them," she said.

She smiled at Dee and added, "It's not far—we'll only be gone a few minutes."

Soon the three were on a trail, moving alongside the leafy growth above the river's bank. A steep drop led to the dark water that was thick with shadows.

Rob stepped towards the river and leaned over, trying to spot a crocodile.

Sorcha clicked her tongue, her green eyes sparkling as she said, "Careful there. If you get eaten, I'll catch hell from my dad."

Dee steered them back to the trail, and they had just reached it when a large man came charging towards them from several paces away. He wore only shorts, and his leathery frame looked too weathered to belong to a human.

He inhabited the centre of the trail, was moving fast, and appeared to have no intention of stepping aside for Rob. By the time the American looked up and saw the man, it was almost too late.

Rob dove to the side, disappearing into a bush.

Back at the rest area, the remainder of the Douglas family was waiting. Shay kicked a soccer ball that seemed half his height, and Keira had ice cream all over her face.

Steve handed over three cones that were on the verge of a meltdown. "I got lucky and flagged down the ice cream truck, so I'm glad you three didn't linger."

"Did you see any wildlife?" asked Sally.

Sorcha smirked, "Did we ever! Tarzan ran Rob right off the trail!"

Rob scratched his head. "Wait a minute—that's the wildman you were telling me about?"

Steve nodded, glad the excursion had been productive.

Rob looked like his pride had been stomped on as he said, "That guy had no intention of sharing the trail."

Steve laughed. "He always runs, never walks. But he's been living here for over forty years—he probably made that trail."

"Well, he was a bit of a train wreck," said Rob. "And he was covered with dirt and grime."

For a moment, Steve sat quietly, thinking. Finally, he said, "I can't imagine it's easy living the life he does. I've heard he prefers to be alone in nature, and he's willing to sacrifice all the comforts we're used to, just to do that."

Then he clamped a hand on Rob's shoulder and said, "And imagine what you'll look like running shirtless down a trail when you are close to seventy."

Dee giggled, "I bet that would be a scary sight, too."

"I know he gave you a scare," said Sally, "but he really is harmless."

Young Shay puffed up his six-year-old chest and said, "That's right! Tarzan don't hurt nobody. You see him by the edge of the highway, and then – pfft! – he's gone."

Sally glanced at Sorcha and asked, "And what do you think?"

She said, "I'm glad he's happy living in the jungle and all, but maybe someone should give him a bath."

Steve nodded and grinned, "Okay, a bath wouldn't kill him, but for now, we should all be glad we saw him. Not many people would go to the extremes that he has to be one with nature. That man has found his dream—he's living as true to himself as anyone I know."

They all looked towards the river, hoping to get another glimpse of Michael. Even the kids were quiet as they imagined what his life was like. A breeze ruffled the trees around them, dragging with it the faint smell of the river mixed with that of the nearby sugar mill.

Chapter Twenty-Three

Michael's Story – Age Seventy-Nine
(Mount Sophia 2009)

*M*ichael's last camp was well hidden in a dense palm forest near a river. It was off the beaten track, and the trail he used to get there had numerous false leads that usually threw off the curious.

A large strangler fig dominated it. Over the last few decades, he had sought out the giant trees. They provided shelter from the rain, privacy from humans, and in season, tasty fruit. And there was one other reason why Michael liked the trees so much — he thought they were magical.

Strangler figs are one of the rainforest's fastest-growing trees. They begin as a simple seed in the cleft of a branch, pooped out by a bird or other animal. Eventually, they send out tendrils and wrap themselves tightly around the host tree, gradually forming a lattice frame that surrounds the trunk. At the same time, the fig sends some saplings reaching up towards the light, while others travel downwards to the ground, where they eventually take nutrients from the soil.

This plundering of sunlight and water sometimes causes the host tree to die, but by this time, the strangler fig is strong enough to stand independently. As the host tree perishes and decomposes, it can at times leave air pockets and empty chambers inside the fig's structure. Because their trunks are gnarled, knotted and hollow, strangler figs are often the only trees standing in areas that have been intensively logged. This worked in Michael's favour.

Michael slept among the fig's many branches. In some trees, he crawled into passages that led deep into the core; in others, he climbed up into the loftier reaches and woke to birdsong. He always felt a mutual awareness when alone in the trees.

Sometimes Michael would wake in the middle of the night, alone in the dark, and for some inexplicable reason, feel that he was twenty-seven again. In the darkness, he would run his fingers along his body, and what had been old, wrinkled skin and sagging muscles by daylight would suddenly seem young and strong.

His mind felt sharper when he lived in the figs. It seemed to reach out through the branches of the magical trees to embrace the night. During those moments, he often felt he was watching himself from above.

He was never alone when living inside the tree, either. Throughout the year the giant fig was visited by tree kangaroos, lizards, possums, snakes, tree frogs, numerous birds, and just about any animal that could enjoy a ripe fig.

Every so often, he would wake to find a creature staring at him—a cassowary perhaps—that had paused while searching the ground for food. There were plenty of snakes in the trees, but they never bit him. The trees were filled with fig wasps too, but he rarely got stung.

On other nights, he would suddenly wake for no reason and lay there, snuggled against his living home, while he remembered his journey to Dutch New Guinea. He would relive it all, only finishing as the sky lightened and sleep slowly took him.

Sometimes he heard voices in the trees and saw inexplicable things.

On several occasions in the last few months, he'd awoken to a sound and looked up to see Caly, the wild pig standing nearby looking at him. It had been over fifty years since their battle, but somehow, he was there, looking strong and fearsome.

Michael had stared at the beast, half its left ear blown away, and blinked at it repeatedly. His knife was still there, protruding from his shoulder.

"Caly?" he asked.

The pig had not reacted other than to sniff around for a few minutes before disappearing into the darkness.

Michael did not doubt that if he walked a few paces and stared down into the dark river he lived beside, he would see Poseidon slowly cruising by.

On other nights, he heard his family or friends talking to him.

"Mike, it's me," Inessa would say out of the darkness. Then, referring to their escape through Manchuria, "We made it, baby! We made it!"

Or it might be Nina Oom yelling at the doctors. "He's not insane, just different, and nothing you've done here has made him any better!"

Many were the nights that he woke from his youngest sister, Renee, whispering into his ear, "What did you find out there, Michael?"

On other evenings his father disturbed his sleep with excerpts from *The Odyssey*. He thought of his dad and wondered what he would think of this strange life in the wilderness. The odd bits of conversation that floated down to him in the dark whispered that he approved.

His friends at the Wujal Wujal Aboriginal community joked that he might be a Yara-ma-yha-who, the mythical creature thought to inhabit fig trees in the coastal rainforest.

The little being was reputed to be about a metre tall, with a huge head and red scaly skin. According to the legends, instead of fingers and toes, it had octopi-like suckers that it used to drain its victim's blood.

Michael thought the fruit bats were a closer match to the Yara-ma-yha-who than he was. When figs ripened, their massive colonies took over the tree, screeching and chattering, while they feasted. Some had bodies the size of foxes, and initially, he feared waking to find them draining his blood, but they left him alone.

It seemed that almost all the residents of the massive fig trees let him be. The home they shared was big enough for all of them, and there was no need to fight.

When Michael first arrived in Queensland, he had lived on the banks of a river in Deeral, about fifty kilometres south of Cairns. There he made his first canoe and began his life-long enchantment with the beautiful — and perilous — rivers of Queensland.

The property was later purchased by Bruno and Jutta Jung. They had two sons, Harold and Ingram, who later developed an interest in Michael Fomenko. Harold first met Michael in 1990, and they remained friends for twenty years. He spent much of this time researching and documenting Michael's life, accumulating a vast bulk of material.

While Harold busied himself researching Michael's past, his brother, Ingram, worked to publish the story.

In 2009 Harold Jung slowly followed a narrow path through the palm forest, ducking under creepers and avoiding deep muddy pockets. If he'd been on his own, he would have travelled faster, but he had an older man behind him, so he erred on the side of caution.

Ingram had contacted the Cairns Historical Society to find a writer who would condense all his brother's research into a book — and this was the bloke they had sent.

Peter Ryle looked fit at sixty-eight, and as a resident of Cairns, he was used to the hot, sticky weather. When he'd been fifteen — in 1957 — he had met Michael at the Mulgrave Sugar Mill. He'd been intrigued by his story ever since and jumped at the chance to write a non-fiction account of Michael's life when asked by the Society.

He had heard stories about the hidden trails Fomenko used to reach his hideouts. So far, he thought this one was obvious. It led through a beautiful palm forest that seemed to belong to another time. He drifted along while trying to imagine what it would be like to live in such a place.

Five minutes further down the trail Harold pointed to the left, just after they passed a large palm. The path they were on continued, but instead, Harold moved left and took a step close to the palm's trunk and then another away from the trail. Suddenly they were on a different trail, albeit one that had seen far less use.

Peter asked, "How lucid is Michael? He must be eighty."

Harold stopped and rubbed his neck. "Sometimes he's very present and reminisces about his great voyage — but other times it's like talking to a young child."

In a quieter voice, Peter asked, "Do you think that's a result of what they did to him at Sandy Gallop?"

Harold shrugged. "It's hard to say at this point. He came to this area in 1957 — more than fifty years ago — and has spent most of that time living in the wild."

Peter nodded. "I've looked through your research — especially the newspaper clippings from the last few decades — and it seems like Michael doesn't realise he has aged."

For a full minute Harold stared at the ground. Through all his research, he was aware of the strains that had pulled at Michael's life, but also the brief moments of glory.

Finally, he said, "There's no doubt the shock treatment left him diminished, but he settled in a place where a firm grasp on the passage of time didn't matter so much. Michael wanted only to merge with an awareness — his Jungle God — and for that, he didn't need to be aware of the passing of years. He grew old without noticing."

Harold turned to continue, but only a few steps later stopped and added, "I'd recommend sleeping alone under one of those giant strangler figs. I have, and you'll see that the concept of time slowly fades away."

Ten minutes later they stood before a massive strangler fig. Roots, thick vines and dangling saplings formed a trunk that was as wide as a house. A dense canopy overhead sheltered them from the sun, and from within its branches, a flock of parrots squawked riotously.

In the shadows at ground level, an old man leaned back against the tree. Michael's leathery frame, covered with grime, matched the tree's bark. His hair had turned white, as well as his whiskered chin, and he wore only a faded pair of khaki shorts.

"G'day," said Michael when he glimpsed Harold.

Harold smiled wide. "Hi, Michael. I hope you don't mind that I brought a friend."

Michael's bushy eyebrows scrunched together as he eyed Peter. After a moment he shrugged and slowly climbed to his feet.

Peter thought the old man was moving to shake his hand and stuck his own out, but Michael passed him and picked up his sugar sack. He shuffled back to Harold while one hand rummaged inside the sack, searching.

He pulled out a Coke and handed it to Harold, and said, "Here you go. I stopped at the shop the other day and picked up some treats."

Then he took out and unwrapped a white chocolate bar and gave some to each of his guests. Peter tried to refuse, but Michael gruffly kept gesturing for him to take it until he did.

"How have you been?" asked Harold.

Michael nodded, "Very well. I'll be doing fine until the rains come."

"What will you do then?" asked Peter.

Michael scratched his head and said, "I might go down to Sydney to take a few college classes—I've learned many wild ways to treat sickness, but it wouldn't hurt to learn some traditional medicine. I'm still young, you know, I have plenty of time."

The parrots overhead kept up their din, and the men leaned closer to Michael to hear him.

Michael smiled. "You should hear it when the figs are in season and the fox bats show up."

Suddenly a small fig wasp landed on Peter's nose. Before he could brush it off, it flew away.

"Did it sting you?" asked Michael.

Peter shook his head. "No."

Michael laughed. "They know who they like. They don't sting me either."

Peter admired a few of the wasps he could see on a nearby root.

He turned to Michael and said, "Did you know that fig wasps are the only insect that can pollinate a fig tree? The wasps also can only reproduce inside fig flowers. And for most species of fig, there is only one species of wasp that pollinates it."

Michael had sat back down and now stared off into the jungle.

He appeared not to have heard anything that Peter had said.

Instead, he replied, "I've been thinking of returning to Sydney to see my parents. It's been a long time."

Peter turned to Harold and whispered, "Didn't I read that both of his parents have been dead a long time?"

Harold nodded solemnly.

Peter asked, "Do you like this life? Are you happy?"

Michael stared off. The birds had settled down, but now the cicadas shrilled.

He leaned against the tree and wiggled his back until he was comfortable. He appeared to be part of the tree — like he'd always been there. He glanced at the canopy, and then the men, and said, "I've had a good life. But it wasn't always easy — it took guts."

"It sure did," said Harold. "Is there anything you need?"

Michael thought for a minute and replied, "I could use an upside-down jib sail — one fitted for an eighteen-foot canoe."

Harold nodded, not sure he wanted to help the old man get out on the water where he might easily die. He'd have to think on it.

"Do you have other plans?" asked Peter.

Michael gazed back into the palm forest.

Harold recognised the look and sensed the visit was over, but for Peter's sake, he asked one last question.

"Michael, before we go, I was hoping you might talk about your great canoe voyage to Dutch New Guinea. Peter has read all about it, and it would be great if you could tell him what you remember."

Michael's gaze drifted slowly from the forest to the two men and then back to the forest.

After a few minutes Harold said, "Okay, we should go."

While they walked off, Michael listened as Peter asked Harold, "Do you think he still remembers any of the details of crossing the Torres Strait? I'd love to know how he rigged his sail."

Michael shut them out and didn't listen for a reply. Instead, he leaned back against the tree and exhaled. Company always exhausted him.

He closed his eyes and thought of his great voyage and chuckled at Peter's comment. Of course, he remembered it. When it came to his Odyssey, he remembered all of it.

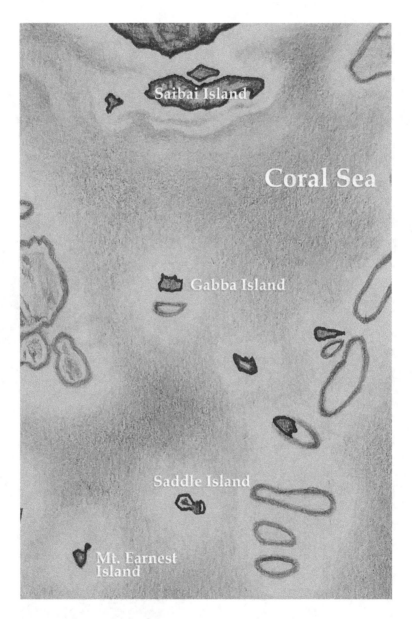

Map 7 – Saddle Island to Dutch New Guinea.
Illustration by Tom Fish.

Map 8 – The coast of Dutch New Guinea.
Illustration by Tom Fish.

Chapter Twenty-Four

The Odyssey XII – Saddle Island
(November 1959)

Michael grinned like a crocodile when he set off from Nagi Island. He'd never been so well-stocked. *Tortoise's* hull was packed with three plastic jugs containing twenty-five litres of water, plus tyre tubes loaded with sugar, rice, flour, salt and tea. He also had plenty of rope, fishing gear, a helmet full of wongai plums, and a basket with eight coconuts.

By his side were several lengths of bamboo that he planned to use as fishing poles and also a sturdy stick with his old cane knife mounted on it.

The other cane knife he wore around his waist.

Although still disgruntled by ranger Dale's request to leave the island, he knew there were plenty of other isles within striking distance. To the northeast he could see Suarji and Getullai Islands, both less than ten kilometres away.

The only thing working against him was the weather. The November sunshine was blinding, and it was as hot as Hades. If he'd had a spare sail, he would have used it now to make a canopy to hide under. Instead, he put up the one he had as a gentle breeze blew from the southeast.

Dale watched from the shore as Michael tightened the sheet and the canvas filled with air. As the canoe moved forward, he gave a farewell wave, but Michael was busy using his paddle to point his craft and didn't see him.

In no time Michael and *Tortoise* were on their way. The canoe skipped along, the bow slowly shifting towards the northwest until Michael paddled hard on the port side to turn the boat. He let out the sheet and adjusted the boom some more. He stopped when *Tortoise* was perpendicular to the wind and pointed northeast.

He had to constantly use his paddle to keep *Tortoise* pointed in the right direction, but he was making good time and heading straight towards the islands.

He spent a few days on Getullai Island. The modest island was only a half kilometre by one-and-a-half kilometres and lay surrounded by a circular reef. He came in at high tide and had no problems.

Even though he had plenty of provisions, he still spent considerable time searching the island for more supplies. He found plenty of coconuts and a sweetwater spring not too far from where he first landed. He revelled in the fact that he encountered no human footprints.

He camped on the north side of the island, where he had a view of Suarji Island, less than two kilometres away. After his last disastrous attempt at crossing the strait, he decided to practice and planned to make several trips between the islands until he felt more confident.

He was also determined to be smarter when he voyaged. He remembered how saltwater crocodiles moved from place to place when in the sea. They weren't great swimmers, so they waited for the conditions to be in their favour; when wind or currents opposed them, they hunkered down and stayed put.

Now Michael did the same.

When he first arrived on Getullai Island, a southeasterly breeze had accompanied him, but soon after, it shifted to the northwest.

He'd expected that, as the monsoons were due sometime in the next month—but it seemed early.

He waited for a day when the wind was very light, then pointed his craft north and began paddling to the smaller Suarji Island. Through a combination of sail and strenuous paddling, *Tortoise* cruised there with no issues. He nearly made a complete circle of the island before finding a sandy beach where he pulled ashore.

Michael stayed on the island for the night. A thorough search in the morning revealed no water, but he did find some wongai plums.

He crossed back to Getullai Island the next day.

Over the following days, Michael made this journey several more times. His confidence grew, and he wondered where he might go next. He hiked to the highest point on Getullai, and under the bright, merciless sky, he scanned the seas around him.

To the east he sighted—barely—what he believed was Saddle Island.

He squinted at the low smudge on the horizon, roughly twenty kilometres away. He knew Saddle Island sat eighty kilometres south of Dutch New Guinea—his final destination.

The winds are blowing in that direction. I'm sure I could make it, thought Michael. But with the monsoon due in the next month, bringing a wind from the northwest, he feared he might be there a while. Without a good southerly wind to continue north, he could be stranded for the duration of the wet.

Still, a voice in his head kept him moving.

If I can make it to Saddle Island, I'll just have to hunker down and wait for the right moment, he thought.

Michael completed the journey to Saddle Island on a quiet morning with the rising sun in his eyes. He sailed slightly north of east and made the crossing by mid-day.

The island was not large—three hundred metres by seven hundred metres—although it had two sizeable hills. One mound sat on the southern end of the island where jungle crept right down to the water, and the other in about the middle. A few derelict fenceposts hinted that some islander had once tried to graze livestock on the northern end where white sand beaches enclosed three sides.

Michael searched the northern half of the island upon arrival. It wasn't easy as the brutal sun made the sand nearly too hot for even his weathered feet. He had no shoes, so he followed the shore where he could.

A few days after he arrived, the clouds blocked out the sun, and the humidity soared. He set out in the morning when it was a little cooler and was overjoyed at what he found. There were two sweetwater springs, several groves of wongai plums, as well as plenty of coconuts. On the beach, he found turtle eggs and shellfish, and the coral reef that surrounded the island offered plenty of good fishing.

He stayed on the leeward side of the island, on a northeast-facing beach, where it was quieter.

His bamboo poles and tackle came in handy now, and soon he was grilling grouper and coral trout over a fire. In the shallow waters of the reef, he also collected crabs and shellfish. And to make it all feel luxurious, he tapped into his supplies and made lots of sugary tea.

The wongai plumbs were in season and he gorged on them while filling a basket with the date-like fruit. Then, when he noticed much of his horde might spoil, he boiled them down into a paste that he mixed with sugar. This turned into his nightly dessert.

One night while licking the sweet sticky substance off his fingers, he had an idea. He had grilled a fish earlier, cooking it directly on the coals after wrapping it in a fat leaf. Now the fire lay spent, a trickle of smoke spiralling casually from the white ash.

Michael grabbed the Japanese helmet and inside it, mixed a ball of dough out of flour, salt and water. He set it aside while he scooped out a depression in the ashes. Then he grabbed his container of wongai jam, poked a hole in the dough ball, and began filling it with the sweet substance.

He pinched the hole shut, flattened the ball into a pancake, and then set it in the firepit. After placing white ash and hot coals over the dough, Michael rubbed his hands together.

This would be a dessert like no other! He was beginning to think that if it weren't for the stifling, oppressive weather or the impending monsoon, he might have been content to stay forever.

In the morning, he baked two loaves of the new jam-filled damper. He'd eaten the entirety of the experimental loaf before going to bed but loved it so much he woke up craving more.

Soon after the dampers were ready, he set out to explore the southern, jungle-covered end of the island. He tossed one of the hot loaves into a sugar sack, along with a plastic jug of water, a coconut and some rope.

He drifted along the northeastern edge of the island, not rushing in his exploration. Two sea turtles frolicked offshore, and he ate the coconut in the shade while watching them.

He eventually followed the beach southward until it disappeared, leaving him with a knee-deep passage along the shoreline as it skirted the jungle.

He was up to his waist when he glimpsed the southwestern tip of the island. The palms and low brush fell away on the small peninsula that extended into a sand bar.

At the end of the land, facing south, lay an enormous crocodile. This time Michael didn't guess but instead knew it was Poseidon.

The croc didn't appear in a rush to go anywhere. Michael glanced at the heavens to the north and knew what Poseidon was waiting for—the monsoon rains. The dark, humid skies and nearly unbearable temperatures hinted that they weren't far off.

The wind and surface currents would be heading towards the southeast when the monsoon rains arrived, and he'd get a free ride home. Usually, Michael would look forward to the rains at this time of year as they'd lessen the heat. But now, he swallowed a lump in his throat because he knew if he didn't complete his crossing before the rains arrived, he'd be stranded here for months.

When he turned back, the rising tide made following the shore impossible. Instead, he climbed through the thick jungle that lined the shore and searched for a way inland.

Before long he was relieved to find a trail that led north and uphill. It had not been used for a long time, and there were no human tracks, but it was man-made.

While he hiked up the hill, he wondered what tribe of Islanders had used the island and if they'd been friendly. Or could it have been people from Dutch New Guinea? The islands along Dutch New Guinea's southwestern coastline are known as the Top Western Islands and are inhabited by the Asmat people.

The Asmat practised cannibalism and headhunting. In 1901, a missionary came across a longhouse with over a thousand heads stacked inside. The missionary was further horrified to discover that the Asmat used human heads as pillows, and they ate the brains of animals right out of the halved skulls.

Could they have ventured this far?

Michael would later learn that the year after his voyage, twenty-three-year-old Michael Rockefeller disappeared in New Guinea. Eventually, theories circulated that he'd been killed and eaten by Asmats from the Otsjanep village.

Michael reached the top of the hill and looked around. The sun lay hovering over the horizon, marking west clearly. He realised the island was aligned northeast to southwest, not north to south.

Dutch New Guinea lay to his north, although the massive island was too far away to make out. It seemed strange that he couldn't see the land because of the earth's curve, yet he knew the world's second-largest island lay dead ahead in the water.

In the skies above, he could make out monsoon clouds stacking up.

Behind him lay Australia, about sixty-five kilometres away, where blistering summer temperatures had heated the land to such an extreme that it produced a low-pressure zone. This drew in warm tropical air from the seas, and over the months leading to the monsoon, the moisture fed the building clouds.

He stared at the clouds, watching them churn.

He turned back and gazed towards Dutch New Guinea.

Halfway there, there should be an Island. He'd seen it on the map at the ranger station at Nagi Island. He squinted and shaded his eyes but could only make out the hint of a landmass.

Gabba Island, he thought hopefully, *and a bit before it, and further east should be Lama Island.*

He glanced down at the southwestern tip of the island and saw Poseidon, still there facing south.

I guess I still have a little time, he thought nervously.

Over the next week, he made several trips to the hilltop to check on Poseidon and the monsoon clouds. During this time, a strange calm settled over the sea. The wind blew less, and the currents seemed to stop altogether. The sun disappeared, too, behind a layer of grey clouds.

He considered trying to paddle the entire way without a breeze but decided eighty kilometres — or forty to Gabba Island if he could find it — was just too far.

Over the coming days, he prepared *Tortoise* for the voyage to Dutch New Guinea. If the conditions didn't turn in his favour, he might have to rely on help. So, he kept his boat ready to go on a moment's notice in case he saw a pearling lugger coming by, even though that seemed too easy.

The island baked under the oppressive heat, and he avoided the noonday sun. During other hours he worked on his sailing skills — with almost disastrous results.

One morning he decided to test out *Tortoise* and circle the island, but a strong wind suddenly picked up and grabbed the craft, blowing him several kilometres to the east. It took him the rest of the day to get back to Saddle Island.

No matter where he was on the island now, he could see that the monsoon rains were imminent. Saddle Island sat in almost the middle of the sea, and Michael could watch the accumulation of dark clouds over both Dutch New Guinea and Australia.

He still faithfully went to the hill because the view was expansive. And he could check on Poseidon.

One morning he made his way to the top of the hill. The air seethed with moisture, and Michael's skin was covered in beads of sweat.

He glanced down at the croc and witnessed it crouched in a strange position. From his perch on the hill, it looked like Poseidon was sniffing the air.

Michael turned and looked towards Dutch New Guinea and sucked in his breath. The entire sky above the island was dark with brewing storms. They merged and loomed, threatening.

Then the dark clouds seemed to gather inland, pulling everything with them. Suddenly the wind stirred and began blowing lightly from the south towards the storm clouds in the north. Michael didn't understand what was happening – but this seemed to be the wind he'd been waiting for.

He looked down at Poseidon one last time and caught a glimpse of his tail as he headed south.

That's all I need to see, thought Michael as he turned and ran down the trail to *Tortoise*. He grabbed a few things from his camp by his fire, then pushed his canoe into the water.

Michael adjusted the sheet and set *Tortoise* on a northern course. His sail managed to capture enough of the breeze to move them along nicely. The current seemed to have disappeared. That weird calm he'd noted was still in play, and he didn't even have to put out a sea anchor to counter any currents.

He still needed to paddle and use his paddle to steer, but he moved along at a fast enough pace that he began to think he might make it to Gabba Island.

Still, it was a long way – forty kilometres – and he doubted he could get there before nightfall.

When conditions allowed him to let the sail do the work, he rested his arms. The boat cruised along slowly without his additional paddling, but at least it still moved.

He tapped into his remaining supplies during these respites. He still had some sugar and salt but had run out of flour and tea. The day before, he'd baked a few more jam-filled dampers, and he ate one while he cruised along.

In the afternoon he glimpsed the island, and by sunset, he could see it clearly.

Maybe fifteen kilometres, he thought.

In the darkness he paddled along slowly. The wind had died down somewhat but still filled his sail.

He continued cautiously, knowing he couldn't land on Gabba in the dark for fear of hitting a reef. Michael tried to stay awake through the night, but eventually, he fell asleep, collapsing on his pile of supplies in the hull.

An explosive sound woke Michael and he sat up quickly. Ahead of him, a few kilometres away, he could see Gabba Island in the gloomy pre-dawn light. *Tortoise* shifted violently on large waves, and he grabbed the paddle.

When he glanced towards the island again, he suddenly saw something in the water directly before his canoe. *Tortoise* dropped into the trough of a wave, and when it rose again, Michael saw — to his horror — that an atoll lay between him and the island.

It was low tide, and when the wave receded, he faced a wall of coral and stone. Before he could react, the next wave pulled him into the side of the atoll. There was a powerful, crunching impact when the wave hit, and the momentum swept him up, nearly vertical, and then forced his canoe over the top.

Tortoise rolled over the edge of the atoll in a complete three-sixty, smashing the outrigger and breaking the mast. Michael dove into the hull and gripped the mast's base.

When he resurfaced, coughing water, they were inside the atoll.

He listened to the powerful crashing of the waves on the other side. He realised that if they hadn't had enough momentum to roll over the edge of the lagoon, they would have been smashed to pieces by the coral.

The canoe was upright but mostly filled with water. Slowly it floated away from the edge and deeper into the atoll. Coconuts and bamboo poles drifted off as he watched helplessly.

He sat in a daze for some minutes and only looked up when the sun finally peeked over the horizon.

The top half of the mast, most of the boom, and half of the sail had ripped away, but the canoe seemed okay. Luckily, Michael still had Smiley's bucket because it was tied to a rope in case he needed a sea anchor. It took a while to bail *Tortoise* out, and the entire time his fingers trembled.

When the water level in the canoe got lower, Michael was relieved to see his water containers and the tyre tubes still tied down securely. He breathed a sigh of relief when he found his paddle pinned under his feet.

Eventually, he stopped and assessed the damage.

The top half of the mast and most of the boom had been torn away, taking two-thirds of the sail with it. However, there was still a corner of sail, preserved because the grommets held it to the remaining pieces of the mast and boom.

The front end of the outrigger flopped in the water with a half-metre of the log still attached. The canoe seemed okay.

Looks pathetic, he thought, *but it might still help stabilise us.*

The loss of his sail staggered him. He thought he was stranded but then realised he could still paddle, and there was an island only a short distance away.

Michael made his way to the far edge of the atoll. He sat there until high tide arrived and then paddled to Gabba Island.

The north side of Gabba Island had a sand beach and no reef. Michael hauled his canoe out of the water and collapsed. He still couldn't believe he'd rolled *Tortoise*.

After a moment he stood and walked inland. The island was of decent size — maybe one kilometre by three — but had no big hills or other distinguishing features. He found a small rise and walked up it until he was thirty or forty metres above sea level.

Then he turned and faced north, and the view took his breath away.

He could see the mainland now. It was supposed to be forty kilometres away but looked closer. Above, the clouds were stacked up like giant mounds of charcoal. Towering cumulonimbus clouds — thunderheads — filled the heavens, and above them drifted long wispy cirrus clouds.

Beyond even that, a thin layer of cirrostratus clouds tried to block out the sun. The golden shafts of light that occasionally broke through were dazzling, and Michael would have watched the sky all day had he not been so distraught.

While he stared into the distance, a breeze moved his hair, and he felt his body drawn that way. He realised the gentle wind from the south that had driven him from Saddle to Gabba Island had been the monsoon's low-pressure zone sucking in all the air and moisture. It was more robust now.

Such power, he thought. And then his eyes lit up with understanding; the pressure effect was creating a temporary south wind.

He thought of *Tortoise* and her current condition, and in a flash, got an idea.

Michael spent the next hour working on his boat. First, he untied the torn sail from what remained of the boom and mast. Next, he unlashed the boom from the mast and set the pole on the beach.

He now had a pole that reached just over a metre and a small triangular sail. He climbed into the canoe and lashed the pole on top of what remained of the mast, forming a T about a metre above the hull.

Next, he added the sail. Luckily three corners of it still had grommets. He tied one end to the bow and the other two corners to either end of the pole. He gave them enough line that they would ride a metre above the pole.

He thought of John Caldwell and wondered what he would think of his upside-down jib sail. Michael didn't know how *Tortoise* would perform with this diminished sail, but he was going to try. One glance at the skies, and he knew he didn't have enough time to come up with another option.

Across the water, thunder rumbled as he set off again.

The big island of Dutch New Guinea appeared as a long, faded line that sat low in the water. It felt so close it made his heart race. For nearly eighteen months, he'd been struggling to get here.

It was still some distance away, but he could see it now.

The closer he got, the more the mountains grew and the further the coastline extended. He knew the southern coast of Dutch New Guinea to be over two thousand kilometres long, but seeing it first-hand still surprised him.

He remembered Father Gilfeather stating that New Guinea contained between five to ten per cent of the world's species. The man had spent hours discussing the extremes found there, like the largest pigeon, the longest lizard or the smallest parrot.

As Michael approached it now, he didn't care about any of those facts. What he liked about the place was just how much of it was untouched by man. He'd heard that scientists estimated thousands and thousands of species of insects, plants and birds were yet to be discovered in Dutch New Guinea.

But could one lose themselves there instead of being discovered? He wondered now.

What also sucked away his breath was the mass of ominous clouds that now floated above the big island. They reminded Michael of a great monster as it leaned over its victims.

He stared at the clouds in trepidation. The southerly breeze ruffled his hair, and in his mind, he imagined the monster taking in a great inhalation.

The heat and humidity were stifling, but still, that breeze stirred again. This time it lifted his new sail and filled it with air.

Michael whooped with joy.

They were heading north. The sail worked fine but required Michael to use his paddle to adjust their direction constantly. And it wasn't that large, so he knew he'd have to paddle as well, or the voyage would take forever.

He tapped into his remaining supplies and drank a handful of sugar water for breakfast. His remaining loaf of damper had washed away in the accident, and he bitterly regretted it now.

By mid-day, he was halfway there. He could see now that before him sat Sabai Island. The mainland was directly behind it, but he understood now why it had appeared closer.

He aimed for the left side of the isle. Another island sat there — the smaller Dauan Island — and Michael hoped to pass between the two in a small channel.

Rumblings of thunder came to him, floating over the water.

When he got near enough to the channel to glimpse the mainland behind it, he began to get cocky. He knew he was going to make it.

I could swim from here if I had to, he thought.

He stood in his boat and stared up at the heavens. Storms, currents, winds — and even people — had tried to stop him from completing this epic journey, but they had all failed.

He was going to make it.

"You couldn't stop me if you tried!" he shouted.

As if in response, a gust of wind shook his feeble sail.

When he got closer to the channel, he had to throw out a sea anchor to keep his craft pointed straight. And because his outrigger was in such a shaky state, he tried harder to keep the canoe balanced.

A dark cloud from the mainland broke away and cruised over him, soaking Michael with a quick shower. He faced the rain and let the drops wash over him.

When he cleared the channel, the mainland was still seven or eight kilometres away, but it didn't matter. He would get there.

He stood tall, faced the mainland and the clouds, and shouted, "I am the King of the Coral Sea!"

The heavens rumbled a response.

Then he turned and looked across the sea and remembered all the stages of his journey. He thought of the people too — those who had helped him.

He wished they could all see him now.

"I'm the King of the Coral Sea!" he shouted again.

He basked in the energy of his words then, eventually, sat back down.

Over the next few hours, he paddled to the mainland. His exhaustion caught up with him, and he could barely lift his arms, but he kept going. When he got there, he pulled *Tortoise* ashore and collapsed on the beach. He had done it.

Within seconds, he was sleeping.

Michael woke when a wet flicker brushed his cheek. He slowly opened his eyes — and then launched himself into the air. When he landed, he staggered backwards.

On the beach before him lay the biggest monitor lizard he'd ever seen — nearly three metres. When it opened its mouth and a forked tongue darted out between the long, fang-like upper teeth, he knew it was no ordinary monitor, but instead a crocodile monitor, unique to Dutch New Guinea.

The monitors he was familiar with had blunt peg-like teeth and no forked tongue. He grinned at the surprise — and confirmation. This creature was the first thing he'd encountered that made him sense he'd travelled to another place. It made him feel like he was on the edge of the world.

If Odysseus were here, he would call for a sacrifice, he thought.

He glanced again at the large reptile as it turned and sauntered down the beach. He remembered hearing that tribespeople thought them evil spirits who walked upright at night, breathed fire and killed men when the opportunity arose.

It almost scared me to death, he thought and chuckled.

Before the Cretaceous period—130 million years ago—Australia and New Guinea were part of the ancient supercontinent, Gondwana. Because of this, there is a close genetic link with many species of birds and mammals found in both locations.

The plants and trees tell a similar story. The rainforests of Dutch New Guinea have towering pines and beech that are remnants of that ancient landscape, but they are mixed with humid, tropical plants that descended from Asia.

Michael thought this was why he felt both at home and in a strange place. He knew the rainforest that thrived just a few feet away had tree kangaroos, cassowaries and other creatures he'd recognise, but still, it felt alien.

He stepped over to his boat and spent a few minutes examining the hull for cracks. It appeared to be okay, although everything else was a mess. The hull sloshed with water, and despite his efforts, not many of his supplies looked salvageable.

He took stock as he lay it all on the beach to dry.

He had a few cups of sugar, three coconuts, five litres of water, ten metres of rope, a plastic bucket and a paddle. During the roll, he'd lost the Japanese helmet, the pole with his cane knife mounted on it, his fishing tackle and all the bamboo. One water jug had been punctured as well as the tyre tube containing the salt.

He tilted *Tortoise* on her side and emptied the water out, then examined the rigging. The small sail that had gotten him from Gabba island was worthless now, badly tattered, and the grommet near the bow was ripping free. The outrigger no longer functioned in any sense.

He pulled out his cane knife and hacked it all away. He would use his canoe as the New Guineans did—without an outrigger. And he would go without a sail too. He would only paddle now.

Over the next few days, he followed the coast west. The heavens above rumbled and flashed lightning, but so far, the heavy rains held off. He encountered no people or any sign of man. At night he pulled ashore and slept in the sand.

When he had the energy, Michael would collect broad leaves he could sleep under to hide from mosquitoes, but most nights, he was too exhausted and simply collapsed.

His stomach growled constantly. He found a few clams and a coconut tree with fruit he could reach, but he craved something more substantial. He wished his fishing gear had survived the crossing.

Several times he ventured into the dense rainforest he was skirting. Here, the humidity soared even more, and immense trees and a thick canopy blotted out the sky.

A few steps inland were all it took to silence the crashing waves, and he found the solitude peaceful. He missed the rainforests of Queensland, and although this place was different, it still felt like home.

He still sensed that awareness around him — his Nature God.

He looked for food and fresh water on his excursions, but he also took time to sit and listen. There was so much life here!

Birds of every shape and size fluttered around him. Parrots, cuckoos, owls, kingfishers and even birds-of-paradise! They chattered and squawked and buzzed by his head.

The trees and shrubs held an equally beautiful assortment of creatures. Michael glimpsed tree frogs, pythons, chameleons and lizards moving amongst the shadowed branches. Countless butterflies, dragonflies and other insects buzzed through the rare shafts of sunlight.

He always felt a pang of regret when, after an excursion, he left the rainforest for the beach.

After he'd covered around fifty kilometres of coastline, he came upon a large river. It was a kilometre wide and appeared to plunge straight into the vast rainforest. It drew him in, and Michael decided to explore it.

The river flowed strong and flat at its mouth. Michael kept to the right-hand shore to avoid the trickier currents. He saw no people but occasionally heard chickens or pigs and wondered if they were domesticated animals kept in a pen.

He glimpsed longhouses through the foliage a few times, but he kept to himself, not wanting interactions with man. The crossing and his time on the islands had made him even more of a loner.

And he also didn't know how friendly these people might be.

One morning he woke to a young girl's laughter.

He'd tied his canoe to the river's bank the night before and slept in the hull. He peered through the foliage and saw the girl—aged about ten—as she tossed some scraps of food into a pigpen.

When she ran off, he stared at the pigs for a few minutes, imagining how good one would taste after being grilled over a fire. His stomach growled like the thunder above, but he moved on.

I'll starve to death before I steal, he thought, knowing Odysseus would have agreed with him.

He continued up the river, marvelling at the chaotic growth along the banks. It took constant paddling to move forward at a slow walking pace. Gigantic trees leaned over the water, connected through a network of vines and creepers—their branches filled with squawking birds. On the shoreline, cranes watched motionlessly.

Sometimes he'd paddle past walls of earth, thirty metres high, formed recently by the river. He stayed clear of those fresh cuts because, at times, great slabs of the earth would calve off like icebergs.

He sensed he was going back in time.

He didn't notice the rain at first. The air had been so full of moisture that he missed the moment when it first turned to soft droplets. It alleviated the heat for a while, but it wasn't the big deluge that was due. The clouds above simply couldn't hold all the water for much longer.

He passed several natives on the shore. Hidden by the rain's lightly tapping lullaby, *Tortoise* whispered past. One older woman worked on a basket by the riverbank and never looked up, but a young girl with a mop of dark hair gawked at him.

He smiled but continued with his efforts.

The river slowed, eventually, and began to narrow. He started to scan the shore for a possible camp. He figured he'd already gone about twenty kilometres up the waterway. He wasn't sure what he was looking for, but when he spotted a waterfall on his right, he decided to investigate.

The waterfall was only a few metres high, and Michael could see a lagoon behind it. So he pulled *Tortoise* ashore and used a well-worn trail to get up to the higher ground.

He took with him only the cane knife on his side and his remaining coconut.

Golden lilies filled half the lagoon, and flowering red hibiscus lined the banks. The pool sparkled with pristine water, and he could see the bottom. It reminded him of some painting of Eden. It was circular, about fifteen metres across, and on the far side, a narrow waterfall trickled from far above.

He spent the next hour swimming and drinking his fill of freshwater. He also drained the coconut of its juice, then split it open and ate all the meat.

He could feel that this place had been in use for a long time. Several flat logs lay by an old fire pit. The earth was pounded flat by the water's edge. He knew human feet had done that.

When Michael spotted a well-worn trail that led off into the jungle, he decided to follow it.

He walked along quietly, listening to the birds and animals. The oppressive heat left most creatures inactive, but the rainforest was so full of life that there was still much activity.

Under a massive fig tree, Michael came across a large colony of black flying foxes. The large males had a metre wingspan and weighed nearly a kilogram.

They made a ruckus when he appeared. Michael stepped back apprehensively when he saw over ten thousand of them roosting above him.

Their dark eyes glittered from the shadows.

He moved away from them, continuing on the trail that led steeply uphill.

Eventually, he came upon another trail that intersected his on a level spot. He paused there to catch his breath.

Michael listened to fat raindrops sporadically hitting the vegetation. In his mind he heard drumbeats reverberating through the jungle. Rain would make things more difficult now, but still, he wished for it. Anything would be better than this brutal humidity.

The jungle steamed around him, sweltering in the heat. He wiped his forehead and tried to decide if he should continue on the path he'd been following or turn off on the new trail that cut it.

I could go anywhere, he thought. *I am free.*

He pondered what would happen if he lost his way or couldn't get back to his canoe, but the images didn't scare him. He knew he could survive here as well as he had in Queensland.

Suddenly, a man appeared, moving quickly down the side trail.

He wore a headdress with feathers, and his face was painted yellow. When he saw Michael, he stopped dead, just ten feet away.

In the moment that followed, Michael remembered Father Gilfeather stating, "There are eight hundred and thirty-two different languages spoken in Dutch New Guinea, but the fourth official dialect is sign language."

Michael knew a few signs and tried one. He brought his hands out in front of him and wiggled his fingers in the sign for rain.

The Painted Man stared at him and showed no signs of recognition.

Michael tried again, raising his arms in an arc over his head in a backhanded motion—signing "sky"—and then trying the rain gesture.

Now the man frowned. Clearly, Michael was making this worse. He tried just to wave, but something he'd done had angered the man. He watched in horror as the Painted Man scowled and pulled a weapon from his belt.

Michael grabbed his cane knife and they locked eyes.

The man hesitated only a moment and then charged at Michael, but before he'd completed a step, a bolt of lightning crashed not twenty metres away.

Both men jumped and, out of nervousness, let out a short laugh.

They stared at each other again, connected somehow by the lightning. And then time froze, only moving now and then, with Michael's heartbeat.

Boom! It went as he observed the Painted Man's makeup and wardrobe. He saw red lines outlining the yellow paint as well as intricate beadwork and numerous feathers. He appeared ready for some event. Michael could see now that the man was older than him—and he stared back with a curious gaze.

In his hand, the man still held his weapon—a dagger, yellowed with age and made from the thigh bone of a cassowary.

His heart sounded again, *Boom*, and suddenly Michael was the rainforest, looking down at the two men. He felt the trees swaying and the abundance of life. He sensed the unbelievable age of the place. He yearned to see more, but, *Boom*, he moved on...

And then he was the Painted Man, staring at the skinny foreigner. Ready to kill him because of taboos he'd broken, but still not sure what he was. Again, Michael wanted to linger, but *Boom*, he moved on...

Again and again, Michael changed his perspective, and soon it expanded. The next moment he was a tiger, watching a young boy approach the shadowy woods. They stood in a magical silver forest awash in moonlight.

Then, *Boom*, he was a fierce crocodile snapping and angry at the intrusion of a young man. He felt a surge of power as the body of the croc pulsed around him.

Boom, he was an old man with skin like bark, leaning against a giant fig tree. The man was dirty and wrinkled and covered with grime, but he smiled and looked happy.

"I've had a good life," he said, "but it took guts. It wasn't always easy."

Michael felt the man's contentment—his satisfaction with having lived well. There was something familiar about the man, and he wanted to ask more, but, *Boom*, he moved on, continuing to change perspective.

When the last *Boom* sounded, he stood silently while the cicadas and crickets slowly came back to life.

When Michael returned to his body, he still found himself confronted by the Painted Man. The man stood there, looking confused, when suddenly a thunderclap erupted right above them—and immediately after, it began to pour.

Finally, here was the deluge he'd been waiting for.

Now the Painted Man's eyes showed panic. He pointed at the sky and then indicated he had to go. Michael nodded, and the man moved down the trail.

After a few paces, the Painted Man stopped and turned around, but Michael was gone.

Now that the rain had started, there was no stopping it. It poured down through the canopy, flowing off in heavy rivulets. The steep trail Michael descended turned into a stream, and he slid and skidded down it, constantly falling in the newly formed mud.

He felt half-drowned by the time he reached *Tortoise*, and he was just in time. The river had risen quickly and was on the verge of stealing his canoe.

He grabbed the stern and hopped in. There was no use remaining here — all around him, water cascaded into the river. He kept his head bowed and focused on getting downstream.

The trees lining the banks rushed by at a dizzying speed.

On the river, he could see much more of the sky. Above him, great sheets of lightning lit up the darkness. The thunder was deafening. It indeed appeared like there was a battle going on above him.

He began to relax when he was halfway to the sea. *Tortoise* had covered the distance in no time, and now that the river had widened again, it had a chance to flatten out.

Michael took a gamble and crossed the river before the mouth because he wanted to continue west up the coast when he reached the sea. It was a challenging task without an outrigger to help stabilise his canoe, but he was getting the hang of it.

When the Arafura Sea greeted him, he paddled only a short way down the coast before pulling ashore. The heavy rain and ominous skies above made it difficult to tell if the day had even ended yet.

Michael flipped the canoe upside down, crawled under it, and went to sleep.

After that first heavy downpour, the weather followed typical monsoon patterns. It sometimes drizzled in the morning, and a few times, the skies even cleared, but heavy rains found him every afternoon.

He made the most of the lack of storms in the morning and tried to cover what distance he could before the rain set in.

Day after day, he followed the coast without seeing another human. The rain whispered to him as it plunged into the sea, and he found himself lost in conversations about days and years gone by. He argued with his mind over events and decisions that were long past changing.

The fact that he'd reached his destination seemed to be lost on him as he questioned what he was doing. Hunger drained his body, but still, he continued.

One morning he floated on the water while he watched the rising sun light up the horizon. He figured he'd gone nearly two hundred kilometres since leaving the river — two-fifty since reaching the island.

In the distance he could see a village.

A small flock of gulls circled his boat, squawking.

He thought of his encounter with the Painted Man.

The entire experience had been a mystery. Why did his perspective change like that? How had he done it? And how could he stop time in a way that he didn't even need to breathe?

Did time actually stop?

He thought of the other times he'd had this fleeting yet eternal experience — with Poseidon, the crocodile, and the tiger before that.

And then he remembered the old man with skin like bark. He'd never seen him before — in real life or a vision — and he wondered who he could be.

He paddled through that morning with the old man on his mind and only later reached the conclusion that had been there from the beginning.

It was me, he thought. *I am that old man.*

It sounded ridiculous, but somehow, he knew it to be true. He felt it in his core. In some way, he had glimpsed himself as an old man. And not just any old bloke, but one that had lived a hard and wild life. When he thought of the expression the old man wore, he knew it to be pride. And as *Tortoise* floated, he suddenly knew where that pride came from — at least some of it.

For the last few days, Michael had forgotten what he'd accomplished on this journey. He revelled in it now. Eighteen months, countless kilometres; he doubted that any of his classmates at Shore could have made the voyage.

But he had, and nobody could ever take that away from him.

He thought of the gritty old man and said out loud, "You did it, old man, don't ever forget it."

He decided he would never tell anyone about the way time had stopped and moved him. They wouldn't understand anyway. So few people grasped what he was saying when he tried to explain about his Nature God — they would never understand the changing perspective that had accompanied his encounter with the Painted Man.

Instead, he would only tell them about his voyage.

Michael wondered at the future that lay before him. Where would this wild life take him? How many adventures before he became that old man by the fig tree?

He smiled and thought, *This is only the beginning.*

Then he looked over the water, took a deep breath, and shouted: "I am the King of the Coral Sea!"

Michael Fomenko on his great sea voyage. 1959.
Photo credit to Sydney Morning Herald.

Michael Fomenko in 1978.
Photo courtesy of Harold and Ingram Jung.

Endnote

*M*ichael continued to live in the wild until 2012, when he was eighty-two years old! Generations of Queenslanders knew him — or at least of him — from glimpses along the highway. He avoided the worst of the wet in his last few years by staying in economy hotels or empty buildings. But who can blame him? He'd spent more than fifty-five years living in either the wilderness or the fringes of society, and that takes a toll on the body.

He could no longer hunt, fish, or climb for coconuts, and even the locals noticed as his lope slowed to a trot and then to a shuffle. Those who had known Michael in his prime watched him age with a sense of nostalgia and perhaps some sadness. Thankfully, he still had a pension and many friends who were willing to help.

No matter how well he was set up during the rains, he would return to his jungle home when they ended — back to his remote fig trees.

When suddenly people noticed he hadn't been around for a while, they contacted the Innisfail Police Department. Gone were the days when they would threaten to arrest Michael, and only a few were old enough to remember his great sea voyage.

Now they simply wanted to make sure he was alright. Senior Constable Scott Hayes said, "We got regular patrols on the roads looking for him — and we're checking his camps. Don't worry, we'll find him."

He was located at the Gympie Cooinda Aged Care Facility.

Michael spent the last six years of his life there. In the beginning, he talked to a few journalists, but then he retreated into silence.

He was comfortable with silence.

I like to think there was a place there where he could listen to the birds and cicadas.

He died on 17 August 2018, at the age of eighty-eight.

Author's Note

I set out to tell Michael Fomenko's story on a foundation of historical facts, but still, it is told as a legend. I think Michael would have liked that. All evidence suggests that he was a fan of *The Odyssey*, and even saw himself as a modern Odysseus.

The original *Odyssey* has twelve chapters, so I told his great sea voyage in twelve. *The Iliad* was the prequel to *The Odyssey*, and it too has twelve chapters. The name means "Troy's story". This tale also contains twelve chapters under the heading "Michael's Story" and provides glimpses into various periods of his life.

Whenever I could, I related Michael's journey to *The Odyssey*, be it an encounter with a crocodile named Poseidon, a clap of thunder, or a standoff with a cyclops in a cave.

There are plenty of other areas where I took liberties, but I found myself unable to resist. An example is how Michael ate his flour. He always purchased it with his supplies, but there is no account of what he did with it. After consulting with a friend, Paula Morris, she determined that he must have been making damper. Throughout the later chapters, Michael cooks damper regularly, but we have no evidence that he did.

Another side of this story where I've had to project my thoughts is how he voyaged up the Queensland Coast and then across the Torres Strait. I'm no sailor, and I had a very poor grasp of sailing basics when I began writing this story. Luckily a fellow Explorers Club member, George Kalan, helped piece it together. First, we examined the winds and currents on the dates Michael was at known locations. Then, after consulting a half-dozen photos of Michael's canoe, George helped me figure out how he might have rigged a basic sail and used it. Google Earth aided us, but without a skilled sailor like George helping, it would not be such a believable narrative.

The cover depicts a man in a canoe on rough seas. This image is a composite, created by Andrew Holman, not an actual image. Although Michael saw plenty of rough weather (up to Gale Force 6 or 7), he most likely was never on the water for a Gale Force 8 or worse, which I'm told this photo borders on.

There is also the matter of what Michael called his Nature God.

I don't claim to know what was in Michael's mind — or anyone's for that matter — but I have felt an awareness in nature. I am not a religious person, yet I have stood in the wilderness and sensed that I was not alone. In Michael's case, I tried to follow that thought.

Lastly, I would like to acknowledge my American readers. This book is written in Australian English and metric. It's an Australian story, and it deserves to be told that way. Below is a conversion chart.

Conversions and facts

1 kilometre = .62 miles

1 metre = 1.09 yards or 3.28 feet

1 degree Celsius = x 1.8 + 32 = Fahrenheit

1 knot = 1 nautical mile per hour,
1.151 miles per hour or .514 miles per second

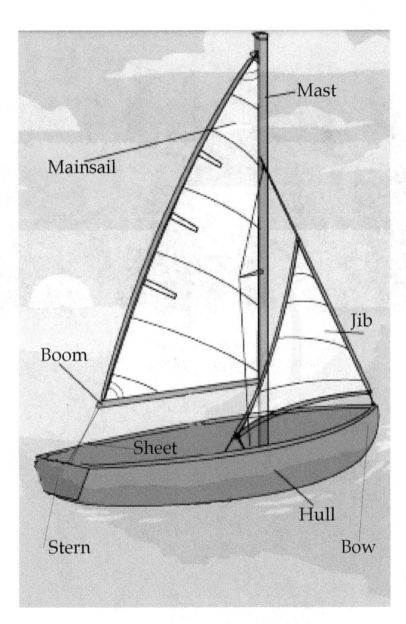

Michael Fomenko with the crew of the *Yola*. 1959.
Photo courtesy of Sydney Morning Herald.

Robert Louis DeMayo

Acknowledgements

Tales like this don't get told without help. I should begin by thanking the story's editor, Alison Starratt. Alison proved invaluable to this book, helping me to tell the story clearly, weed out any American slang, and keep me on track.

Former Disney artist, Tom Fish, completed the maps that I later labelled. Andrew Holeman designed the cover by combining several images.

A special thanks to George Kalan for his help with the sailing sections. Without his assistance in understanding how Michael sailed his canoe through some challenging waters, I would have been stranded. Following Michael's progress for well over a thousand kilometres was a great adventure for both of us, and I was sad when it ended.

Another special thanks is to Paula Morris. Paula helped me understand how Michael kept himself fed while on his incredible journey. She currently runs Happy Home Chef, a successful catering business out of the Brisbane area. Over the years, friends have shown her various Aboriginal cooking methods — like making damper — which likely came in handy for Michael when island hopping.

Thanks also to Anthony Hadleigh for his assistance in piecing together some of the history and geography of Cape Flattery.

Perhaps the biggest help has been from friends who talked at length about some of the challenges Michael faced. Among them, Steve Donavan, Bob Brill and Peter Muller have been incredibly helpful. In addition, fellow writers Kim Boykin and Claire Obermarck were invaluable, and I thank you both for the hours you spent listening to various chapters.

I've mentioned the Douglas family before, but I have to do it here as well. Thank you, Steve and Sally, for opening your home to us on our visits and showing us what is unique and special about Queensland. Shay Douglas runs Earth Heroes and was very helpful in connecting me with conservation groups.

My parents, Pat and Ron, always heard early chapters from my novels, and this one was no different. The day my father made his final trip to the hospital, he sat and listened to a few sailing sections I'd been working on with George Kalan. He seemed to enjoy them, and for a few minutes we were on the water together, sailing *Tortoise* across the Coral Sea.

I would also like to thank my wife, Diana, and daughters, Tavish, Saydrin and Martika. Since the beginning, you've listened to this story, and I'm eternally grateful for your encouragement and suggestions. Saydrin was the first to finish reading this one.

Lastly, I would like to acknowledge the people who looked after Michael when he was still with us. Throughout my days researching this story, I was moved by the outpourings of kindness and generosity directed towards him. Something about his epic dream connects us, and I've tried to include as many of you as possible in this book. Please forgive any small changes I've made to fit it all together.

I welcome you to join me in remembering Michael. *Tortoise* may not be that large, but in this case, I think it can fit us all, at least in this moment.

Dugout canoe under construction.
Photo courtesy of Harold and Ingram Jung.

Harold Jung by one of Michael's canoes. 2008.
Photo courtesy of Harold and Ingram Jung.

Ingram Jung, Harold Jung & Peter Ryle.

A Special Thanks

*I*n the previous section, I thanked people who actively helped me write this story, but I honestly feel I would never have completed it if it weren't for three men.

They are Harold and Ingram Jung and Peter Ryle.

Harold Jung spent twenty years researching Michael with the intention of writing a book about him. They were friends, and this lengthy acquaintance allowed him to patiently let Michael reveal his past. He visited Michael at many of his haunts, roaming all over the north. He always carried a camera and documented the hidden hideaways. The photos of Michael about to disappear behind a bamboo grove or embankment seem to capture his elusive nature.

Harold collected newspaper clippings and magazine articles, wrote to officials requesting documents, and accumulated a room full of photos and memorabilia associated with Michael Fomenko. He travelled to the National Archives of Australia to source further information and interviewed a lot of people who knew Michael — including his sisters and friends — many of whom are no longer living.

When Harold died in August 2011 at age forty-four, his brother Ingram took over the quest to honour Michael's legacy. Over the years, he tried to get others interested and talked with filmmakers, TV channel stations, and documentarians. Ingram eventually contacted the Cairns Historical Society to find a writer to compile the research in a non-fiction book.

Peter Ryle wrote the book using the Jung research, and I can imagine it was no easy task. Luckily they still had all the interviews and documents, which was fortunate because most of the newspaper articles were filled with exaggeration and hyperbole. If I'd had to write a book based only on them, it would seem more Marvel Comic with tales of Michael wrestling pythons, narrowly escaping piranhas and killing crocs with his bare hands.

Even Michael himself became an unreliable source as he grew older. Whether this was due to his time in Sandy Gallop or fifty-plus years living in the wild, we'll never know. But many times, his statements only confused things.

There is still much about Michael Fomenko's life that we don't know, but thanks to *Michael Fomenko – The Man Who Dared To Live His Own Exotic Fantasy*, we can say a few facts about his life with certainty.

By using the Jung research as a compass and then weaving a story around it, I hope that I've made a narrative that's entertaining and still somewhat truthful. I used his own words when I could, and I believe it's the tale Michael would want people to hear.

Michael Fomenko in 1990.
Photo courtesy of Harold and Ingram Jung.

Robert Louis DeMayo and family.
Sedona, Arizona.

Biography

Robert Louis DeMayo is a native of Hollis, New Hampshire, U.S.A., but has lived in many corners of the planet. He travelled to nearly a hundred countries before he was thirty, crossing many of them overland.

His love of Australia began in 1990 when he hitchhiked from Darwin to Sydney — and back six months later. Subsequent visits to the Cairns area over the last thirty years have led to lifelong friendships and a seemingly unquenchable desire to see more of Queensland.

He took up writing at the age of twenty when he left his job as a biomedical engineer to explore the world. His extensive journaling during his travels inspired five of his novels and far-reaching work for the travel section of *The Telegraph*, out of Nashua, New Hampshire, as well as the *Hollis Times*. He is a member of The Explorers Club and chair of its Southwest Chapter.

His undying hunger for exploration led to a job marketing for Eos Study Tours, a company that serves as a travel office for non-profit organisations and offers dives to the *Titanic* and the *Bismarck*, Antarctic voyages, African safaris and archaeological tours throughout the world.

For several years following that role, Robert worked as a tour guide in Alaska and the Yukon during the summer and as a jeep guide in Arizona during the winter. He was made general manager of the jeep tour company but eventually left the guiding world to write full time.

Robert is the author of eight novels that have collectively won ten national awards. His printed books and eBooks are available on Amazon, KDP and Ingram. In addition, several of his stories are available as audiobooks on ACX.

He resides in Sedona, Arizona, with his wife Diana and three daughters: Tavish Lee, Saydrin Scout, and Martika Louise.

Also by Robert Louis DeMayo

Pledge to the Wind, the Legend of Everett Ruess

In this compelling narrative of a young man's travels in the 1930s, Robert Louis DeMayo has taken journal excerpts, poems, and letters Everett sent to family and friends, and turned them into historical fiction. Through this recreation of Everett's travels, we are given rare glimpses of the young artist as he explored the southwest. Everett travelled alone, accompanied only by a dog named Curly and a couple of burros, but he often stayed with Navajo or Hopi.

His letters about these experiences, flushed out in this story, show how unique his time in the southwest was. Upon reading it, Brian Ruess wrote, "In this work of fiction ... I saw Everett for the first time, as he might actually have been."

★★★★★ -*"Reading this exquisitely written work should inspire anyone to want to live a simpler life with endearing respect for nature. It is almost unfathomable that someone as young as Everett Ruess could have such a profound look at society and the way it can strangle the purity and life out of so many. Robert Louis DeMayo captures both the country's beauty and an individual's quest for beauty in its simplest form. This book makes one want to pack up and visit the glorious beauty of the southwest similarly, to try to even remotely see life through the unadulterated eyes of a young man who dared to live life on his own terms."* – Tim Glover

Historical Fiction.
Wayward Publishing.
Available in print, eBook
& audiobook.

Also by *Robert Louis DeMayo*

Pithecophilia

The powerful true story of one man's quest to unravel the mysteries of the world's primates.

From the steep slopes of the Virunga Volcanoes to the steamy jungles of Sumatra, *Pithecophilia* explores author Robert Louis DeMayo's life-changing search for ape encounters as he discovers the secrets of their history, biology, and what they can tell us about ourselves.

Touching on the efforts of the world's leading conservationists and scientific institutions, you'll also discover how the early exploration of Africa and Asia's untamed wilderness shaped our knowledge of apes and how their efforts to document our planet's wild animals eventually led to efforts to save them.

Imbued with touching memories, humorous anecdotes, and over fifty years of wondrous, magical, and sometimes terrifying experiences, *Pithecophilia* paints a beautiful picture of how primates are, in many ways, windows into our own souls.

★★★★★ -"This book would make an inspiring gift for any young person who is a fan of Steve Irwin, David Attenborough — or Indiana Jones."

★★★★★ -"Insightful and informative [...] It made me want to pack up and travel the world!"

★★★★★ -"One can live vicariously through DeMayo in the comforts of home with a mind

Memoir-based Non-Fiction.
Wayward Publishing.
Available in print or eBook.

CPSIA information can be obtained
at www.ICGtesting.com
Printed in the USA
BVHW030049011022
648434BV00008B/72

9 781736 598481